PUFFI[ ]

Editor: Kaye Webb

JAMES COOK, ROYAL NAVY

In this memorable re-creation of the boyhood and early voyages of Captain James Cook, George Finkel (himself an ex-naval officer) has succeeded in bringing to life one of the most famous men in the history of exploration and the sea.

As we follow Cook's childhood in Yorkshire, his early training aboard the Whitby colliers, and his growing interest and skill in navigation and charting (his work led to the charting of much of the Canadian coast and he was present at Wolfe's siege of Quebec), it becomes clear how this experience combined with his strong determination and personality to make him the right choice to command the Admiralty's extensive voyages of exploration into the Pacific, to Australia and to New Zealand.

Besides the dominating figure of Cook himself, the story is peopled with other well-known characters: Joseph Banks, the brilliant, selfish young naturalist; Lieutenant Hicks, whose death came as such a blow to Cook; Hugh Palliser, who helped him in his career – and, of course, Elizabeth, James' young wife patiently waiting for her husband to return to their London home. Here is a vivid impression of James Cook, explorer, circumnavigator, seaman.

For readers of eleven and over

Cover design by John Mason

JAMES COOK,
ROYAL NAVY

George Finkel

Decorations by Amnon Sadubin

PUFFIN BOOKS

Puffin Books,
A Division of Penguin Books Ltd
Harmondsworth, Middlesex, England
Penguin Books Australia Ltd, Ringwood, Victoria, Australia

First published by Angus & Robertson 1970
Published in Puffin Books 1973
Copyright © George Finkel, 1970

Printed in Australia for Penguin Books Australia Ltd
at The Dominion Press, Blackburn, Victoria
Set in Intertype Fairfield

Contents

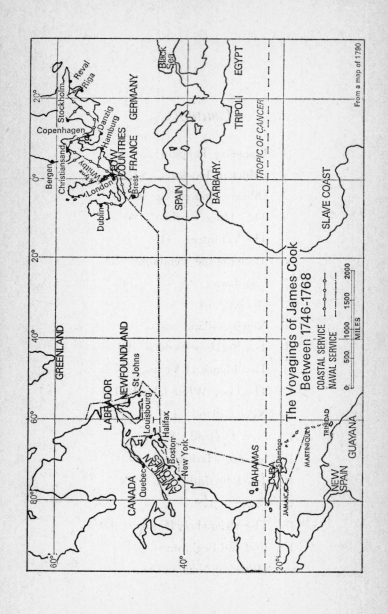

The Voyagings of James Cook
Between 1746-1768

COASTAL SERVICE ——○—○—○——
NAVAL SERVICE ——·——·——·——

0   500   1000   1500   2000
MILES

From a map of 1790

I   *Roseberry Topping*

'The twenty-ninth of May
Is Royal Oak Day!
If you don't give us holiday
We'll all run away!'

The words of the old schoolboy's jingle rang out between pauses for breath as two boys scrambled up the smooth turf to the summit of Roseberry Topping. Breathless, for they had hurried over the half-dozen miles from Ayton-in-Cleveland up the lower slopes of the miniature mountain. It was Royal Oak Day, a holiday, a sweet May morning, in the year 1739. James Cook and his cousin Jonty Emery laughed as their heavily nailed shoes slithered on the turf; they solved the problem by unbuckling and hanging them round their necks by the straps. A very few minutes saw them to the sloping plateau of the crest, and for a while they stood silent, gazing on the country laid out before them.

Many generations of lads had gazed over the same wide view, which was little changed over the centuries. Roman-British boys had stood here on watch for the approach of heathen pirates. Nearer in time, a beacon had flared to tell the people of the Tees Valley that the Spanish Armada was off the Channel coast. And nowadays, every boy in the district climbed Roseberry Topping at least once before he left childhood behind him.

Larks sang; the air was sweet with the tang of gorse-blossom. The cousins gazed out over an immensity of gold and green and blue, stretching away in the clear air of early summer. Almost at their feet, it seemed, lay a little village with a triangular green.

'What place is that, Jonty?' James asked. His cousin, at
thirteen, was two years older, so of course he knew everything.

'That? It's Newton, of course, where Aunt Alice keeps the
alehouse – that square house you can see beside the green,
with the yard at the back.'

'That's where father said we were to go and get a ride home
with Mr Barr, the carrier.'

'Plenty of time for that,' Jonty said, squinting at the sun.
'It wants a good while to noon yet and we'll go down quicker
than we came up. Let's stay here for a while.'

They made themselves comfortable a little way back from
where the edge tumbled down in a fall of shattered boulders,
and attacked the girdle cakes spread with damson jam they
had with them, washing them down with watered ale.

James knew that his cousin had stayed with Aunt Alice last
year, to help get her hay in. Aunt Alice was a widow, and
childless. Her husband had been lost at sea, and the Walker
brothers, whose ship he had been in, had made over the inn
to her as a tenant. There were twelve acres of good land with
it, and she kept two cows and a hundred head of poultry, pro-
ducing butter and eggs as well as looking after the inn.

'I think you could see to the end of the world from here,'
James said dreamily. 'You can see a lot of places, anyway.
Whereabouts is Yarm, Jonty?' He knew Yarm; it was the
farthest he had ever been from home, when his fathter had
taken them all to the Cheese Fair six months back.

'That's Yarm – I think.' Jonty pointed to a smudge of smoke
by the silver flash of the Tees. 'And that will be Stockton,
that bigger place farther on. I went to Stockton Market once,
and saw them building ships by the river. It took all day to
get there.'

'And what lies beyond?'

'Oh, there's Durham, and then a great place called Newcastle, and after that Scotland, where my mother and your
father came from.' Jonty stood up and swung his arm around.
'And over there is the sea, with a whole lot of other places on
the far side of it. Foreign places.'

James had never seen the sea before. Now he gazed upon it

eagerly. It was very distant, but he saw the North Sea at its very best, like a smooth sheet of blue-green watered silk. 'You'll be going to sea next year, won't you, Jonty?'

'That I will! I am promised a place in one of Mr Walker's ships. Next March, at the beginning of the season.'

'There's a mighty lot of it,' James said wonderingly. The sea was bigger than ever he had thought it could be.

'There's more sea than land in all the world, so they say. There are places where a ship can sail for weeks without sighting land.'

'Is that where you'll be going?'

'Not I! I'll be in ships sailing to London, or the Baltic, where there is trading to be done and good money to be made.'

'Is that what Mr Walker's ships do?'

'Aye. He and his brother have a good many ships, and each captain has a share in the ship he sails. Some of the mates, too. They say he's a very good master.'

'He must be rich.'

'He'll not be wanting for much, my father says. He'll be a warm man – and so shall I, when I'm a man grown, after I've served my time.'

'Seven years!'

'What of it – it will pass!' Jonty shrugged off more than half his total lifetime carelessly. 'I shall be no more than twenty-one by then, and probably rated as mate. I'll live very carefully, and it won't be long before I'm skipper. Then I'll begin to take shares in other ships, too . . .'

'Is that what Mr Walker did?'

'Aye. There were three Walker brothers at one time, but one was lost at sea.'

'Lost?' James repeated.

'Aye. That happens, too. But I'll not let it happen to me!'

James could not imagine storms or shipwreck taking toll of this confident cousin. Obviously, to be lost at sea implied some fault in the man who was drowned.

'The Walkers have a farm in Ayton, as well.'

'That they have – and a good one. But I don't think I shall have a farm when I am rich. It isn't easy to find honest bailiffs to run a farm. – Unless you'd like to be my bailiff, James?'

That was what James' father was – bailiff of Airyholm Farm. James frowned as he thought over Jonty's suggestion. 'I don't want to be a bailiff, Jonty. I don't know what I want to do, but I don't want to stay on a farm all my life.'

'Then I won't have a farm. I shall build a fine house in Whitby and spend the winters there, making plans for the next year's trade and taking wine with my captains!'

James thought it sounded a fine thing his cousin intended to do, but he was not sure that he would want to do the same. He looked out at the glimmering sea, where the sun, halfway to noon, cut a gleaming pathway toward the south. It was so bright that his eyes watered, and he turned them towards the cool north out of the glare.

'Aye, that is what I mean to do,' Jonty concluded. He sounded very satisfied with the prospect.

James thought some more about his cousin's ambition. Perhaps – perhaps there was more to life than making money by trade in the summer and drinking wine in winter.

'Shall you not take a wife?' he asked.

'Oh, yes – in time, for a man must have a wife. And I shall need one more than most, to look after my great house in the summer while I am away at sea. But I shall not wed until I am thirty, at the least, and only then if I can find a wife with a good portion.' Jonty pulled a stalk of grass and gnawed at the sweet tip. 'Have you thought what you will do, James? When you are grown, I mean?'

James shrugged.

'I don't want to stay on a farm, but I've not thought much about it. To be a carrier, like Mr Barr, would be a good life. There has been talk of my being made 'prentice to Mr Dutton, the wheelwright, when the time comes. But I don't know.'

And just then the thought came to James that if he could stay on Roseberry Topping all by himself, for a long time and think and think, then he would know what to do with his life, and how to set about it.

'Why not come to sea, like me?' Jonty asked.

'I might do that,' James told him doubtfully.

'I'll tell you what. Follow me to sea, and you could be mate

– aye, and skipper in time – of one of my ships! I would always
be able to make a place for you. How about that?'

'I think I would rather go to sea than become a wheelwright,' James said slowly.

'Well, then! We could start making plans now. It's not
too soon.'

James nodded. After all, he was eleven now. 'No, I suppose
not. But if I went to sea, Jonty, I don't think I'd want to sail
in colliers or coasters, as you are going to do, and as my uncle
did.'

'What would you want to do, then? What else could you
do?'

'I don't know. I would like to sail on the seas you spoke of
– where you can sail for weeks without seeing any land. I
would want to sail to the Indies, the Americas, to Africa. The
hot countries, where there are elephants and wild men.'

'You would not make much money doing that!' Jonty
sounded disapproving.

'I don't think I want to make all that much money. I'd have
to make enough to live on, I suppose. But if I could get that,
then it would be a fine thing to sail right round the world, and
see things no one had ever seen before!'

'You'd have to go a long, long way. I doubt if there is anywhere left that no one has ever seen.'

'There will be some place I could find!' James answered
obstinately.

Jonty was a kindly lad, and he realized his cousin was still
very young. 'Aye, that's right!' he said. 'I daresay there are
some places – islands, and such – that no one has seen yet.
You might as well find them if you can, James. And when you
have, come to me and there'll still be a skipper's berth for you
in one of my ships!'

In after years, James often recalled this conversation between his cousin and himself. The mild May morning, his
first glimpse of the sea from Roseberry Topping, Jonty's easy
plans for the future . . . they made together a long moment
in his childhood which he did not forget.

2 *Reluctant Huckster*

If James' father – James Cook the elder – had been the tenant of Airyholm Farm, he would have been a passing rich man. Since he was only the bailiff he lived well enough, but he had little chance of ever saving money.

He had migrated south from Scotland during the Jacobite troubles of 1715, and he had the Scotsman's belief in the virtues of education. It was not easy, but he was determined to see that his sons had as good a start in life as he could give them. From his eighth year, young James went to school, attending the classes held by Mr Pullen, the curate, who made his pupils proficient in the three R's for the sum of fourpence the week.

School was held in the church vestry every day, except Sundays and Yarm and Northallerton market days. These last were not holidays, but it was an understood thing that the pupils might be expected to help their fathers with droving on these days. Neither was there any school at sowing or harvest time. Mr Pullen gave very good value for the fourpences he received, and his pupils graduated after three or four years able to read, write and figure. And to say their catechism, of course, and be confirmed in the faith of the Church of England.

So James learned to write a passable hand and to spell reasonably well, to read print, and became proficient in the first rules of arithmetic. He was not very enthusiastic about the readings from the poets – Mr Pullen was a great admirer of Alexander Pope, in spite of the latter's Catholic religion, and James made little sense of the *Essay on Man*. In his twelfth year, James was coming to prefer fact to fancy.

The sea and ships were frequently in his mind. He knew now that there was other trade in the world besides coal from the Tyne and pitch and pit-props from the Baltic. His favourite arithmetic problems concerned calculation of the tonnage of ships, or profits on a trading voyage. In these, goods were exchanged for foreign moneys with magical names: maravedis, ducats, pesetas. In his mind he saw the counting houses where these coins lay glowing by the sackful, the richly clad merchants who owned them, and the rich smell of the spices they traded for them.

Like many a stay-at-home parson, Mr Pullen had a passion for books of travel, and sensed the dawn of similar tastes in a few of his pupils. To these few he would lend a volume of Raleigh, Dampier, or Hakluyt, and this way James made acquaintance with that wider world he had sensed from the sight of a summer sea, viewed from the crest of Roseberry Topping.

Jonty had been a sea now for a good while, and James had told his father that he would like to follow him. But he never spoke of his desire to sail into the great seas far from land. He knew he would have to start his seafaring in coasters or colliers, for they were the only ships that came to the little ports on the Yorkshire coast. It would be time enough to change to a deep-sea ship when he was a man grown and clear of his articles.

Indeed, his seafaring had advanced beyond the realm of talk. Mr Walker had been approached and had agreed to make a place for James as soon as he had turned fourteen.

'I know well that some owners ship lads at twelve,' Mr Walker said when James and his father went to see him. 'But twelve is over-young for most lads to begin seafaring. At that age a lad needs good, regular sleep, which he will never get in a collier. But when – James, is it, after thy father? – when James is fourteen I will ship him for a month, to see how he shapes. Then we can talk about his articles, and I'll not be hard on thee in the matter of a premium.'

For a while, James went about the chores at Airyholm with

a light heart. That was the year 1741; he was thirteen in the October. Suddenly his fourteenth birthday seem much closer. Only two more winters and a summer in between, and he would be at sea with Jonty! For he had no doubt that he and his cousin would serve in the same ship. What times they would have, both at sea and ashore! He was all impatience for December, when Jonty's ship, the *Bobby Shaftoe,* would be laid up in harbour for the yearly refit.

But Jonty never came back to port. The *Bobby Shaftoe* was sailing north in ballast on her last passage of the season. Out of the Baltic howled a black easterly gale. Black Tuesday, they called it afterwards, when five stout ships were driven on to the fangs of the reef known as the Black Middens, that graveyard of ships that lies between the mouths of Tyne and Wear. Of the crews of these five ships, only eight lived to reach the shore, and three of these died soon after. Jonty was not one of the five survivors.

James grieved for the loss of his cousin, but it never occurred to him to change his mind about seafaring. Men were thrown from horses and killed, but it did not stop any-one from riding. And during the year that followed, the sharp edge of the loss of Jonty became blunted – though he would never forget his cousin.

But there was something else, affecting James himself. At thirteen, no one would have thought him tall for his age, but in the spring following Jonty's loss he began to shoot through his clothes, growing as fast as a beanrow in early summer. He outgrew his strength, his sturdiness vanished; he had fits of utter weariness he could not fight.

They took him to see Master Sheldrake, the village leech. 'I do not think it is a green-sickness,' he pronounced. He was tooth-drawer, apothecary and physician for man and beast alike in those parts. 'He has outgrown his strength, which is no great matter at his age. Keep his feet dry, his head cool, his bowels open, and let him eat what he will except of salt meats and vinegar pickles – and keep him out of the night air! In a year or two you will have forgotten that anything ever ailed him.'

'It was intended he should be 'prenticed to the sea,' James'
father said. 'But that is a year and more away. Will he be
recovered by then?'

'Find his strength again in a year, you mean? To be
'prenticed to the sea?' Master Sheldrake might have been
speaking of the Black Death, such was the horror in his voice.
'Do you want to kill the lad? Did you not hear what I said?
Keep his feet dry, and let him eat what he will except salty
meat and vinegar pickles! If he goes seafaring, will his feet
ever be dry? Will not every bite he eats be soused either in
brine or vinegar? To send a lad in his condition to sea would
be to write his death-warrant!'

And that, it seemed, was the end of James' seafaring plans.
It would be a landward life for him after all; nor did James
care much at the time; he felt too weary. One thing cheered
him: if he was not to go to sea, neither was he to farm ashore.
It is almost as difficult for a farmer to keep his feet dry in the
winter as for a sailor.

Then, just as James was about to be apprenticed to Mr
Dutton, the wheelwright, a new opening appeared in his life.

The village of Staithes lies a few miles from Ayton, on the
Cleveland coast. It is so remote from other parts that the folk
there almost speak a language of their own; its streets are so
steep that many of them become flights of steps. The lower
windows of some houses look clear over the rooftops of their
neighbours lying downhill. Most Staithes folk live by fishing,
although some have holdings in the sheltered little valleys
behind the village.

William Sanderson, who kept the village shop, was a
cousin of James' mother. He was not a Staithes man by birth,
and after a thirty-year residence there he still felt something
of a johnny-come-lately. As a lad he had suffered from weakness of the chest, and had been prescribed sea air and a diet
which included fresh fish daily. That weakness had long been
cured: William was now a red-cheeked man in his early fifties
who had not ailed a thing for years. This happy state he put
down to taking a daily walk and eating a fresh fish dinner at
least four times a week. He could not always get fresh fish

in winter, but to offset the eating of stockfish or salt beef he
took an apple or a winter-pear daily, as long as they lasted.
After that he would eat a sliced raw onion, and relish it, as
he said he also relished the great spoonful of raw fish-oil
which he took daily. These last made him stink most wonder-
fully. He was grocer, huckster, haberdasher and ship-chandler
all in one. Indeed, his was the only shop in Staithes.

James was past the age when most lads were apprenticed,
but William Sanderson was glad to have him. Not many lads
in Staithes were willing to serve in such a clamjamfry of a
shop as Sanderson's, but James did not worry about this. He
felt as though he had been released from a prison – for a
prison the farm at Airyholm had become to him for a year
past. He had done his duty by his father, and he was com-
petent at the tasks within his strength, but his heart was not
in the land.

It was in the spring of 1744 that James walked over the
moors to Staithes, carrying his spare clothes in a bundle at his
back. It was the season when the sky is high-piled with towering white cloud and the land dappled with sun and shadow,
days loud with birdcall and fragrant with fresh-growing things.
He put on a mighty hunger as he walked, and came to Staithes
in time to eat a great dinner of cod-steaks, boiled potatoes and
onions. Fish was rare at Ayton, and he had never sat down to
such a great platterful before. The flesh came clean away from
the bones in sweet milky flakes, and James ate until his waist-
band creaked.

'Eat hearty, lad!' his cousin-employer urged him, and
Emma, his wife, smiled her approval of James' appetite.

Then there was sleep, in his own little room up under the
eaves, with a window to give him a view over rooftops to the
sea, and a bed to himself. It was the first time James had not
had to share a bed with a brother or two, and he enjoyed the
luxury of it. He felt he was really setting out in the world,
that the shop at Staithes was the first step on his way to
fortune.

Spring merged into summer, and James filled out visibly as
the year advanced. The shop work was not hard. In a town-

ship like Staithes very little business was done over the coun-
ter. Every Wednesday, if the weather served, Tommy Barr
the carrier arrived, with a loaded wagon and a summary of
the latest market prices from Northallerton and Yarm. Over
the next three days, Master Sanderson would ride out on Jess,
his old grey cob, with four pack-saddled Galloway ponies
behind him. In this way he did by far the greater part of his
business. He carried tea, sugar, spices and sometimes a few
bottles of brandy picked up at sea from a French fisherman,
with a pannier or two of laces and buttons and ribbons and
suchlike. He came back laden with eggs and butter, cheese
and bacon, all credited to the seller at the current market
price. Soon James was commissioned to do some of the trading around the nearer farms on foot, with two pack-ponies.
This exercise, coupled with the bountiful table at the Sandersons', soon made him lose the spindly look of the lad who has
outgrown his strength. James looked forward to the weekly
rounds and the friendly welcome he met at each outlying
farm.

So a year passed. James was grown tall now; he would be
seventeen at his next birthday. Like many another before
him, he seemed fated to spend his life in an occupation for
which he had little heart, but his mind did not dwell too
long on this. At that time he was only too glad to have escaped
the drudgery of the farm at Airyholm.

It was the events of the late summer of 1745 that gave a
turn to events and set James' mind to thoughts of the sea once
more.

That was the year Charles Edward Stuart landed on the
Moidart shore and rallied the Highland clans to his banner.
By the middle of September he had beaten all the Hanoverian
armies in Scotland and held the royal city of Edinburgh. Up
and down the east coast of England there was talk of little
else; ports like Leith and Dundee which had been friendly
for nearly one hundred and fifty years were suddenly in the
hands of a rebel prince. The folk of Whitby and Staithes had
known many years of peace under the house of Hanover;
now, talk of armies and battles in the near north reminded

them that their strip of coast was part of a larger world, and
that if Charles Edward Stuart invaded England and made for
London, there were only two roads he could take: either by
Carlisle or Newcastle. If he came by Newcastle, his road
south would lie through Northallerton – one of their own
market towns.

Every Wednesday the Staithes folk got the clash of the
countryside from the carrier, but a week was a long time to
wait between bulletins in such stirring days. William Sanderson and James formed the habit of walking to Whitby on
Sundays, hoping for fresher tidings. In the town they would
separate, William to take his ease at an inn among skippers
and mates, and James to walk among the barks and brigs and
their crews down at the port. Slowly his old dream of the sea
reawakened; he realized that to be a huckster in a fishing
village was not for him.

Whitby built the best ships in the world for the coastal and
Baltic trades – Whitby men themselves were not slow to tell
you that – and in the first three months of the year the port
was thronged with ships laid up for the winter and refitting
for the next season. But with the turn of the year the seamen
departed and the flow of news dried up, and Master Sanderson no longer took his Sunday walks to the town.

But the ships a-building were there still, and that was all
the excuse James needed. He had struck acquaintance with
some lads his own age, and lacked neither someone to talk to
nor employment for his hands. He was quick to learn the
seaman's craft – he had only to be shown once, for instance,
how to tuck a splice into a rope, and he was a welcome guest
in any rigging-shed. So he met many a 'prentice seaman, and
discovered a strange thing: that while he envied them their
life at sea there were some among them who envied him his
ashore. James could not understand this.

There was a battle up in Scotland at a place called Culloden
in the April of '46, and after that there was less need than
ever to go to Whitby for news on a Sunday. There was no
more war in Scotland, although many of the rebels were still
at large, and no chance that they would invade England by

any road ever again. Yet every Sunday after church, James
still walked to Whitby.

One Sunday at the end of March, as James sat learning a
long-splice in a rigging shed he looked up to see Henry Walker
standing before him – the man who had promised him a place
in a ship. Master Walker was soberly dressed in grey with
very plain linen. As a Quaker, he saw nothing wrong with
work being done on a Sunday, so long as it was from choice
and decently conducted.

'I know thy face, lad,' he told James. 'Does thou not come
from Ayton way, and did I not once talk with thy father
about making thee 'prentice in one of our ships? What happened – did thee change thy mind?'

'No, Mr Walker. Did my father not tell you?' James fought
back a strong temptation to use Mr Walker's own Quaker
form of speech. 'I fell sick of a growing-sickness, and Master
Sheldrake said I should seek a landward occupation.'

'Whatever ailed thee seems to have gone,' Mr Walker said.
'Thee looks as likely a lad as ever I saw. And what is it thou
art doing, when th'art not sitting in my rigging shed splicing
cable?'

'I am 'prenticed to Master Sanderson, the merchant at
Staithes,' James answered.

'So! That suits thee better than the farm, eh?'

James nodded. 'I am – content enough there,' he said.

Henry Walker was a shrewd man; he sensed there was
something in James' mind that he had not spoken. 'They say
Master Sanderson is a warm enough man, and that without
going five mile from his own fireside. And he has no living
child, as I hear. Thee could have done worse, friend James;
in time thee might do very well for thyself.'

'Aye, so I suppose.' From the tone of James' voice it was
clear that he did not regard the prospect with much favour.

Mr Walker had gained a position in the world by his own
efforts, but he had been helped at the outset by a kindly
master and he had never forgotten it. Unlike some, he had a
great feeling for lads at the outset of their lives; he knew that
if they were not truly happy in their work they would never

make a real success of it, nor achieve happiness. 'What is it thee would do with thy life, then?' he asked James quietly.

James looked up at the square face under the low-crowned hat, seeing the understanding in the eyes. 'I think you know, Mr Walker. I would go seafaring. When I was still a little lad you promised me a place, then I fell sick and could not take it. But I still want to go to sea.'

'That I can guess, else thee would not be sitting in a rigging shed of a Sunday, tucking splices for the love of it.'

'But I am bound apprentice to Master Sanderson,' James went on.

'Maybe that is something that can be resolved, with friendliness on both sides. Say that there was a lad in one of my ships that was not so happy with the sea as thou might be – a lad with a weakness of the chest, maybe – something might be done. I would have to see thy father and thy present master, and I can promise nothing unless they gave their blessing on the plan.'

'Oh, if you would, Master Walker!'

Mr Walker smiled. 'I felt the same as thee when I was a lad. And th'art not likely to change thy mind at thy age. Happen I'll do us both a good service by speaking to thy father.' He paused, then said: 'Thee is sure thee is shot of thy old sickness? Thee does not lose thy breath on a hill, nor sweat in the night? Thee is not troubled with a cough?'

'Why no, sir! If I were, Mr Sanderson would soon cure me of it, with his fish-oil and onions.'

'Thy father is still at Airyholm? Then happen I will ride over and visit with him. I could look in at Staithes on the way back and see Friend Sanderson about transferring thy articles, if thy father gives his consent.'

James could hardly believe his own ears. 'So quickly as that?' he said.

Henry Walker looked at him. 'Thee might not realize it, but th'art near on six feet tall. Thee will be a man grown in two or three years. Already thou art some years behind in thy seafaring. If we are going to do anything in this matter at all, then it must be done quickly.'

3   Diligent Apprentice

The bark *Freelove*, out of the Tyne with sea-coal for London, came ghosting up the Thames with only the faintest of easterlies to stir her canvas. She lost the tide off Blackwall, but Sam Outhwaite, her skipper, did not set the hands to kedging. He would reach his usual berth of Wapping almost as quickly if he waited on the tide and set the hands to aid the drift with the sweeps. Meanwhile, after six days at sea on watch and watch, it would do the crew no harm to have a twelve-hour spell of idleness. Set them up nicely for the unlading, in fact.

It was midway through the forenoon watch when the anchor roared down, and Sam had the hands piped to an early dinner. With a steady ship under him the cook excelled himself, and the dinner of sea-pie and duff was washed down with a quart of ale for all hands, to celebrate the conclusion of another passage. Then all hands turned in to catch up on their sleep. At watch and watch no man ever gets more than three hours sleep at once; after a few days the body craves for a longer rest as a miser craves for gold.

All slept aboard the *Freelove* that afternoon except for the anchor-watch. James Cook, as befits the last-joined apprentice, was the junior hand of the watch; his watch-mate was Andrew Ferguson, the cook – usually known in the dialect as 'Andra'. Not that a cook had any obligation to keep a watch, but the *Freelove* was that sort of ship! Sam Outhwaite was loved and respected by his crew.

James' first passage had been pure joy, once the filth and dust of coaling had been swabbed from the decks, and now he was perfectly happy to stand the watch. He had not come to his first ship as an utter stranger: his waterfront rovings had given him a knowledge of ships and of seamen and their ways.

21

He was able to pull his weight from the start. It was summer, and the passage had been easy. His berth was comfortable, and the Walker brothers fed their men well. Unlike most colliers, Walkers' ships carried one man as cook, and unless the weather prevented a fire being lit there was at least one hot meal a day.

The anchor watch had nothing to do except keep a look-out. The sails had been given a harbour-stow while the sea-pie was cooking, and the hatch-covers were already off and whips rove at the yard-arms ready for unloading. It was warm, and a perfect afternoon for doing nothing.

'Well, there was no great hardship in that passage,' James remarked as he and Andra settled themselves on top of the deckhouse. 'Apart from the watchkeeping – and the washing down at first – there was very little to do.'

'The hardest part is yet to come – when we are anchored in the Pool of London,' Andra said, taking a good look up and down stream before hacking himself a chew from a pig-tail of twist tobacco. He was a man in his fifties, a seaman with some affliction of the feet that prevented him from going aloft. 'So take your ease while you can, lad. You'll need all the strength you can muster when it comes to swaying coal out of the holds.'

'So I've been told.' James refused a chew of the proffered twist. 'How long will that take?'

'This time of year? We'll work dawn till dusk, so it should take about two days.'

'Two days? Well, that will pass.'

'And another day to take in the gravel ballast, then down-stream on the next tide. It's little you'll see of London, James boy, this trip at any rate.'

'Nay, Andra, I did not expect to see very much of it,' James said, rather absently. He had been figuring in his head, a trick he had learned while calculating in terms of eggs and butter and market prices on his farm rounds for Master Sanderson. He had just resolved that if they carried four hundred tons of coal, then every man of the crew would have to shovel a ton every hour to get it out of the hold in two days. He should be able to manage his share of the work, with his hands hardened as they were now. 'Any road, I have already seen a great deal.'

'You've seen nothing yet, lad! Wait till you see Fleet Street and the Strand, with an inn at every third door, and every inn full of arguing philosophers, all busy improving the world. But the end of the sailing season is the time for sightseeing, when we've discharged cargo and lie weatherbound in the face of an easterly.' He spat a jet of tobacco-juice over the side. 'Tell me, what do you reckon to have seen up to now?'

'Oh, a deal of things! Flamborough Head on a fine morning and the Dutch Indiaman the skipper hailed, the King's ships at the Nore, and Greenwich, and that –' he pointed to a flush-decked ship of twice the *Freelove*'s tonnage, chequered black and yellow along the side with a row of gun-ports. 'Another frigate, isn't she?'

'That's what they call a Blackwall frigate,' Andra said, 'an East Indiaman – one of John Company's ships. Out to Fort George they go, with a landing of Brummagem goods and Whitbreads export ale – ah, grand stuff that is, to be sure! – to the nabobs in India, and return back-loaded to the hatch-tops with silks and tea and spices. The skipper of a ship like that makes a fortune in four years, they say. All the officers can make their own private trade, the bos'n makes a fortune from their old rope, and even the foremast hands cannot be pressed into a king's ship. Ah, they're the ships to sail in!'

James' eyes glowed. 'It must be a fine thing to sail in such a ship and see the world.'

'Aye, but it's not for the likes of you and me. Nearly all their foremast hands are lascars, from the Malabar coast. Dark-skinned little fellows, that don't look strong enough to blow the froth from an ale-mug – but they say they are prime seamen all the same. Few of the topmen are English, and the gunner and his mates are mostly old Navy men. Some of those ports are quakers, but there are cannon behind most of them.'

'Quakers?'

'Aye – false gunports painted on to give a ship the look of having more force than she really has.'

'Then some of her company are Englishmen like us.'

'Not very many, and the places go by favour – you have to know the right man to get a birth. You can forget John Company, lad; you're like to be in colliers for a long time. Coal to the Thames, and pit-props from the Baltic – that's your life, and you may as well get used to the idea.'

Andra shifted his quid and spat again, then tilted his raw sennit over his eyes. He did not sleep – he was too old a hand to sleep on watch – but neither did his attitude encourage further talk. James knew the signs, even after such a short acquaintance. He was content to keep silence. There was much to look at in the London river on that fine afternoon.

Midway through the forenoon next day James felt as if he had been shovelling coal since the beginning of time. The kerchief tied across his mouth and nose did not prevent him drawing in coal-dust with every breath. Sweat ran down his back so that his shirt chafed, and his hands were not so hard as he had thought; he suspicioned the beginning of blisters. His thoughts were set on dinner time, and the prospect of a quart or so of smallbeer. If coal-heaving did nothing else, it produced a noble thirst.

There was some sort of commotion on deck, but he paid no attention and went on filling the skep that had just been dropped into the hold. A hand gripped his shoulder; he turned to see the grimed face of Billy Hawthorn, the senior apprentice. 'Skipper wants thee!' Billy yelled. 'Up on deck! You can leave the shovel.'

In the blessed fresh air of the deck James saw a group of his shipmates helping a middle-aged man in shore clothes towards the ship's side. His face was drawn with pain, and his right arm was held in a rough sling.

' 'Tis the tallyman,' Skipper Outhwaite told James. 'He got himself knocked neck-over-croup into the scuppers with a coal-skep. Broke his shoulder, by the look of it – and three Walker ships in the river at once! You said you could write and figure?'

'That I can, skipper.'

'Then here's thy chance to put your learning to good use. You can keep the tally-sheets – the mate will tell what's to do. It would happen on a day like this!'

Jeremiah Swales came up to James with the tally-sheets pinned to a board. ' 'Tis simple enough if you keep your wits about you,' he said. 'We are discharging cargo to four merchants, and there's one tally-sheet for each of them. You find out from the lightermen as they come up which merchant employs them, and you keep tally of the quantity they take, by the skepful. Smartly, now! We've been idle long enough.'

There was a lighter alongside either side of the *Freelove,* and a whip rove to either end of the fore- and main-yards. James asked the ownership of the lighters, found the right sheets on the tally-board, and began his tally. A vertical stroke for each skep up to four, a horizontal stroke for the fifth, then begin at one again... It seemed to James that the art of writing and figuring were not really necessary to a tallyman – anyone who could hold a pencil and count up to five could do it. But the task did require a sharp and quick eye and quick wits and a certain agility. There was no single place on deck where he could stand clear for more than a minute or two from the hands manning the whips; and it was tiring to be continually dodging the swaying skeps. But the air was sweeter and the dust was less, and the time passed in a flash.

In the cuddy that evening Skipper Outhwaite was well pleased with his new tallyman. The line totals were neatly noted in the margin and the full sum shown at the bottom of each sheet. Laboriously the skipper checked one or two sheets, then realized that he had no need to. From then on the *Freelove* carried her own tallyman, nor was he ever known to make a mistake.

But if James never shovelled coal again, it was a different matter when it came to stowing ballast. This was stinking stuff, dredgings from the river-bed, and he wielded a shovel in amongst it with the rest of them. Sometimes the stench was so fearful that they worked in it only half an hour at a time, levelling it off and securing it with coamings so that it would not all slip to one side and alter the trim of the ship. And it would all have to be shovelled clear at the Tyne, to free the holds for the next lading.

Then it was northward ho! again, to ship the ballast ashore on the Ballast Bank at North Shields, and warp under the staithes when the holds were clean. Once more the *Freelove* would settle deep in the water as four hundred ton of Walls-end coal thunder into the holds. Deep-laden and steady she ploughed south, light in ballast and tender she shuttled north, and the novelty soon wore off the passages as far as James was concerned.

Not once in that first year did James set eyes on the much talked of sights of London. He was ashore only three times – and once was at the Shields – and he might have been in a foreign port for all he understood of the quick Cockney twang of the folk in the streets around Wapping. His whole world was the *Freelove,* his whole contact with mankind was with her company.

Then came a Sunday at Wapping in late August, warm and still, when they had finished unloading on the Saturday too late for the lighter-loads of ballast to come out to them. They had roused out that forenoon with a pleasant air of holiday, hosing down the decks under the pale-blue skies with a good deal of skylarking and squirting with the hoses. Andra had given them shore bread and bacon and pease-pottage for breakfast, and had arranged for half a pig to be roasted for them in a cookshop for dinner. In addition there was to be apple-sauce and sage and onions; James looked forward to this feast in store. He had shifted into his best clothes in honour of the day; as he stood idly gazing shoreward, the captain's voice broke into his thoughts.

Sam Outhwaite was a good family man, who took his duties by the apprentices very seriously. He saw to it that they were worked no harder than the rest of the crew, and that they were not only shown what to do but told the reasons for doing it. Also, he had a one-quarter share in the *Freelove,* and was more than well disposed towards James, whose skill as a tallyman had saved him the hire of a longshoreman this last few months. That James was a good tallyman was clear. There had not been one dispute of any note with the shore merchants of late. Seeing what skinflints they were, this was remarkable.

'Ha, James! It's blithe to see you in a shore-going suit and all. Art going to church, then?'

'I had not thought of it, sir. I do not know the churches here.'

'Well, I know the churches, and I am so inclined! Let us go together.' He summoned a wherryman with a blast whistled between his fingers, then marked a certain downcast look on his apprentice's face. 'Never fear, James,' he said, 'we shall be back in time for dinner. I have a share in that half-pig myself!'

Wapping and Whitby had much in common at that time, for all that they lay three hundred miles apart. The northern speech was as common on the streets as the Cockney twang, and many a seaman out of the collier barks had taken a Wapping girl to wife. Some had swallowed the anchor and settled there. Such a one was Robert Batts, who worked as factor for a group of north-country shipowners.

James and the skipper ran into him as they were leaving the church. 'What cheer, friend!' Sam Outhwaite hailed him. 'I have not seen thee for months.'

Sam and Robert had sailed together as mates in the *Free-love* before Sam had gotten the command. Then Sam pushed James forward. 'This is James Cook, my latest apprentice.'

Robert offered his hand. 'Your servant, Master Cook, You look somewhat older than usual for a new apprentice. Belike you transferred your articles, and this is your second ship?'

'No, sir. The *Freelove* is my first ship. I came to the sea somewhat later than is the custom.'

'And shaping well enough, too,' Sam broke in, especially as a tallyman! It is something to have a lad on the half-deck

who is a bit of a scholar. But what do we do, gossiping at the
church-porch like a pair of Cullercoats fish-wives? Bear up,
and let us take a pot of ale at the *Prospect!*'

'Eh, Sam lad, that I cannot do. I have another bit of
business on first.'

'Of a Sunday? Fie on thee, Robert!'

'This is Sunday business – a christening. My daughter
Elizabeth.'

'Of course! You have wed again – did you not lose your
first wife three or four years ago?'

'Four years ago, nearly. And I tell thee, Sam, a man needs
a wife when he has three young bairns on his hands. So I
married again – Janet Stowe, she was, a widow with two
bairns of her own.'

'And this child is your firstborn by your new wife?'

But Robert shook his head. 'The little maid is nearly four.
Dorcas, my first wife, died at her birth. She was a Quaker,
Dorcas was, and did not hold with baptism. So none of our
three were ever christened. But Janet is a stout churchwoman,
and believes in baptism, so the child is to be christened today.
The others were christened a fortnight since, but the little one
had a flux at the time. Ah, here comes Janet now!'

A pleasant faced young woman came up, shepherding a
brood of children and attended by a servant girl. Elizabeth,
who was to be the centre of the impending ceremony, was
a dark-haired child, wearing a dress that was almost a miniature copy of her stepmother's, her ringlets partly covered by
a straw bonnet trimmed with red rosebuds. Her father bent
down to her.

'There now, my poppet! There's naught to be afraid of.
No one is going to hurt thee!'

'If you talk like that to her, Robert, she will think that
someone *is* going to hurt her. She is only strange to all the
bustle, and two strange men –' Mrs Batts broke of smiling.

'Your pardon, my love – I had forgot! May I present my
old shipmate, Mr Outhwaite and one of his 'prentices, Mr
Cook.

They exchanged courtesies, London fashion, James making his leg clumsily enough. The little maid laughed, and ran from behind her step-mother's skirts to stand in front of him.

'Come back, child – do not bother Mr Cook. He is not used to children.'

'Nay, ma'am – I assure you! She will not faze me – I was used to little ones at home, being the eldest. Please let her be.'

The child took his hand and said: I'm 'Lisbeth. In church today they will make me one of God's children.'

'Listen to the lamb!' said Mrs Batts. Robert Batts turned to Sam. 'Instead of going down to the *Prospect*, why do you not attend the christening with us, and then drink the child's health. And Mr Cook also, of course.'

'With the best will in the world,' Sam said.

James smiled down at the little girl and squeezed her hand. She smiled back at him from beneath her bonnet.

'That settles it, then,' Robert said. 'One more thing. Mistress Batts is to be one godmother to Elizabeth, and the parson's lady is to be another. Would you be godfather to the bairn?'

Sam looked to where James was hunkered down to bring himself level with Elizabeth. The two were having a very serious conversation, though there was the ghost of a smile on his apprentice's lips. 'Aye, if you like,' he answered. 'But would it not be better if James stood sponsor for her? They seem to have taken to one another. A lad his age needs responsibility to steady him, especially in the seaman's trade. I can testify to his good conduct and sobriety, and he has such a good head on his shoulders I would not be surprised if he did very well indeed for himself in a few years' time.'

And so it was that James Cook attended the christening of little Elizabeth Batts, and became her godfather.

4   The 'Three Brothers'

The diminishing shape of the *Freelove* stood away to south-ward; James turned his eyes towards the Whitby jetty. Above him the grey herring-gulls wheeled and mewed. He had said his goodbyes to Sam Outhwaite and his mates in the *Freelove*. The coble from the shore was bearing himself and Andra Ferguson towards his new ship, the *Three Brothers*. An odd name, James thought; something more Dutch than English about it. He turned to Andra.

'*Three Brothers*', he said. A queer name for a ship, and I cannot see a reason for it. She's brand new, so they say, so she cannot be named for our owners. There are only two of them.'

'There were three of them once-over,' Andra reminded him. 'The third was drowned when he was just a lad. And that will be the ship itself, at the fitting-out wharf.'

James peered under the sail, to see a new-painted ship standing very high out of the water, with only her jib and mizenmast stepped. He followed her with his eyes until the boatman, sail and rudder balancing one another to a hair, swept alongside the Town Steps. Henry Walker was waiting for them on the quay.

'Well, lads, there's thy new ship!' He gestured towards the ship James had been looking at. 'And thee will be pleased to know, Andra Ferguson, that there is a galley in her.'

'I am. Mr Walker – 'tis something every ship should have.'

Henry Walker turned to James. 'Well, lad – I suppose thee is wondering what all this is about. Sam Outhwaite spoke very highly of thee.'

'I am right glad about that, sir. I have always tried my best.'

'To be sure. That is why I have had thee drafted to this new ship.' Andra had come up with a handcart, and James had not been idle as they spoke. He slung in his duffle bags, settling his chest of books and instruments more carefully. 'Sam tells me thee can take a sight as well as any, and work it out from the tables quicker than most.'

'I can claim no great credit for that, sir – the figures seem to run into my head in a kind of pattern, and all I have to do is to set them down. And that ability I have to thank you and Mistress Walker for. It was you who gave me the snug little chamber backing on to the chimney breast, so that I have warmth and light to study during the laying-up time in winter.'

'Pshaw, lad, thee makes much of a very small thing. It is a pleasure to aid the diligent. But I did not have thee brought to this new ship because thee could work out a sight.'

'No, sir?'

'No. I had in mind to promote thee. Hark'ee, James. Like all colliers, the *Three Brothers* will carry six or seven 'prentices, and some of these will be first-timers. Of them all, you will be head 'prentice, and you will get to know them during the fitting-out.'

'Aye, aye, sir!' James wondered what was coming.

'A ship as big as the *Brothers* could well carry a second mate, but thee is still under articles and there is nothing I can do about that. But I can advance thee to bos'n's mate, and pay thee for it, for if I do that there would be no need to ship a bos'n. But I will put it to thee fairly. Cans't cope with the extra duty and keep up thy studies at the same time? For I would not be the one to stand in the way of a young man at his books.'

James considered a while. As a third year 'prentice his wage was four shillings a month and all found, and it was impossible to save on that. But even if they only paid him the able rate of thirty-two shillings a month a bos'n's mate, he would be able to start putting away some savings, though as yet he had no notion what he would do with them. It did not take long for him to make up his mind.

'The winter lay-up is the only time I can study,' he said, 'at watch-and-watch during the rest of the year I contrive not

to forget what I have learned, that is all. Being bos'n's mate
will not affect that side of my life one way or t'other. I thank
you for the offer, sir, and I will do my best to serve you well.'

With the ship still in the rigger's heads, Andra and James
were the only two living on board, since someone had to be
ship-keeper. While there was no fear of theft in a place like
Whitby, there was the ever-present danger of fire in a wooden
ship, a greater risk than ordinary with the ship so new and
oakum and tar and tallow lying around where caulkers and
riggers were working during the day. They cleared a couple
of berths for themselves in the half-deck, and settled down
to a few weeks of comparative ease and comfort.

After supper that first night, they took their ease on deck.
Tomorrow, James thought, he would get out his books and
spend an hour or so with them after supper. But not this
evening: it had been a long day and there was a pleasant
weariness in him that made idleness attractive for once. They
talked, naturally enough, about their new ship.

'She'll be one of the biggest in the trade,' James said. 'I had
a look at the builder's drafting of her, and figured she must
be more than six hundred ton. Why, there are Indiamen not
much bigger than that.'

'They'd be a deal faster, I'll warrant,' Andra said lazily.
'But they could not have a better galley!'

'And that's another thing,' James said. 'Why a galley complete with stove? You did us well enough with sea-pie and
lobscouse over a brazier on deck.'

' 'Tis a sign of the times,' Andra said. 'Seamen are demand-
ing a galley now; next thing it will be a table to set at, and the
lord knows what after that. Then, the wars with the French
are over for a while. She'd get a better charter from Government with a galley.'

'A collier chartered to Government service?'

'Why not? It happens at the beginning and end of every
war. There are more colliers than anything else afloat in the
Narrow Seas; they make good transports for either men or
warlike stores. When these wars began colliers took thousands
of soldiers across to the Low Countries – that was before your

time at sea– and while there are not so many to bring back, there are still a great number. Some ships will be on charter for a year or more.'

Andra was speaking of the Peace of Aix-la-Chapelle, which marked the end of the wars fought over the question of the Austrian Succession. These had gone on so long that most folk had forgotten why they had ever begun. Neither side could be said to have done well. The French had gained in the Low Countries, but failed in Piedmont against the Austrians, and done badly at sea. Everyone was tired of the war.

'I was still a little lad on the farm when the wars began,' James said.

Andra drew on his pipe. 'I was in the *Speedwell*, and she was taken for a transport. If we are so chartered, please God we carry stores and not soldiers! With soldiers, the ship is at one time crowded and lightly laden, and she'll roll like a bucket. Every last soldier will be sick as a pig, and the bilges will stink to high heaven for weeks after we land them. Soldiers! I'd sooner carry beef cattle, or horses.'

James laughed. 'You cannot mean that, Andra! Every soldier cannot be sick. Besides, we might get a smooth passage, even if we are chartered as a trooper.'

'It could be a passage as smooth as a pond-crossing or the Tyne ferry on midsummer night – but the soldiers would be sick. They start puking as soon as their feet feel deck-planking under them. You'll see.'

James rose and stretched his six feet of height. 'Maybe. Let's take a turn round the 'tween-decks now, to make sure there's no gleed left glowing. It's dark enough to see a spark in the gloom.'

'I've known the Walkers advance a 'prentice to bos'n's mate before,' Andra said after they had done their fire-rounds and settled down again. 'It's advancement for you, true, though you might get as many kicks as ha'pence out of it at first. If you do well, you'll get a mate's berth as soon as you're out of your articles. Meanwhile, they get a keen young bos'n dirt cheap. But there's the Whitby owner for you! *If tha does owt for nowt – do it for thisen!*'

'I had not thought of that – nor do I agree with all of it,'
James told him. 'I do very well out of it, too – I am better paid,
for one thing. And, as you say, there could be a mate's berth
at the end of it.'

'Aye, and a command with a sixty-fourth share a few years
after that. If that is what you want.'

'That is what my cousin Jonty wanted, when we were lads
together – before he was lost at sea. I wanted to sail farther
and see more than anyone had done before. I'll never do that
in a collier.'

'No – but you'd have a chance of finishing up with a fine
house in Grape Lane, Whitby, like the Walkers. I mind
you've spoken of the other thing quite some number of times.
Maybe you could do it, too. There are ways to anything, if a
man has the will – and if he is prepared to give up other
things to get what he wants.'

'I wish you would tell me of them! I confess I cannot see
a way of getting out of the colliers – except to swallow the
anchor and get a living as a tallyman.'

Andra thought for a while before he spoke again. 'This
peace, now. It will not last – no peace ever has. There will
be war again with France in five or six years' time. Then you
could take the bull by the horns and up and volunteer into
the Navy.'

'What! Who in his senses would do such a thing?'

Andra silenced him. 'I ken well – the seaman's pay is bad –
still the same as it was in old Charles Stuart's time, they say.
But get into a channel cruiser at the outset of a war, and
there'd be prize-money for sure. If you were mate in a collier
you'd be able to ship as master's mate in the service. Pay,
prize-money and perks – you'd maybe do very well in a five-
year war.'

'I might fall to shot or splinter, too.'

'And you might be struck down by broken tackle or lost at
sea in a collier. Say you entered the service. At the war's end
the Navy would pay off its ships and put you on the beach.
You'd have more than enough to kit yourself up and gain a
berth in an Indiaman. They ship old Navy men when they
ship anyone on this side.'

James frowned thoughtfully. ' 'Tis a desperate thing to do. Once signed on, there's no release from that service while the war lasts.'

Andra shrugged. 'Others have done it. Frankie Drake, for one. He was an Essex man in colliers at the start, but he took the old Queen's service, and did well enough out of it, too. Devon claims him now, of course, but he only lived there after he made his fortune.'

'There must be few enough who do as well as he did.'

'Very true. And few who have done so well in the coaling trade as the Walkers. But why should you not be one who does well? You are strong, a good seaman, and you have a head for figures. There are plenty who can claim the first two qualities, but not many with the third as well.' He pulled at his pipe. 'Besides, there's the press.'

'The press cannot take a 'prentice in articles, unless he was articled from a poor-house.'

'You'd be well out of articles by the next war. They'll be laying up the Navy ships now; there'll be masts and yards thick as bulrushes at Deptford and Chatham next time we pass. Come a new war, and they'll be getting them in commission again as fast as they lay them up now. The press don't ask many questions at the start of a new war – there'll be hair an skull flying while they fit the Fleet for sea.'

James was thoughtful. 'It would seem that a man like me would have little chance of escaping the press. So why volunteer?'

'For this. A pressed man goes to the guardship, and has no say where he serves, or under what captain. And I don't need to tell you that there are bad captains and good. But a volunteer can nominate the ship and captain he will serve – and the best captains are known all up and down the London river. If war comes, do as I say. Choose a good captain, go for a berth as master's mate – and take your chance of fortune!'

Andra Ferguson's words sank into the back of James' mind, to be almost overlain by other and more present matters. Just over a month later the *Three Brothers* was stretching her new canvas at sea, with coal from the Tyne to the London river.

After they had run a second cargo she was chartered as a transport, as Andra had said she would be. They lay for a few days in the Thames while the articles were being drawn up, and both watches went onto day work. There was plenty to do, taking on extra water, sweetening the holds with coats of limewash and rigging canvas windsails for ventilation.

The skipper, John Waller, shook his head. 'I'm feared it's soldiers we'll be carrying,' he said, 'by the look of those water casks.'

When he had a free evening, James spent it ashore with the Batts; his friendship with the family had grown over the years.

James' god-daughter was now a grave child in her eighth summer, with a sweet, gap-toothed smile. This time he took her a wooden Dutch betty-doll he had got from a Rotterdam smacksman at the Shields. He was astonished at how she had grown in the six months since he had seen her.

'Elizabeth! I declare that soon you will be too great a girl for dolls! And what will cousin James bring you then as a gift?'

'Mamma says that a lady may accept flowers, comfits, or gloves from a gentleman,' Elizabeth said gravely. 'You may bring me flowers.'

'Why not gloves or comfits?'

'Because I already have mittens and a muff to keep my hands warm, and comfits make my teeth ache. Also, I have a great love for flowers.'

Then they might take tea together, and afterwards, he would play spillikins with her and the other children, until they were called to bed.

The *Three Brothers* lay alongside the quay at Flushing. They had been there two days when her freight of soldiers – a company of the Thirty-Eighth Foot – marched down from Middelbing. Flushing to Dublin, and three weeks on the passage. They were light in ballast and the ship rolled and

rolled. They had light winds, and those mostly adverse. As
they got over their sickness the soldiers were friendly enough;
some even lent a hand with the endless trimming of the sails
necessary on such a run. But to James the chief interest of the
passage was that it took him away from the Tyne and the
London river for the first time.

Dublin he found to be a smaller London, transplanted and
shabby, an English city set on the fringe of papist Ireland.
They were more than a week there, so he had time to slip
ashore.

'I had thought to find it different,' he told Andra, as they
drank a pint of porter and ate cockles in an alehouse. 'The
voices are different, and that is all.'

'Make no mistake – it *is* different, lad. This is not Ireland,
only the doorway to it. As my old father used to say – never
judge a land by its seaports. What idea would you get of
Whitby, if all you had ever seen of England was the London
river?'

They sailed for Liverpool in the second week of November, with another company on board, this time of the Forty-
Seventh Foot. The soldiers were overjoyed when they heard
of their destination, for most of them were Lancashire men.
Had the westerlies which had plagued the *Three Brothers* on
her outward passage held they would have made the Mersey
in two days, but the wind backed easterly. They were ten
weary days on that passage.

While they were making good storm damage and sweetening the ship in the Mersey, John Waller saw the Government
agent and obtained leave for the ship to winter at her home
port. The passage from Liverpool to Whitby took five weeks.
Five weeks of bitter winter weather, north-easterly gales, ever
shortening hours of daylight and longer and blacker nights.
They came to Whitby two days after Christmas. They had
scarce strength enough to secure the ship, but now there were
friendly hands ashore to aid them, and afterwards they could
tumble into berths miraculously still and sleep like dead men.

One of the mercies of the seaman's life is that he tends to
forget the bad times and remember the good. As far as James

was concerned, the hazards of the last part of 1748 were
soon over-ridden by the ease and comfort of the beginning of
1749. He hired a horse and made the journey to Airyholm to
see in the New Year with his family. When he came to
Whitby again there were leisurely hours working on the
refit of the ship, and the snug comfort of evenings at the
Walker's house in Grape Lane, when he sat in a quiet corner
with a candle and his books, and explored the ever-expanding
wonders of the world of mathematics. It was a good winter,
after a bad beginning.

They sailed in the second week in April for the Tyne, to
take on coal for the London river. Officially, the *Three
Brothers* was still on charter to the Government, but the
Walkers had their ears to the ground and were pretty sure
the ship would soon be given a clearance. His Majesty's
treasury were not likely to pay the hire of a ship a minute
longer than necessary.

So it proved. John Waller reported his ship to the government agent in Deptford and got his clearance, then they took
on a cargo of bricks and leather and sailed for Bergen. It was
very different to their last passage the year before, for the
winds were light and they had clear skies and sunshine almost
through the twenty-four hours. They found the Norwegians
folk very like themselves, their language oddly akin to the
sing-song Tyneside dialect they used to hear at the Shields.

The trade in pit-props and pine-tar had been greatly hampered by the late wars, and during the next three seasons the
Three Brothers made almost as many voyages to Norway or
the Baltic as she did between Tyne and Thames. Often it was
coal to the London river, a mixed cargo to Scandinavia, with
tar and timber back-loaded to the Tyne. Some of the passages
were sheer pleasure, those in early or late summer mostly, but
some of the midsummer passages were hot and slow, with fit-
ful winds or no wind at all. These were times when the tar
in the deckseams softened and bubbled in the heat. The

winter passages would be a sheer misery, a hell of cold and griping fear.

There was one such passage in late October when fifteen colliers left the Tyne, slipping past Tynemouth Abbey on the same tide. One day out, and the little fleet was well scattered when a sudden north-easter blew chill out of the Baltic. All hands were set to take in sail; bare-poled, the *Three Brothers* drove and clawed its way off a lee shore for three days. It took three weeks to make the Thames that time; of the fourteen ships that sailed with them, only four others berthed off Wapping or Barking.

That was the last autumn that James sailed as 'prentice, acting bos'n's mate. James faced a board of skippers and owners at Whitby in March of '52 to get his rating as Able Seaman. There would be no further examinations for Mate or Master after this; the berths went to those judged best fitted to hold them. After three gruelling hours he satisfied these most diligent examiners that he was fitted to draw the pay of forty-two shillings a month and all found of an able seaman (the pay had been increased only during the last year) and was duly given his clearance from his articles.

He continued as bos'n's mate in the *Three Brothers*, but not for very long. Two months later he was advanced to mate in a slightly older and smaller ship, and since it was advancement he took the berth. He had mixed feelings about it, for it meant parting from men he knew and trusted, and in particular leaving his kindly old sea-mentor, Andra Ferguson. But that is the way of the sea.

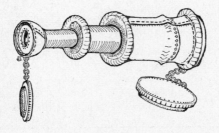

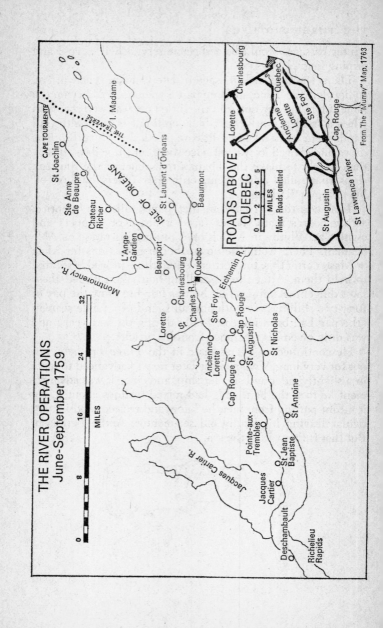

THE RIVER OPERATIONS
June–September 1759

MILES
0   8   16   24   32

Montmorency R.

CAPE TOURMENTE

St Joachim

Ste Anne de Beaupre

Chateau Richer

L'Ange-Gardien

Beauport

ISLE OF ORLEANS

I. Madame

THE TRAVERSE

St Laurent d'Orleans

Beaumont

Lorette

St Charles R.

St Charlesbourg

Quebec

Ste Foy

Etchemin R.

Ancienne Lorette

Cap Rouge R.

Cap Rouge

St Augustin

St Nicholas

Jacques Cartier R.

Pointe-aux-Trembles

St Antoine

St Jean Baptiste

Jacques Cartier

Deschambault

Richelieu Rapids

ROADS ABOVE QUEBEC
Minor Roads omitted

MILES
0 1 2 3 4 5

Charlesbourg

Lorette

Quebec

Ancienne Lorette

Ste Foy

Cap Rouge

St Augustin

St Lawrence River

From The "Murray" Map, 1763

5   The Volunteer

Bos'n Cook, balancing easily on the low poop of the tender *Eagle*, slipped a rope becket over the tiller to give the little ship a shade of weather helm. Sails balanced by rudder, the vessel slipped easily over the Atlantic swells outside of Brest; he knew she would continue thus as long as the wind held. There was coffee aboard, taken from a French prize; while she held so steady as this it might be possible to light a fire and brew up for breakfast. Well-sugared black coffee, in James' opinion, was one of the little things that made the duties of the Inshore Patrol bearable, though on a morning like this it was pleasant enough. Over to larboard lay the dim line of the French coast, visible every time his command rose to the swell; over to starboard three almost translucent rect-angles of sail could be seen from the masthead. They were the tops and t'gallants of *Eagle*, Captain Hugh Palliser, the parent ship of this and half a dozen other small craft all bent to the single task of sweeping the seas clear of the French.

James was lucky in his captain. At first sight, Hugh Palliser seemed to have all the fashionable affectations of a London macaroni — though he stopped short of the quizzing-glass — so that to some he might appear a fop and a fool. He was neither; he had been trained by the great circumnavigator, Admiral George Anson, and he was a fine seaman and a seasoned fighter at sea, two qualities that did not always run together.

Young Levett, the most junior of James' seven-man crew, stuck his head above the hatch. 'Breakfast, skipper! Shall I bring it up top?' They might still be serving in colliers, thought James, so easy was the lad's manner towards his skipper.

'I'll eat it here.' James surveyed the plateful of pickled
mackerel mashed up with biscuit. 'What about some coffee?'

'Only enough charcoal to cook dinner this afternoon.'

'Running out of charcoal, are we? You should have let me
know two days back, you young rascal! We'll have to drop
down on to *Eagle* tonight and re-vittle.' They carried stores
and water at ordinary rations for a fortnight, but sometimes
helped them out by fish caught by themselves or by stocks
taken from small prizes.

No set watches were kept aboard the *Eagle* tender, since
they hove-to on fine nights with two men of an anchor-
watch. There was little risk in this; James, like all old watch-
keepers, slept with one eye open. His berth was right on the
water-line; there was only an inch-and-a-half of planking
between him and the sea, and the hull of the ship was a
sounding-board for the harping of the wind in the rigging.
Any change in the note, or in the sea-thresh so near his ear,
would bring him instantly awake – and all the rest of them,
too.

As James ate he watched the morning bustle about the deck
of his first command. Though called a sloop, the ship had
two masts, the mainmast a little the taller. She was fore-and-
aft rigged on both, with a loose-footed foresail. She carried
short topmasts, with square top-sails on both, so that she was
something between what would be later known as a top-sail
schooner and a brigantine. Neither topsail was set at the
moment, and the look-out at the main-top had been there
since before sun-up. The look-out would tell him if *Eagle*
should shake out her t'gallants, which would be the signal
for James to set his own square-sails to keep pace with her as
well as he could; this was his duty at all times. James' command was on *Eagle*'s larboard side between her and the
shore. His was one of three small craft so placed. The others
were out of his sight, ahead and astern, but they too could
see *Eagle* and she could sight them. There were three more
cutters and sloops to starboard of *Eagle*, so that the sixty-gun
ship sailed in the centre of a circle three leagues in diameter,

with her consorts set at intervals on the rim. In clear daylight *Eagle* could thus keep watch over seven hundred square miles of ocean.

Martin the gunner was cleaning the four six-pounders, heavy metal for such a small craft. Captain Palliser did not believe in burnishing guns in wartime; he held that a burnished gun, while delighting the eye of an old-fashioned admiral, could dazzle the eyes of the gun-layer and put off his aim. As a result the four guns, cleaned daily and wiped with linseed oil, glowed a warm brown like well-used pennies against the weathered oak of their carriages.

Finishing his breakfast, James went below to shave. Or half-below, rather, since there was barely four-foot-six of headroom in the tiny cabin. He stood under the open hatch, head and shoulders out in the weather, his polished bronze mirror propped against the coaming. It was a good face that looked back at him. James was now eight-and-twenty. Peering into the mirror, he frowned a little as he fancied his hair was retreating up his forehead. He wore his hair drawn back and dressed in a short pigtail, as most seamen did. This style went well with his grave eyes, strong nose and chin, and a mouth schooled to a certain firmness.

A full year in the service now, he thought, as the razor rasped across his beard. It had passed quickly enough; already he had served under two captains. It was lucky that the first, a man called Hamer, had been put sick ashore, for he had not been up to his task. For all that he had rated James up to master's mate a month after his entry, James had felt no great affection for Captain Hamer. He never would have respect for any man who fell short of his assigned task.

There had been no war when James entered the service, though it was obvious that it was not far off. He had spent the evening before he went to the depot at the Batts', and small Elizabeth – now rising thirteen – had wept at his going. She was getting to be too great a girl for James to take on his knee, and it *was* gloves or a lace kerchief for a visiting-gift now, instead of a doll or comfits. He had cheered her with jokes that he felt himself were unfunny, for though he had decided to enter the Navy of his own free will, now that the time had come he had felt strangely queasy about it.

For three years – ever since he was quit of his articles – he had been mate in the *Friendship,* and he knew he was almost certain to get the next command the Walkers had to offer. But what, after all, did command of a collier mean? Fifteen or twenty years of labour in the North Sea, with more foul weather than fair, and a modest living ashore on his savings at the end of it. If he survived so long, that was; James had no illusions of the chances a coastal seaman had of seeing old age.

So he had volunteered for the Navy, one jump ahead of the press-gang. For all that he had served his articles and had his discharge as a mate, the highest rate he could enter the Navy was as able seaman. However, that was higher than any other that joined at the Deptford depot with him, and as a result he had the responsibility and the interest of taking a draft from Deptford to Portsmouth by coach to join *Eagle.* It was the longest land journey James had ever made, through a country greener and richer than he had thought possible. After that there was the chaos of the *Eagle,* fresh out of ordinary, and being rated up to the master's mate within a month of joining.

The old hands declared that the first seven years of any war were the worst. If his first few months in the service were an earnest, James was inclined to agree with them. Bringing *Eagle* to be fit for seas was a nightmare, made no better by a captain who should have been invalided from the service years before. The master was a good seaman, but some of the master's mates were drunken wasters and most of the fore-mast hands had never known the feel of a deck underfoot before. Entered from workhouses or the assizes – as an alternative to a jail sentence – they were slow, feeble, and clumsy. With such a captain and crew, it was not to be wondered at that the *Eagle* had some sprung spars and damaged top-hamper in the first of the autumn gales.

Captain Hamer needed no further excuse. Making no effort to refit at sea, he put about at once from his station off

Brest and ran for the shelter of Torbay under reduced rig.
With insufficient sail aloft to steady her the *Eagle* rolled like
the proverbial bucket, so that the lower masts loosened in the
steps and she nearly lost the mainmast. She was so strained
and unseaworthy that a Court of Enquiry sat on her, in secret
as all such Enquiries were. James was called to witness to the
state of the rigging, and was nervous at first. But when he
found that the Court – three post-captains in blue and white
and gold – were both men and seamen he forgot his fears and
spoke up and answered the questions as well as he could. He
never had any fear of a senior officer after that.

So Captain Hamer left, and Hugh Palliser took over the
command. He had been one of the officers of the Court, and
within a month of joining James found himself advanced to
bos'n. And that, in turn, led to his being given command of
the little sloop as soon as the spring weather was fit for the
small craft of the Inshore Patrol to take to sea.

The lookout shifted his quit of tobacco and let his eyes
roll around the horizon. He saw nothing, yet missed nothing,
his eyes sweeping past the three pale trapezoids of the *Eagle*'s
top-sails, then suddenly swung back to them. They were
slowly foreshortening, merging into one. James was just putting his razor away when the hail came.

'Ahoy, the deck! *Eagle* altering course to west'ard – *Eagle*
altering course to west'ard!'

James ducked out of the cabin and finished dressing by the
tiller. For a moment he held his course, for to keep station
broad on *Eagle*'s beam meant he had to make a wide sweep
to the south before he altered course to the west. He had the
chart brought on deck, and studied it carefully. Well astern
of him now was the Point St Matthew, and that other head-
land fine on the larboard bow would be the Point du Raz.
James knew to within a mile exactly where he was.

Captain Palliser could only be attempting to head off a
French prize, and apart from Brest there were half-a-dozen
ports she might make for. Lorient, St Nazaire, Quiberon – a
mort of others, great and small. James' prime duty was to give
warning of French ships coming out, but it was equally his
responsibility to try to prevent them slipping in. Captain

Palliser would approve of anything he did to prevent this, short of losing the sloop.

'Lookout, there! How lies *Eagle* now?'

'Steady on the new course. She has set her t'gallants.'

So *Eagle* was putting on speed. James eased the sloop a point or two to the south-west. 'Let me know when we drop her topsails. I want to keep her t'gallants in sight.'

James called the gunner to him. 'I want all the guns loaded, Martin, and the aftermost pair handed aft to the sternports. Leave the for'ard pair as they are.'

'Barshot, skipper? You a' going to try to slow the chase?' Martin had no doubt there *was* a chase.

'If we can, lad. *Eagle* must have sighted a prize, and we must lie between the prize and the shore. We must try to slow her if we have to.'

Barshot and chainshot were used against the rigging of ships to slow them down, but chainshot – two hollow hemispheres linked by a fathom of steel chain – needed a twelve-pounder at least to be effective. James had no twelve-pounder and no chainshot, but he had barshot, which was said to be a French invention. It looked too childishly simple to be so effective – a hemispherical nosecap, with eight iron bars linked to it like the ribs of an umbrella to the stick. Folded back and secured with a twist of spunyard, these were rammed down on top of the wadded powder charge like a long segmented cylindrical shot. The bars spread wide after firing, and the contrivance howled through the air like a hallowe'en ghost. James had yet to see it in use, but he could imagine the havoc it would wreak in the maze of lifts and sheets and halliards that made up the rigging of a ship.

All hands except James and the look-out went to the task of shifting two of the guns. Inside half an hour the sloop had a sternchase where before she had a broadside, with all four guns loaded and ready.

'Prime and light linstocks, skipper?'

'No – belay at that. We'll wait as long as we can. Stop the vents and put the tompions back.'

There was good sense in this. Gunpowder absorbed moisture, especially the fine priming powder, which made it slug-

gish in firing. And if linstocks were lit too early the glowing
end became choked with a layer of ash. Martin stopped his
vents and slipped in the tompions. There was little he could
be taught about keeping powder dry.

'Deck, ahoy! Second sail in sight! Broad on to the starboard
bow!'

The chase, James thought, with a tightening of the chest,
as he gave the helm to Martin and ran up the shrouds to the
maintop. The look-out gave way to him, and he braced himself against the topmast with an arm through the shrouds,
then sought the newcomer in the tiny field of his telescope.
The motion of the ship was much greater here, thirty-five feet
above the deck; for a while he saw nothing but dizzy circles
of sky and sea. Then the image swept past his eye; he lost it,
then found it again. A tiny segment of white sail showed
above the rim of the world, which resolved itself into the
t'gallants of a fair-sized ship. She was headed slightly across
James' own course, and would be making good speed with a
soldier's wind almost dead astern. He turned to the look-out.

'Never mind the *Eagle* now, lad – watch the newcomer!
If those topgallants aren't French, I'll eat my hat.'

'Aye, skipper, I'll not lose him!'

'Good lad! D'you want the telescope?'

'Not I! I might drop 'un. I see pretty near as well without
'un anyways.'

James slid down the back-stay to the deck and gave the age-
old order for the first. 'Clear ship for action! All hands
shift into clean clothing!'

There was little to clear, for they had no fire lit or partitions
to strike down, so it was a matter of filling the water-buckets,
keeping the decks wet with the pumps, and scattering sand
for foothold. Three and four at a time the crew went to the
fo'c'sle to don clean shirts and drawers. A splinter wound
almost always drove a rag of clothing into the flesh, and if
this were dirty it festered and poisoned. James had shifted his
rig that morning; now, as he strewed sand with the rest, a
nice little problem in mathematics ran through his mind.

His problem was two-fold. The first part – what course
must he steer to bring himself a mile ahead of the prize? The

second part – when this was done, where would he be in rela-
tion to *Eagle*, other things being equal? Not that the answer
to the second part greatly mattered. *Eagle* would be somewhere within sight, provided he was still between the quarry
and the shore. And there he would surely be, for on such a
day of wind and sunshine, this required only a certain fortitude of mind.

Three hours later, James needed that fortitude. The chase
was dead ahead of him, about a mile distant, and coming
down fast. Ten minutes at most, and he would have to do
something, or be either run down or left astern. And to be
left astern meant he would have taken the Frenchman's broadside in passing. She was a French Indiaman, they thought,
built on much the same lines as a frigate. She'd be well-armed,
but only for defence against pirates in eastern waters. Probably no bow-chasers, but a fair broadside and some heavy
metal in the stern-chase. For all her gunports and war-like
looks, it was not her task to seek trouble, but to run from it
and try to fight it off.

James' orders were already given. Three hands were told off
to handle sheets and braces at need, Martin and three others
to serve the guns, and he himself would be at the tiller and
direct the fight. Any minute now!

Eagle could be seen from the deck, still hull-down, and
unlikely to overhaul the chase before sundown unless James
could slow it. One of the other sloops was in sight, but it was
up to James and his crew to do all they could. To all intents
they were alone, at least for the next hour. Which, after all,
was all that mattered.

His belly felt full of wind; he wanted to swallow and
swallow. It was a hellish temptation to open fire, but he knew
Martin's carefully loaded barshot could do no damage at this
range. He steeled himself to wait until she was within a
cable's length – a hundred fathoms – before he opened fire.
Although that would also bring her to within long musket
shot, and she just *might* have a few three-pounder swivels
for'ard.

She had. Twin clouds of smoke billowed from her heads,
and a column of spray rose from the sea a hundred feet astern.

James failed to see where the second shot went – and they were still out of the range he had set his mind on. He eased the sloop off the wind a little, thus taking avoiding action and closing the range at the same time. Half-a-minute to load those swivels – which he was sure they were. That splash had been a very small ball. He counted out a half-minute under his breath, bringing the sloop back to her original course. As he did so, the quarry fired again, but he saw the fall of neither shot.

'Put him off nicely, skipper! I reckon we could try some long hops ourselves now!'

'Wait until after he has fired again. I'll only change course once this time.'

He eased off the wind again, watching the Frenchman as he came on at a slight angle to their course, looking as big as the Tower of London. The grey clouds of powder-smoke erupted from his bow again, one of the balls striking a dozen feet alongside of them.

'Now, Martin! Fire at will!'

There was a double crash from astern, and everything was suddenly blotted out in a cloud of bitter smoke, under cover of which the guns were sponged and rammed and loaded again. James eased back on to the old course, so that the stern-chase was just a shade off the target. Martin ran to the gun on the larboard side forrard, which was already trained as far aft as the wide port would allow. The gun roared and the smoke blew forward so that James saw the effect of the shot: a huge rent in the enemy's forecourse.

'Good shooting, Martin! A shade more wind, and that sail would flog itself to tatters!'

'It's a fair start, skipper. But what we want is spars about their ears!'

James brought himself stern-on to the Frenchman once more, and again his little stern-chase thundered its challenge. All his qualms had gone now. His belly no longer fluttered; nothing mattered except bringing down the enemy spars. In his mind's eye he saw the two ships like two chessmen moving on a board, unequally matched, a knight against a queen per-haps. Again he was blinded by the smoke of their own dis-

charge, and bore off on the other tack to give the starboard
forrard gun its chance. As he did so, a ball from the other's
chase ricochetted from a wave-crest and scored a long groove
in the deck. James scarcely felt a qualm.

'A miss is as good as a mile!' he sang out, cheerily. 'Give
them some of their own medicine, Martin!'

But there was no visible sign of that shot striking at all, and
the running fight continued. Loading and firing, twisting and
dodging, James contrived to keep in and out of the Frenchman's course, always between the quarry and the shore. The
Frenchie would never make Brest now, that was certain, and
every mile they took him along the coast gave *Eagle* a better
chance of catching up. They ran through the splashes of a
dozen near-misses, and one or two balls came inboard so that
there were minor splinter wounds to tend. A hole appeared
in one of his own top-sails, and a halliard parted with a whip-
like crack. James gave the order to cease fire, to give the hands
a chance to reeve a new halliard, and then Martin fired one
last defiant shot, almost at a venture.

Intent on their own affairs, and gulping down draughts of
cider to ease their powder-parched throats, they saw only the
last of the fall of the Frenchman's topmast. Slowly, taking the
t'gallant with it, the towering spar folded forward like the
blade of a clasp-knife into the haft, and as it did so the un-
balanced ship flew up into the wind. The fall of the forward
masts took the man t'gallant with it, and the great ship slowed
up, hampered by the raft of tangled rigging that cluttered her
larboard side.

James had no time to admire the sight. As the chase slewed
and slowed her broadside came around, and the sloop was
right in her centre. Her gunports erupted in smoke towards
her gadfly of a tormentor, but the list she had with the wreckage of her other side caused the guns to point high. Howling
like banshees, the round shot passed overhead, and it took all
James' determination not to duck, for all that the old hands
said that you never hear the shot that strikes you.

Hastily he brought the sloop round and out of the way,
while Martin sucked his teeth at the poor gunnery of their

foe. Well out of range, he gave the orders to heave-to, and stood by to watch *Eagle* bring the foe to terms.

'One hand to the look-out!' he said. 'We don't want any *chasse-marée* coming down on us unseen. And get a fire going Levett – I don't care if it is the last of the charcoal. I feel like a pot of coffee tonight, if ever a man did!'

6 *Master of the 'Pembroke'*

James approached the quarterdeck, hat in hand as custom decreed, and waited to catch Captain Palliser's eye. The captain was talking to the shipwright; he was hatless and in his shirt sleeves, his sword still hanging from a lanyard looped about his wrist. Like most naval officers, he preferred to go into action unencumbered by belt or scabbard.

The shipwright saluted with his hat, and turned away about his business. 'Ah, bos'n! Saw your holding action. Very pretty – very pretty piece of work indeed. Did you sustain much damage?'

'Very little, sir, and all made good, pretty well, except a shot-hole in one of the top-s'ls. Sloop fit for sea, sir, but we do need vittles and charcoal.'

'And the butcher's bill?'

'Two men slightly wounded by splinters, sir. We've gotten the splinters out and treated them ourselves. The men are fit for duty, sir.'

'Excellent. They must see the surgeon and get a hurt certificate – never know when they might need it to get a Greenwich pension. But you did very well. If you hadn't hung on so and cut up her rigging, I declare she'd have got away – been in Quimper or Lorient tonight, sure as eggs! You used bar-shot, I suppose?'

'Aye, sir. Couldn't think of anything else that might stop her, sir.'

'Mention it in your report. Nasty stuff, bar-shot. Not gentlemanly, eh, bos'n? But then, we're not gentlemen – we're seamen! All the same, your efforts have set me a pretty problem. You've half-dismasted the prize, and she has to be sail back to the Thames. Let me think!'

James, conscious that he still had to find the purser and get some stores for the sloop, stood and held his peace. The captain turned. 'You're an old collier hand, bos'n – mate, wasn't it? So you must know the entrance to the London river pretty well?'

'That I do, sir.'

'And you must have handled craft pretty well as big as that Frenchman. What about you taking her in? I can make you acting-master for the passage.'

'And the sloop, sir? She needs vittles and firing.'

'You'd like to take your own crew, I suppose?'

'Aye, sir. They're good lads, and we know each other. But I'd need a few more for yon ship, damaged as she is.'

'To be sure. I can spare you four seamen, and six marines to guard the prisoners. I'd gladly let you have more, but I'm devilish short as it is. It's the best I can do.'

'I'll manage very well on that, sir. With permission, I'll get my gear together, and warn the lads in the sloop.'

'Pray, do so. See my clerk in an hour; he'll have all your papers in order, including the acting warrant. Oh – and bos'n! As prize-master with an acting warrant, your share of the prize-money may be quite a sum, especially as I shall enter you and your crew for double shares, at my expense. Have you a prize-agent?'

'No, sir. I had not thought it necessary.'

'Nor is it for the ordinary Jack, who boozes his share the minute he gets ashore. But this may be a long war, and you may go quite a way up the ladder before all is done. I'll give you a note to my own man – Simmons, in Church Street, Deptford. He charges ten per cent, but he gives good value for it – after all, the more he can get for you, the bigger his own cut! No, don't thank me – glad to do it.'

Acting-master! James could scarcely believe his good fortune. This would mean he would get an officer's share in the value of the prize, for the captain took one third, the officers one third split between them, and the lower deck the remainder. He would not have been a Yorkshireman of Scots extraction had he not felt a certain satisfaction at being maybe as

much as two hundred pounds richer as a result of one long
day's work. Damaged or not, short-handed as he might be,
nothing was going to stop him taking the prize into Deptford.
He hurried back to the sloop, to give the good news to his
crew.

'Then you have no regrets, James – none at all?' Robert
Batts and James were emptying a tankard apiece at the
Prospect Inn. The passage to Deptford was accomplished,
the prize safely brought in. 'I must say you look well enough
on it.'

'I do well enough and I think I have prospects. I've had
one acting-warrant, but what I really need is a permanent
warrant. Then I think I might do quite well, one way and
another.'

'I might drop a line to Joe Osbaldeston about that, and get
a few others I know of to endorse it. We could ask for a lieutenant's commission for you, which should give you a flying
start. Captain Cook, Royal Navy! I like the sound of that!'

'I do not aim so high, Mr Batts. And who is this Mr
Osbaldeston? I never heard of him, though it sounds a right
Yorkshire name.'

'And Joe's a right Yorkshire tyke! He's the member of
Parliament for Scarborough – that includes Whitby, of course
– and he's always strong to help the sea-faring fraternity.'

'I see.' James took a pull on his tankard. 'Well, his help can
certainly do no harm, but if you write, tell him to ask for no
more than a master's warrant. You have to serve six years
before you can be made lieutenant, and I'm better fitted to be
master, anyway. And there's another thing that you can do
for me, if you will.'

'Aye, if I can – just name it.'

'I was made acting-master to bring in a big prize, so I shall
get an officer's share of the prize-money. What it will be I
don't know – it depends on how the cargo sells – but even the
ship will bring a good price, for she's a French Indiaman. I've
got an agent to see that I get my rights in the matter of prize-

money. Would you be so kind as to take it over from him and put it to use?'

Robert Batts nodded. 'Yes, I'm willing to look after your funds for you. What do you say if I put it into house property? Houses always go up in value when there is a war on.'

James knew he could trust the other's advice. 'Just so long as the money is in something reasonably secure and not lying idle.'

'Nothing so secure as house property, James! A house or two will never come amiss. . . I suppose you'll be wanting to marry one day.'

'So I might – but if I do, it will not be for some time yet.' James paused. 'Speaking of that, there's something on my mind. Elizabeth is fast growing up.'

' 'Tis a habit young maids have. One minute they're nought but gap-toothed bairns, the next thing they've grown and wedded and flown the nest.' Robert Batts looked keenly at his young friend. 'But what of it, James?'

'I am no lady's man, and I doubt if I've much chance of becoming one. But the thought of Elizabeth marrying another troubles me.'

'James, lad! That cannot happen for a while yet! The lass is but fourteen!'

'I know that well enough. I also know I'm well-nigh old enough to be her father. But you might as well have it straight, Mr Batts. If I do not marry Elizabeth, I fancy I will not marry at all.'

Robert Batts sat silent for a while, pulling slowly at his church-warden pipe and looking out at the shipping in the crowded river. Then he smiled. 'Well, you've known Elizabeth long enough, and you are old enough to know your own mind. In five or six years' time she will be a woman grown, and you will still be on the sunny side of thirty-five. She's a serious minded lass, no vapouring flibbertigibbet. Aye, you'd make a right handsome pair. I'd have no objection, so long as you promise me one thing.'

'And that is?'

'That there's to be no word of marriage between you until

Elizabeth is eighteen – and if she should fancy another by
then, she's to have her choice and you won't blame me.'

'Fairly spoken, sir – we'll drink to that, in wine. Tapster!
Two glasses of Madeira!' The wine came, and James raised
his glass. 'Rely on it, sir! I'll do naught to fill Elizabeth's head
with fancies, but do my best to have her think me the best
man she knows. To our closer relationship, Mr Batts!'

The next two years were hard but profitable ones. James
sailed either in *Eagle* or in one of her sloops or cutters, and
took more than one prize back to Deptford. *Eagle* was never
part of a fleet, and any fights were single-ship actions. Of these
the last and most memorable was against the frigate the *Duc
d'Aquitaine*, off-shore from Brest. This vessel had been built
as a French East Indiaman, and had slipped a cargo of silks
and spices into Lisbon and then run light in ballast to Brest.
She was big for a frigate, some 1,500 tons, but this great size
fitted her admirably as a commerce raider. The French Navy
in Brest had taken her over, brought her up to strength in guns
and men, and the intention was that she should use her size
and power to harry English trade in the Indian Ocean under
the golden lilies of royal France. Like British Indiamen, she
carried a large crew of lascars, and the French admirals
thought these would not be at their best anywhere except in
their own home waters.

So the *Aquitaine* took advantage of a late summer fog to
slip out of Brest, being given an offing of nearly a league by
being towed out behind two shore-galleys. With the fog there
was only the lightest of airs, and after the galleys left, the
great ship, almost becalmed, drifted off-shore with all sail set.
During the forenoon the fog lifted, and by chance the *Eagle*
was within sight of her, less than three miles away.

James was in the *Eagle* at the time, which was cruising in
company with another ship of equal force, *Medway*, commanded by Captain Agnew. The morning fog had been low
on the water out at sea, and the two ships were within quarter
of a mile of each other, in full sight from the mastheads.

Captain Agnew had taken advantage of this to pay a visit
to his brother captain. They were on the quarterdeck together
when the first sighting of the *Duc d'Aquitaine* was reported.
At the same time the first stirrings of a breeze was felt.

'A breeze, by gad!' Hugh Palliser declared. 'Kind Neptune,
do but strengthen it a little, and I have that Frenchman.'

'Nay, Hugh – *we* have him, surely?' Captain Agnew
prompted. 'You don't think to take on a ship that size single-
handed?'

'Why not? I'll grant you she's big, but there's little enough
in her. Those teak-built Indiamen only have scantlings to
carry eighteen-pounders – and I have twenty-fours on my
lower deck. I'll warrant she has nothing but lascars for topmen, and they're naught but rabbits until they get to their
own warm sun again. As for her gun's crews, they're at sea
for the first time, some of them, and they've not had time to
do a gun-drill. No doubt she'll knock a few spars about our
ears, but if we both engage her we'll both suffer damage.'

'There's something in that. And you're the senior. But –
what will folk say when they hear I stood to one side and let
you go in single-handed?'

'We'll toss a guinea for the honour – winner to engage the
Frenchman, loser to stand by and provide a prize crew.
Whichever way it goes, I give you orders in writing. We'll
use my lucky guinea – here it is. What do you call – head or
spade?'

It was as hard an engagement as James had known up till
then, for all that *Eagle* brought heavier metal to the fray than
Aquitaine. There was enough wind when they came up to
each other to give steerage way, and Captain Palliser had the
weather gauge. He crossed the T – that is, took *Eagle* across
the stern of *Aquitaine* – and raked the enemy through the
sternports with his larboard battery. Against most ships this
would have been enough, since the shot of five-and-twenty
heavy guns passing end to end through a crowded gun-deck
would have wrought terrible havoc.

But *Eagle's* carefully aimed broadside wasted its force on a
well-nigh empty space, as they found later on. The *Duc*

d'Aquitaine carried her batteries high, the gundeck being less than six feet beneath the spardeck, with a spacious 'tween-deck space above the holds. With a great hole blasted in her stern the *Aquitaine* swept on, bringing her helm over to come on to the same course as *Eagle,* and set about doing as much damage as she could with bar-shot.

James and his bos'n's party had a hectic hour splicing shot-through halliards and lifts and clearing wreckage that could not be quickly repaired. The *Duc d'Aquitaine*'s batteries were concentrated on the rigging and the spar-deck, so that the gunners in the hot, red-painted gun-decks suffered little loss. The Frenchman was intent on crippling *Eagle* and so making her escape. The fact that *Medway,* undamaged and watching, could prevent this did not seem to occur to the French captain. Perhaps, thought James, since the action must be noticed from some high point ashore, he was counting on assistance from the *chasse-marées* – those heavily armed shoreboats crammed with men, half-galley and half-lugger. This was easily the hottest action James had ever been in.

Much the same thoughts came to the mind of Captain Agnew on *Medway,* and while he had no doubt of the ultimate outcome, he felt the sooner the engagement was settled the better. He sent his launch and cutter across with a boarding party – half marines and half seamen – and the eighty men in the two boats made all the difference. Hooking on to the larboard chains – the *Aquitaine*'s disengaged side – they poured over the mizen rigging and took the quarterdeck. With her captain and most of the officers in enemy hands, the fight went out of the Frenchman, and the lilied banner of France came down to the sound of British cheers.

The butcher's bill showed the way the fight had gone. Fifty-four Frenchmen had died, and she had two hundred and more wounded, some of whom died that night. *Eagle* had ten dead and two and thirty wounded. It was the end of the fighting season; of the five hundred odd who had sailed in her from Portsmouth in March, only three hundred and forty remained. Battle, wounds, and sickness had accounted for more than a third of her company in less than half a year. Now she was a crippled ship, not fit to hold her place in the line until she had been refitted and her crew brought up to strength. That meant a return to Chatham or Portsmouth.

Late in the season though it was, the seas were calm. As the sun set there was an off-shore wind. *Medway* watched over victor and vanquished as they crept out to sea, making repairs as they sailed. Through the night they buried the dead – there was a Popish chaplain in the *Aquitaine* to read the burial service over the dead Frenchmen – and tended the wounded and did what they could to the rigging. It was a long weary haul back to Portsmouth, where *Eagle* paid off into dockyard hands, and James found himself, for the first time in years, a seaman without a ship.

On the morning of October 27th, 1757, the day being his twenty-ninth birthday, James walked from the Batts' house in Brick Lane to call on the Admiralty agent to see if there were any orders for him. He had been told that Mr Osbaldeston's efforts might be meeting with some success, and that already he had been named for a warrant as Master on two occasions. Both were for sloops-of-war (not to be confused with the sloops of the Inshore Patrol) but both had sailed before he could be fetched from *Eagle* to join them. It was, then, with hope in his heart that he went this day to the agent.

He had Elizabeth on his arm that morning, a slightly built girl of almost seventeen, dressed soberly but well, as befitted the daughter of a rising merchant. She wore silk gloves and carried a bearskin muff, both items having found their way to the house in Brick Lane from the freight of French prizes. James, true to his word to say nothing of marriage until Elizabeth was eighteen, was on affectionate but cousinly terms with her. To the passers-by it was obvious that the girl had the greatest regard for the tall young seaman who was her escort.

The agent's clerk had a missive for James, handing it over in exchange for a signature in the correspondence book.

Elizabeth wrinkled her nose when she saw the paper. 'Oh, fie, cousin James! Sailing orders already, and you have been with us but a few days!'

James laughed. 'These are not sailing orders – at least, not

ordinary ones. For a lower-deck sailor such as myself, sailing
orders are a list of names on a parchment, bidding you which
ship to go to.' He sliced his penknife under the fouled-anchor
seal and unfolded the stiff paper. He held it so that Elizabeth
could see – for she had been taught her letters – and they read
it together:

*Know by these Presents that My Lords Commissioners for
the Office of Lord High Admiral of England present their
Compliments to Mr James Cook, presently Serving as Boat-
swain in His Majesty's Ship 'Eagle', Captain Hugh Palliser,
and by this Warrant do advance Him to the rank of Master,
Royal Navy. The said James Cook, Master, Royal Navy, is
directed to repair on board His Majesty's Ship 'Pembroke',
her Captain not yet being appointed, and to take up His
Duties not later than Noon on the Tenth day November this
year of 1757. And he is further Directed to acknowledge in
Writing to their Lordships that he has Received and will
Carry out these Orders.* It was signed with a single name –
Anson. James looked at the signature of the circumnavigator
with awe. He had never expected to receive any communica-
tion signed by such a great one.

He passed it to the clerk, who nodded and said: 'My con-
gratulations, Mr Cook! *Pembroke* is one of our newest two-
deckers, so at least all your gear will be sound. Do you wish
to write your reply here? I have copies of a formal letter that
only require your signature.'

'Thank you! I will gladly write my reply – but in my own
hand. If I might borrow your copy to get the trick of the
phrasing?'

Elizabeth was delighted. 'Oh, James! How wonderful this
is! Not to go until the tenth of next month! That is almost
two weeks you can continue your stay in our house!'

James often smiled to himself afterwards when he recalled
Elizabeth's reaction to his first Warrant, but in fact he needed
those two weeks to get together the uniform and equipment
fitting to his new rank. The clerk at the agent's paid him the
twelve pounds clothing allowance, but it was as well that
James had his savings to draw on, for the allowance did not

cover half of the things he found he would need. Hitherto, he had not been required to wear a uniform dress. Some captains rigged out their crew in a uniform, at their own expense, but this differed from ship to ship, and was often pretty fancy. The usual lower-deck rating wore duck trousers, often made from a worn sail, with a canvas smock as a working rig. On his rare shore leaves, he would be clad in those same trousers with a shirt and coloured neckerchief, short jacket, buckled shoes and a rounded varnished hat.

Never again would James wear this free-and-easy rig. Now he had to have breeches and stockings – of silk for dress occasions, a long waistcoat and jacket with gilt crested buttons, and a tricorne hat. Where once he had fought with a standard three-pound naval cutlass, he was now required to possess his own sword, and to wear it at all times. Two weeks was little enough time to get all this new gear.

'But it should have been a lieutenant's commission,' Robert Batts commented. 'You have earned it, James, if ever a man did.'

'I'm just as happy it is not,' James replied. 'This way, under the captain, I am chief man in the ship. I have no wish to be just another fighting-man at sea. As master, everything except the guns, powder, and small-arms is in my charge. And I shall have a cabin to myself.'

Maybe this was the thing he looked forward to most in his new appointment: his private cabin. He knew it would be small and would not have headroom for his more than six feet, but it would be his to work in and study in his off-duty hours. It would be the first time that he had had his own place since those far-off days when he was 'prentice to William Sanderson, long ago in Staithes.

By dint of taking a hackney coach from Barking to the Strand, and from there an outside seat on the *Highflyer* coach, James did the journey to Portsmouth, all eighty-six miles of it, in just over fifteen hours. If the mail-coaches improved their speed at this rate, James thought, he might be able to get north to see his family one of these days. Maybe as a wedding trip, in a few years' time. His father had given

up farming now, and was in the building trade. He had
written to tell James about the house he had built at Ayton.
James had not seen any of his family these last four years and
more.

At the staging halts where the horses were changed the talk
was all of the new phase of the war which had been pro-
claimed: to hold the French on this side of the Atlantic, and
drive them out of the Canadas on the other. It was news to
James that *Pembroke* was to be one of a powerful fleet intended to cross the ocean to that end – thrilling news. He was
a master, Royal Navy, on his way to take up his first officer's
appointment, having served at sea for eleven years. This
would be the first time he had ever been away from the North
Sea or coastal waters.

James knew as little as most Englishmen about the Americas, except that the French and their Indian allies had been
a sore trial to the English colonists farther south. French-
provoked Indian raids had been going on for years, even when
there was peace between England and France elsewhere in
the world. Now that there was a general war, England had
decided to make an end of the French on that side of the
world once and for all. James had always been one for listening
rather than talking, and he did some rare good listening during that journey to Portsmouth.

Pembroke, when he found her, proved to be a graceful
sixty-four gun ship, finishing off a refit and storing ship at the
same time. A few days after James joined her, she moved from
the fitting-out basin to a berth in the harbour, near the victualling yard on the Gosport side. The captain had not yet joined
and James and the first lieutenant, Jeremy Clarke, a man about
his own age, shared the responsibilities between them. They
had but a skeleton crew at this time, bos'ns and gunners'
mates, all older men and staid hands, and a few score half-
mutinous seamen, from the Press Office. It seemed to James
he was everywhere at once, now checking some item of rigging with the bos'n, maybe condemning a cask of salt beef
with the cooper, or authorizing an issue of slop clothing to
cover the near nakedness of a draft of felons, sent by the Press

Office from Winchester Assizes. The snug cabin was there all right, but he only saw it to drop exhausted on the cot and sleep before turning to for another seemingly endless day.

They completed the provisioning and moved out into Spithead, to an anchorage midway between the mainland and the Isle of Wight. They received another draft from the Press Office once they were away from the shore and had some chance of keeping them inboard. The mess-decks were the usual bedlam of doxies and sailors' women. They were still one hundred and ten short of complement when Captain Palliser joined from the *Eagle*.

'This will never do, gentlemen,' he said, as he was going over the watchbills with James and Jeremy Clarke in the comparative peace of the great cabin. 'Much as I dislike it, there's only one thing to be done. We must put on our own Press. You agree?'

'I agree,' said Jeremy, while James nodded. 'The taverns, sir?' There were over eighty taverns between the dockyard Main Gate and the Unicorn Gate, all of which did a good trade. 'They have often enough been pressed, I know –'.

'Not the taverns!' said the captain, firmly. 'All we'd get there would be watermen and dockyard hands, every manjack with an exemption certificate. While you gentlemen were about your duties this forenoon I took a boat and had a look at the commercial basin. Gentlemen – what riches! At least forty sail of coasters!'

'They won't have above a dozen hands in each, sir,' James said. 'And some of them will be 'prentices that we can't touch. Still, two or three from each, and our problem is solved.'

'My thoughts exactly, Mr Cook! And tonight's the night – before *Centurion* or *Northumberland* get the same idea. I see you smile, Mr Cook?'

'Aye, sir. I was just thinking that I did well four years back, when I volunteered to avoid the Press. I don't like it – but, as you say, sir, it's the only thing to be done. And this way we are sure of getting prime seamen.'

Thus it was that James took part in his first and last Press. Both the commercial basin and the town jetty were thronged

with ships, and with a slight pang of homesickness James saw
a few colliers among them. He managed to leave the boarding
of these to Mr Clarke, having no wish to impress an old shipmate.

Almost inevitably in that small seafaring world, one such
was caught up. Ninety in all they took, which, with another
score of felons from Chichester Assizes, would complete their
crew. The ninety unwilling recruits were read into the service
the morning after their taking, and as he and Jeremy Clarke
were re-making the watch-bill, James heard a familiar voice.
Looking up, he saw Andra Ferguson.

'Andra, old friend! I'm blithe to see you, but sorry it has to
be like this.'

Andra grinned, showing tobacco-stained teeth. 'You're no
sorrier than I am – sir! It looks as if I would have done better
to take the advice you seem to have profited by.'

'Old shipmates, eh?' Jeremy Clarke said. 'Ah, well – it
happens!'

'Rather more than that, James told him. 'Ferguson, here,
was my sea-daddy when I was a raw 'prentice. I'd appreciate
it if I could have him in my part of the ship.'

'To be sure, Mr Cook. After all, I shall get most of the
felons tomorrow from Chichester. I can afford to be generous.
What did you sail as, Ferguson?'

'My feet trouble me, and I've shipped as cook or sailmaker
these past few years. I can make a passable shift at either, sir.'

James smiled suddenly. 'You can take my word for this, Mr
Clarke: last night's work will make us the envy of the fleet.
We have just shipped the only cook I know who can make
salt beef taste like a *fricassee* of fresh veal!'

7 Louisbourg

Bedford Basin lay wide under the May sky, the bluer by contrast with the dark conifers in the woods ashore. The morning air was fragrant with the tang of salt and resin. The fleet in the Basin was rousing to a new day; the ships outnumbered the houses in the little settlement ashore.

Eight bells sounded through HMS *Pembroke*, and a marine bugler stood at the quarterdeck guardrail and sounded a strident G. James, in time with everyone else on the upper decks, turned aft and swept off his hat. There was a stillness as the ensign was run up to the peak of the gaff, and the bugler sounded another G. The great flag spread in the morning breeze, hats were clapped on heads, and the ship stirred to life. Officially it was now the forenoon watch. A new day had begun.

Glancing up at the white ensign, James reflected that but a few days ago it had been the red, but now that Admiral Boscawen had arrived, *Pembroke* had been promoted to a place in the van, and had changed her colours. The admiral had been lucky in his passage from Portsmouth – under four weeks from England to Halifax. Sailing last December, *Pembroke* had taken nigh on three months; but then, she had brought a troop convoy, and had been two weeks refitting storm damage at the Azores.

It had been a rough passage all right. One in ten of the soldiers had not survived the journey, and they had lost two transports with all hands. *Pembroke* had lost forty of her six-hundred-odd crew – but that was only to be expected in a new-commissioned ship. The remainder would be all right. If a man survived his first twelve months at sea, it took a good deal to kill him after that.

65

There was a fine smell coming from the direction of Andra Ferguson's galley, and James ate a hearty breakfast of fried salt pork and shad roe, soft shore bread and coffee. He mopped up his plate with a crust of bread, had a second cup of coffee – he cared little for small-ale at breakfast these days, unless there was nothing else – and went to make his morning report to the captain.

'I doubt if he will be able to spare you time, Mr Cook,' Saul Pascoe, the captain's clerk, told James. 'He has just now been bidden to the Flag, to eat breakfast with the admiral. I was about to ask you to have the gig ready.'

'Thank you, Mr Pascoe. I'll give the orders for the gig, and await the captain's pleasure by the entry-port.'

The gig's crew looked very smart, James thought, as the bowman hooked on at the foot of the ladder. The boat was painted in blue-and-white, and the colours were repeated in the rig the crew wore: white duck trousers, tight in the seat and flared to the knee, blue shirts and a white neck-cloth, topped with a round white hat girdled with a blue ribbon. Vanity, of course, and all paid for from the captain's pocket. The same vanity that had prompted himself and Jeremy Clarke to purchase leaf for the gilding of the ship's name above the stern-windows. But it did enable *Pembroke* to show a good face to the Fleet.

The side-boys stiffened to attention, and he turned to see Captain Palliser, stooped under the deck-beams. James' hand snapped to his hat-brim and the captain flapped a negligent hand in acknowledgment.

'Good morning, Mr Cook. All ready, I see. It would not do to keep the admiral waiting, would it? I suspect I will be with the Flag most of the forenoon, and I suggest you discontinue your sounding of the harbour. It might be better if you stayed on board.'

'I was intending to do that, sir. I have soundings enough to work up into a tolerable chart of the eastern end of the Basin. I noticed the ship a trifle down by the head yesterday, and I had it in mind to shift stores on the orlop to correct it. By your leave, of course, sir.'

'By all means, Mr Cook. I need not ask that you'll put a guard on the spirit-room?'

'There'll be no cask broached if I know it, sir!'

'To be sure! Well, let's hope I bring some sailing orders back with me, or I'm damned if we'll not be aground on a reef of our own beef-bones!'

'You think it will be Quebec, sir?' James spoke low, for a dozen pairs of ears were eagerly cocked to catch their conversation.

'Ah, only the Admiral can answer that one! But we'll be sailing against the French one way or another. The Horse Guards haven't sent twelve thousand soldiers all this way to catch coneys in the woods.'

The captain was piped down the side with all due ceremony, and James turned to the matter of trimming the ship. Below, the decks rumbled and creaked while the crews were at gun-drill, the guns dummy-loaded with bags of sand to simulate powder. They were run out through the ports, run back on to the breechings to simulate firing, unloaded, reloaded, and then the whole operation was carried through again. Time after time, until the series of movements were so automatic they could be done by a man half-senseless from noise and smoke and wounds in the heat of battle. To ensure the gunners still remained thinking men, the drill would be suddenly varied: starboard and larboard guns' crews would change places, or forward would go aft, or one battery of four guns would run a relay race against another, while the disengaged crews stood round, offering advice and making small wagers. Amid this inferno James was glad of the fate that had made him master and not gunner, so that he at least enjoyed the fresher air of the upper deck when in action.

Aloft, some of the topmen were exercising in the rigging, the bos'n standing on deck with a watch in his hand, timing the setting-up of the three t'gallant masts. He saluted as James approached.

'Morning, bos'n! Not much trouble with your part of ship, I see.'

'Not much, sir!' replied the bos'n. 'Those lads out of the

last press in Portsmouth be coming along to be right proper
seamen now.'

'And only eight months at sea – it is a great credit to you
and your mates, Mr Stimpson. Let us hope for some good
prizes, so that you will all be well paid for your trouble.

'By the way, Mr Stimpson, I have a feeling we might get
sailing orders very soon. When you've got those t'gallants set
up again put on sufficient hands to cross the yards, and then
set a party to shifting stores. I want ten ton shifting from far
for'ard on the orlop to as far aft as you can. Oh, one more
thing. Just in case we get our orders, see that the hands have
an early dinner.'

There was an agreeable warmth in the sun now, and the
light danced and reflected from a thousand wavelets. James
thought with pleasure of the task he intended to perform for
the rest of the forenoon; the conversion of a series of soundings and bearings to make a chart of Bedford Basin. Until
nine years ago, this coast had been French. Both Halifax
and Dartmouth were very new settlements. The Acadian
French had never made charts of their harbours, relying on
pilotage and local knowledge. James snorted as he thought of
it. In these modern days, charts were a necessity so that trade
might be free. He had no time for skippers hugging local
knowledge to themselves, and making a trade secret of it.

He had strong memories of the day of wind-driven sleet
only three months ago when *Pembroke* had helped bring in
the shattered convoy, five weeks on passage from the Azores,
with relays of leadsmen taking soundings, soaking wet from
the lead-line. Well, that would not happen again; he had
obtained permission to take soundings for a chart, and other
masters had been instructed to assist him. He felt not a little
satisfaction over this. Though really, it was no great honour,
he reflected, as he ducked under the deckbeams of his cabin.
He had only been given the task because no one else wanted
it. He hooked the deadlight of the scuttle back, and set the
port open. The reflections of the sunlight danced on the deckhead. Ashore he could see the shingled roof-tops and the shin-
ing spires of the two little churches in Halifax. He wished
he had been present when the churches were built. The land

was almost virgin, and they could just as easily have been laid out so that the line of them made a good sailing mark.

He got out his instruments and set up the board with his chartwork pinned to it. He filled a pipe, sharpened all his pencils, then fell to work. He hummed the tune of *Bobby Shaftoe* under his breath, unconscious that he was doing so. James was happy.

Some time later he heard the cry '*Pembroke*', a warning that the captain's gig was returning. He stepped off with his dividers against the scale the position of his last calculation, and pencilled it in with a tiny cross. Then he shut the dividers carefully – their porcupine-quill points were easily damaged – put them in their case, and laid his pipe in its rack. Automatically he reached for his hat; it was seldom off his head these days, unless he was eating or sleeping. He reached the entry-port just as the bowman hooked on to the chains.

Captain Palliser came aboard looking as vague as usual, an affectation that deceived none of his officers. 'Ah, yes, gentlemen! Number One, I wonder if you and Mr Cook would be so kind as to attend me to my cabin?'

As they turned aft James heard a little buzz of speculation from the group around the entry-port, instantly stilled by the officer of the watch. He heard also the sound of bugles and drums from the encampments ashore that housed the troops. It was not the right time of day for bugle-calls. Something was in the wind.

'Ah, Mr Pascoe!' The captain's clerk had risen to go as they entered the cabin. 'Please to remain – there may be orders to write. Steward! A glass of wine for these gentlemen – and one for me. I've had a dry forenoon.'

The great cabin of the *Pembroke* was as big and as well furnished as any drawing-room ashore, James thought. The deck was covered with sailcloth, painted in squares of blue and white, with one or two French rugs setting it off. The furniture was mostly gleaming mahogany, there were curtains at the stern-windows, and silver lamps filled with whale-oil, to light at night. They stood by the table and took the glasses of madeira wine offered by the steward. Captain Palliser sank gracefully into a chair and toasted them with lifted glass.

'I give you a toast, gentlemen! Fair winds, fair fighting, and rich prizes!'

'Amen to that, sir! You have our orders, then? Is it Quebec, sir?'

'Not yet, Number One – but that will come, never fear. No, 'tis Louisbourg for a start, that place on the Île Royale we took in '45, and stupidly handed over to them at the Peace. Now we have to take it again.'

'We'll do that all right, sir.' Jeremy sounded very confident. 'When do we sail, sir?'

Hugh Palliser turned to James. 'How are we fixed, Mr Cook? Are we ready for sea?'

'With the next tide, if you like, sir. All stores inboard and secured, complete with wood and water, ship's trim correct, and the hands have been sent to early dinner, sir.'

'Good – good! Ever thoughtful, Mr Cook – ever thoughtful! You two gentlemen had best get a quick meal yourselves, for we've company coming. Two companies, in fact. Fraser's Highland Regiment.'

'Two companies, sir!' James sounded worried. To find accommodation for an extra five hundred in an already crowded ship was no small problem.

'Oh, that's not all, but it's not for very long. We've to receive a brigadier and his staff, too. Thank God it's not a full general, or he'd probably have wanted to bring his horse as well – can't direct a battle without a horse, you know! I'll use my sea-cabin while they're with us, and the brigadier and two of his retinue can be sea-sick in here.'

'A brigadier?' Jeremy Clarke said. 'That ranks with a rear-admiral, sir?'

'Oh, for the salutes, you mean? A brigadier ranks with a commodore – it's an appointment, not a rank. This one is called Wolfe, and a very pleasant fellow he is, although he doesn't look much like a soldier. He wants no gun-salutes, in case there are some Acadians still ashore to mark the ship he's in – though how he expects to conceal any movement with all that drumming and bugling is beyond me.' Captain Palliser turned to his clerk and began to dictate orders.

'Coffee, Mr Cook? I have some ready.' There was neither irony nor servility in Andrew Ferguson's voice. James had got his feet on the ladder of promotion while Andrew had been pressed. That was all there was to it.

'Thanks, Andra – I'd be glad of it. Plenty of sugar!' James stirred the strong brew and blew on it. There was no need of wardroom manners over a mug of coffee with an old friend.

'What's it like topsides?' asked Andrew.

'Tailend of a summer gale and an onshore wind,' James replied, sampling the coffee. 'Do you *never* go topsides these days, Andra?'

'Not often – and not at all since these sodgers came aboard. I cook sixteen hours in the day and need the rest of the time for sleep.' He yawned, obviously needing some fresh air. 'When will the landing be?'

'Who can say? Five days we've been here, and still it's no weather for the boats. In a day or two, maybe, if it continues to moderate.'

'That's not so good. Every mounseer for fifty miles around knows we're here, and why.'

'Oh, they knew well before that, old friend! Though most of the *habitants* were expelled from Halifax in '55 there are enough still there to get word to the French of everything we do . . . for all that Halifax is an English town.'

'It's not so much of a town yet, at that. Tell me, Mr Cook, do you think this land will ever amount to much?'

'Andra, I wish you would call me *James* when we're alone. You make me feel about a hundred years old.' He walked over to an open port and looked out at the rugged shoreline. 'This land already amounts to a good deal – it has fisheries and furs, and the best timber in the world. The farming would be good, too, if it had good English ploughs at it. These shiftless *habitants* only scratch away at the valley bottoms. Why do you ask?'

'There should be some prize-money after we take Louisbourg. My share would not be much, but I've a little bit put by in London I could have sent over. I thought to stay here, and set up an eating-house in Halifax. There's a widow-

woman who would help me, if I could maybe buy my discharge. I'm getting too old to follow the sea, and my feet get
no better. Would you say I had a chance of doing it?'

'Buy your discharge? Offhand I'd say no, not until we've
taken Quebec. I hear that's a very rich place, and there'd be
good prize-money after the taking.'

'Aye, but when would we take it? This year – next year?'

'This year, if we are quick about the taking of Louisburg.
If not, then next year for certain. But I don't think a request
for discharge would get very far until Quebec falls. Unless
you can find a substitute.'

Next year, eh? Ah, well, I've waited this long, so another
twelve-month won't hurt – not in this ship, at any rate. Will
you put in a good word for me when the time comes?'

'To be sure I will!' James told him warmly. There was a
stir of movement on the upper deck, and he drained his mug
of coffee. 'I'd best be going to see what's toward – the sooner
we finish here the sooner I'll be eating roast beef and good
Yorkshire pudding in your tavern at Halifax!'

June 8th, 1758, James wrote in his Journal: *This day we
landed the Brigadier and above Two Thousand soldiers in
Freshwater cove, but they were Repulsed after a brisk exchange of Fire, the French being conceal'd in intrenchments.
Some of Our boats were so shot about we contriv'd to burn
them on the beach. Then we landed our Soldiers at the North
Rocks, they from there taking the Mounseers in the Flank
with such a deal of our Hot Stuff that the French broke and
fled back to the Fortress, leaving twelve pieces of Ordinance
behind.*

Aye, it was all true enough, James thought – but how
could he write down what that day had really been like?
About the boats so riddled with shot that the men had used
their torn-up shirts to plug the leaks, and bailed with their
hats. (He made a *memorandum* to replace the torn-up shirts
of his own boats' crews from the slop-chest.) The sound of
saw and hammer reached him here in the cabin as the shipwrights worked through the night on repairs.

Above the night-noises of wind and sea came the steady pounding of cannon, firing at long range on the walls of Louisbourg. In his mind he saw the windrows of Highland dead, as Colonel Fraser's men had flung themselves up the beach, to be swept time and again by the hidden guns of the masked batteries with a storm of grape and canister shot. Of English bodies awash in the shallows and the surf so stained with blood that it broke in pink waves on the half-moon of sand. Of the proud stubborn regiments backing down the beach to the waiting boats, and of his own Jacks – and himself – dashing ashore to help the wounded men.

The brigadier was last off the beach, as he had been first on. He had walked through the storm of shot as if it had not been there, his face drawn with the pain of his sickness. 'Twas said he suffered of the stone. Certain it was that he suffered badly from something. James had come to have a great admiration for the little round-shouldered brigadier that day, and there was no doubt that his regiments loved him. It seemed that the army had its traditions no less than the senior service.

So they had left the beach to its quiet dead, creeping seaward out of cannon-shot. The brigadier's eager eyes never left the shore, dwelling in particular on the North Rocks. Screened from the beach by the cliffs themselves was a narrow inlet in a flat slab of sloping rock. The tide raced and boiled through it, but the flat rock at a distance had the look of a natural if hazardous jetty.

'I wish we had one of your admirable charts of this place, Mr Cook,' the brigadier told him. 'Do you think the boats could get through that inlet and land us on the rocks?'

'It might be done, sir. You'd have to jump for it.'

'Then we'll try. Please to have a signal made to the others to follow us in. I might be able to take the French in the flank from that cliff-top.'

The French had obviously thought any landing impossible at this place, and their passage through the cutting in the rocks was unopposed. Indeed, it would only offer a passage for about an hour at each rise and fall of the tide, and the tide was making fast. They would have to make haste, James

thought, as he set his own boat straight at the entrance. They
went in like a cork into a bottle, the seamen fending off from
the rocky sides with oars or stretchers.

'We'll not get all the soldiers ashore, sir! The tide!'

The brigadier nodded. 'I can see that, Mr Cook. Let me
have but five hundred ashore, and I think I can make my
mark. The rest can either wait on the next tide, or we may
have carried the beach by then. . .'

'Aye, aye, sir.' The inlet had widened to a lagoon, the water
lapping calmly at the rocky banks. The brigadier and his
retinue landed almost dryshod, two men leaping ahead to
help them. 'Stay there!' James ordered. 'Help the others
ashore as they come up. We'll take you off from the beach
later on.' He had a cutlass apiece passed to them out of the
boat – safer than pistols, he thought; a sailor with a loaded
pistol was more of a danger to friend than foe. 'There'll be
an extra tot for you back on board. Half-a-pint apiece!'

'Aye, *aye* sir!' Strange what sailors would do for the promise
of grog, James thought, as he turned the boat in the pool and
headed it out through the entrance. Lighted of its passengers,
it stood higher in the water and the leaking was much less.
Only four of the crew were baling-out.

Nine boatloads he signalled in to land their troops before
the rising tide filled the channel and swirled over the rocks.
The soldiers formed into half-sections and began scaling the
rocks towards Freshwater Cove. Among the red-hackled bon-
nets and tall grenadiers' caps, James thought he saw the glint
of his own seamen's varnished hats. He hoped he had not
sent them to their deaths.

The climbing figures vanished, and there was a silence, the
rocks deserted as if they had never known man. Doubtless the
men were drawing the charges from their firelocks, and re-
loading with fresh powder. Then – *crash*! The ordered
thunder of a volley sounded from the cliff-tops, and a grey
cloud of smoke drifted back. Fifteen seconds, and *crash*!
again – and again – and again. There was a cheer; James
guessed that the gunners in the hidden battery had either
been felled by the volleys, or had fled.

They were within sight of the beach again; from the cliff-top James saw a group of tiny figures rush cheering down towards the batteries.

He turned to the waiting boats, resting on their oars. 'Give way!' he called to the section under his command. 'Make for the north end of the beach! Follow me!'

That was how the British came to have a firm foothold on the Île Royale for a second time – but it had been no easy landing.

Now James laid down his pen, loosened his neckcloth and slipped off his shoes before stretching out on his cot. No point in undressing in this situation, that he knew. His eyes closed, and he dozed off with the sound of the shipwright's saw and hammer still echoing through the ship.

Off Louisbourg
July 28th, 1758

My dear Elizabeth,
Admiral Saunders has Ordered the Pickle scooner to Portsm'th with Despatches, so there is a Mail and I enclose this in a letter to yr. Father. After a slow start we have Done very well on this coast, having taken five French sail-of-the line as Prize as well as the Fort of Louisbourg with above seven thousand Prisoners. So that the whole of the Atlantic Coast in these Parts is Ours.

Yr. Godfather took his small share in these great Enterprises, tho' I doubt if you will read of him in the Public prints. However, you might well read that the Brigadier Wolfe landed Full twelve hundred men on the Hill-top. Mr Clarke, our 1st Lieutenant and myself were Charged . . . Here James' pen spluttered badly, and he took his knife to trim a new point.

They had been charged with the wet and hazardous business of landing eighteen-pounder cannon from ships' launches, within long cannon shot from the batteries on the Île Marque. For half the distance between ship and shore they were under fire; the fact that they could only be struck by chance at such

range was not really soothing to tensed nerves. Compared to
making this passage with the guns and carriages – they had
to be brought separately, for no launch could carry a mounted
eighteen-pounder – the task of rigging a flying-fox and hoist-
ing them to the cliff-top was soothing, in that it was only
brutal hard work with no particular hazard attached.

They counterpoised the flying-fox with baulks of timber,
and there were one or two minor mishaps in the felling of it,
but nothing that a touch from the tarpot and a tot of grog
would not cure (Ordinary Seaman Harris lost his leg below
the knee as a result of his own clumsiness: he set his foot in
the bight of a rope), and the raft of timbers they had used
in the operation was towed back to the ships to the great delight of the shipwrights after the island fell.

James resumed his writing.

. . . *with getting the guns ashore and setting them up on*
the Cliffs, which we did, and when this was done the Island
Battery soon gave in. We saw with Great Pleasure the Moun-
seers haul down Their golden Lilies, and cheer'd when our
own Meteor Flag was hoist in its stead. And once this was
done the Fort was Completely seal'd off and surrendered to
our Victorious arms two days back.

There, it was said, even if it was a somewhat bald account
of a strenuous three weeks. And now came the business of
ending his letter, a difficult thing now that Elizabeth was
neither child nor woman. Formality would please her, thought
James, formality with warmth and affection. Which was,
after all, just how he felt towards the lass. So –

It is rumour'd that we may essay a Thrust against Quebec
next, to take the whole of Canada out of King Louis' hands.
To do this we will have to sail up the St Lawrence river, and
since this Stream freezes about October I fancy it will not be
attempted until next Year.

James ended it with 'Sincerely' and signed it with his usual
signature, a large and legible *Jas. Cook.* It should do, he
thought. There were some things he could not have set down:
the marine sentry dirked and scalped by French-paid Micmac
Indians, the mash of flesh and splintered wood when a French

cannon ball skipped the surface of the bay and shattered a
whale-boat bringing off victuals to the landing party. It was
better to let the lass dream her dreams, to let her go on thinking that war was a matter of thrilling charges and resounding
cheers, that wounds were always in mentionable parts of the
body, that death always came with a merciful ball through
the heart. God send she never learned anything else.

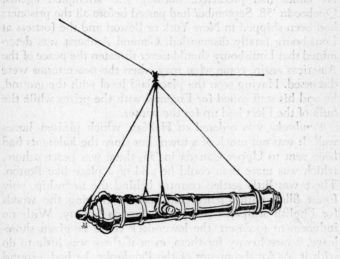

8 Quebec

As James had predicted, nothing was attempted against Quebec in '58. September had passed before all the prisoners had been shipped to New York or Boston and the fortress at Louisbourg finally dismantled. General Amherst was determined that Louisbourg should never threaten the peace of the Americas again, come what may when the peace terms were discussed. Having seen the place laid level with the ground, he and his staff sailed for England with the prizes while the bulk of the Fleet laid up for the winter.

Pembroke was ordered to Halifax, which pleased James well. It was not much of a town, but since the *habitants* had been sent to Upper Canada in '55, there was peace ashore, which was more than could be said of a place like Boston. There was little settled country behind the township, only forest filled with French-paid Indians ranging the woods for English scalps to collect the French bounty. With no inducement to desert, the lower-deck could be given shore-leave, a rare luxury for them, even if there was little to do with it. As for the master of the *Pembroke*, he had a sound ship and a well-trained crew, and his chartwork to hold his interest. Captain Palliser had sailed for London, and the command of *Pembroke* was now held by Captain Simcoe, an excellent navigator.

In the prevailing mood of generosity following the capture of Louisbourg, Andrew Ferguson applied for his discharge. This was granted on the score of age and infirmity – *Worn Out* was the eloquent reason given in the ship's ledger – and Andra quit the service and married his widow. Inside six weeks he had set up a tavern ashore; by mid-winter this had become a regular port of call for the junior officers of the

Fleet. Many a night James supped off boiled lobster or clam chowder, settling the affairs of the world meanwhile in talk with his fellow officers.

It was not only naval officers who used Ferguson's Tavern. After such a successful affair as Louisbourg an affection grows between the services who have shared the task, and the tavern was a place where they could meet. James was there one night in company with Jeremy Clarke when they were greeted by Major Hollands, a military engineer who had been on Brigadier Wolfe's staff. For James this meeting was fortuitous; he had in mind to ask a favour of the major. Major Hollands gave him the opportunity he sought when he asked: 'And how is your chart of the Basin coming along, Mr Cook?'

'My chart, sir? It goes well enough, as far as the soundings and bearings are concerned. But I confess to having some difficulty with the shore-lines – the actual mapping. I am good enough with the lead-line and the bearing-compass, but an indifferent surveyor. All I know of the art is what you taught me in the *Pembroke* when we lay weatherbound in front of Louisbourg. And it is not enough, I find.'

'You would like to learn more?'

'Indeed, I would. If you could see your way clear to give me lessons?'

'Gladly, Mr Cook. If ever a coast needed surveyors, it is this one – and there are precious few with the taste for it. Where are you working on your chart?'

'While we are alongside, Captain Simcoe is living with his lady ashore, and he allows me to set up a drawing-table in the great cabin.'

'I will come and see it tomorrow, and we will settle this matter of the shore-lines together. I need a good chart of the harbour, so that the shore-batteries can be sited properly.' He raised his glass of madeira. 'Here's to good charts of the seas wherever King George's ships can sail – and to the men who make them!'

So the chart of Bedford Basin was made, the first to which James ever set his signature. Eight copies were completed by Major Holland's draughtsmen. Two of these, each in a

separate ship, Captain Simcoe sent to Captain Palliser, and
before that officer returned to Canada he arranged to have
them printed on the press owned by the Royal Society.

When the printed copy arrived, James looked at it with
awe rather than pride. There they were, all the hundreds of
depths and bearings and observations, rendered down into a
proper printed chart, three feet by two. It was as accurate as
checking and double-checking could make it. James prayed
most fervently that no error had crept in. He would never
forgive himself if a keel so much as kissed the bottom from
an error in a chart bearing his name.

The completion of the chart would have left James with a
gap in his life had it not been for the spring refit. It was sure
now that they would go to Quebec. There was little James did
not know about river work, after the years he had spent
sailing in and out of the Thames. Decisions had to be right,
and gear had to be handled more smartly than ever before;
nothing must give way or jam when taking great ships up
a crowded river-channel. Especially one that they did not
know. For, although the French had been in Canada for one
hundred and fifty years, they had never made a chart of the
river.

General Wolfe (he had been promoted during the winter)
sailed into Halifax at the end of March. The *Stirling Castle*
had sailed in a convoy of seventy-eight warships and transports, but it was the second week in April before the frigates
Squirrel and *Diana* brought these in. Surprisingly, not one
ship had been lost on the way, but they had the usual toll
of sickness and deaths.

Diana had laid up for the winter in Chatham, and carried
mails from the Nore. There were two letters for James, one
from his prize-agent and the other from Robert Batts. Enclosed in this was a note from Elizabeth.

My dear Godfather, she wrote, *I was Rejoic'd at having
your letter from Louisbourg of last July, and most Proud to
think that I knew One who had taken part in this great Feat
of Arms. Yours is the first letter I have ever receiv'd from any
Gentleman, and I treasure it greatly and read it daily.* Now

what did I say, thought James, as he read this. What could I
possibly have said, to make a girl write so? Pray Heaven the
lass was not sickening with a green sickness!

Deborah, my eldest step-sister, was wed just before Advent
last, and had me for brides-maiden. I had a New gown for the
day, a blue silk with a petticoat of white Taffety, very fine.
The Groom you will recall, he is Albert Simmons in the
Flourmilling trade. He is good to our Deb, but I do not greatly
like him. I danced at the Breakfast, and wished you had been
there to partner me in the contry-dance.

My Father and step-Mother are well, and wish you kindly,
dear Godfather. I pray each night for the safety of you and
your Brave sailors, and do most devoutly wish for the ending
of the Present most Cruel War.

Your most Affec'ate and Devot'd,
Eliz. Batts.

And what was a man to make of that? James wondered.
The girl was seventeen now, of an age to marry. Did she
think in that way of him? She had wished he had been at
Deb's wedding, and had mentioned the groom in no very
cordial terms . . . was she comparing Albert Simmons in her
thoughts with himself? Then he laughed at himself. Reading
hidden meanings into a pleasant little note from a sheltered
girl! It was time he was either wed himself or else at sea
again, if a few lines from a young girl could set him in such
a tizzy!

Soon enough they were at sea again, a great fleet of over
one hundred King's ships, victuallers, and transports. Round
the north of the Île Royale, with no fortress at Louisbourg
to harbour a fleet to challenge them. North still, round the
Gaspe Peninsular, then into the St Lawrence, headed for
Quebec. All through the last part of May the fleet groped its
way up the St Lawrence, like a blindfold man finding his
way across a strange room. There were, of course, no charts,
and the French had taken up all their buoys and markers.
There were farms and villages along the banks, mostly un-
tenanted. Every able-bodied man from sixteen to sixty had
been pressed by General Montcalm into the army in front of

Quebec, and the women and children had taken to the woods
at the approach of the fleet. Yet there was danger ashore, for
the woods swarmed with Indians. A few watering parties filling casks from creeks were ambushed, tomahawked, and
scalped. Watering could only be done safely under a strong
guard of marines or soldiers.

So they pressed on, coming at last to the Île aux Coudres,
where the main channel ran between the island and the north
shore of the river. Ninety miles upstream lay Quebec, and there
the river was dotted with hundreds of islands, some as large as
English counties. Lying before the city, fitting the channel
almost as snugly as a cork in a bottle-neck, was the Île
d'Orleans. Its western end was just two miles from the city,
almost within long cannon-shot. This was the spot General
Wolfe had in mind for a base.

June 29th, 1759, James wrote in his Journal. *For five weeks
now we have sail'd up this Great river, facing just about every
hazard that can fall to the lot of One in the Naval Service.
Swift tides and Shoals, savage Indians ashore, and a well-
prepared Foe. Last night but one we anchored five miles from
the City, six ships of War and about thirty transports, and
yester-eve were attack'd by Fireships. After some Ado we
tow'd them Clear, hot work and arduous, so that the Fleet
suffer'd no Damage.*

James was glad he was not General Wolfe, who had to
devise a way of taking the place. Yet it might not be so
difficult, for the French seemed to have very poor ideas on the
subject of defence. That place Cape Torment, now. The only
clear channel lay within a half-mile of the foot of the cliffs.
A battery on the heights could have held up a fleet for weeks
with a dropping fire, which would have been very difficult
to answer, except with bomb-ketches. Half a dozen short
eighteen-pounders, with a furnace for heating shot, and the
fleet would never have passed – yet there was not a single
cohorn on the heights. It could not be shortage of men; Montcalm was known to have eight French regiments and thirty
thousand *Canadiens* under him. James wondered whether
those figures included the Indians.

He rubbed his head thoughtfully, thinking of the scalped corpses he had seen. That was a horrid, barbarous custom. Yet it was the fashion lately, so he had heard, for London folk of quality to prate about the Noble Savage, saying that the true nobility of Man was corrupted by cities and civilization. He wished he could bring some of these fine folk and show them a dirked and scalped corpse. There was little nobility about that! The lowest cut-purse from the Seven Dials would not stoop to such a vile practice!

James had come close enough to being scalped himself. He had as little regard for death as any in the Service, but the thought of being gashed and haggled afterwards made his flesh crawl, though he knew the feeling to be illogical. He had been sounding an inshore channel late one afternoon, two boats working together in line abreast. They were working as quietly as they could when James suddenly heard sounds of fighting from the other boat.

' 'Vast sounding, there!' he ordered. 'Pull for the jollyboat!'

They had turned across the current towards the other boat. James had been standing in the bows, and they ran into something that crunched under the impact. Automatically James grappled with the boathook at the obstruction, a canoe half crushed between the two heavier boats. James got the reek of rancid bear's grease that always betokened the presence of Indians, and for half a minute there was bedlam: pistols flashed, and cutlass met tomahawk, men lost their footing in the wildly rocking boats. The curses of the English were answered by the howls and whoops of Indians. James emptied his pistol at a half-seen naked torso, dropped it and drew his sword. But by that time there was no foe to smite. Only the faint lap of water as a second canoe vanished in the gloom, leaving four dead Indians in the jollyboat, and one dead seaman.

There was plenty of work for the Navy that summer. James spent any spare moment on the charts. He was working in the mess one day on the latest reach of the river to be sounded when Major Hollands announced himself.

'Still at your charts, I see?' he greeted James.

'It is a task that grows on me,' James answered. 'This last twelvemonth and more we have smelt our way into so many uncharted places on the end of the lead-line that I have begun dreaming of a Golden Age.'

'You surprise me, Mr Cook. I would not have thought you were given to dreaming.'

'Nay, sir, all men dream sometimes. I had my fill of dreams when I was a lad.'

'And what was it you dreamed? Being captain of your own ship?'

'There was that, of course.' James gave a brief thought to Jonty, and his old dream of being a ship-owner. Had he ever really wanted that for himself? 'But there was something else. I dreamed of sailing farther than a man had ever done before. I cannot mind if I ever thought of the ship very much.'

'And you've not done it yet.'

James shook his head, smiling. 'For ten years I was never out of soundings, never out of the waters between the chops of the Channel and the Baltic. When I came to this side of the Atlantic, it was my first venture deep-sea.'

'Well, there's time enough yet, and the world is wide. But what is your new dream? What is this Golden Age you speak of?'

'I do not think it is impossible. I dream of a day when a mariner can go to a map-makers to buy himself a chart of any stretch of water that would float a ship. To save luckless sailors from catching the rheumatism standing drenched in the chains heaving the lead on a winter night, or from being tomahawked while sounding a channel. That is my new dream, Major.'

'A most laudable one – and surely it will come. That is what I have come to talk about: maps. You will not have seen this one, Mr Cook. Cast your eyes over it.'

It was a map of a part of the St Lawrence on a scale of two miles to the inch. Quebec city lay at the centre, and the map showed the country from the mouth of the Cartier river to Cape Torment. Individual houses were marked, and the streets through the villages, but the river itself only appeared as a plain blue channel.

' 'Tis a good map,' James said, 'and will be of great value to the General, once he gets ashore. Is it French?'

'It is not. It was made by Colonel Mackellar, the chief engineer to the army. He was captured at Oswego in '56, and held in Quebec for near a year until he was exchanged. You can judge whether he wasted his time while he was on parole.'

James stood looking down at the map, 'Now all you want to complete it is a chart of the river – is that it?'

'As you say, Mr Cook. I may as well tell you what our problem is: to bring General Montcalm's main forces out of the city so that we can fight them.' He laid a finger on the village of Beauport. 'Brigadier Townshend thinks we should go in *here*, and attack the city across the mouth of the St. Charles.'

'There's one good reason I know of right now to prevent that plan,' James said. 'The shoals along the bank there extend nigh on a mile out from the shore at low tide. None but the smallest ships could give any gun support to a landing, and they would be high and dry at low tide.'

'The French have fortified the cliffs above the banks, too, and have sunk hulks with guns to cover the crossing of the Charles,' said Major Hollands. 'No, there is no easy way in there.'

'What about a direct attack on what is called the Lower Town? We could cover it by batteries mounted on the Pointe aux Peres.'

'We would be swept away by the fire of the French guns in the Citadel, Mr Cook. I shudder to think of the butcher's bill.'

James wrinkled his brows. 'Then there is left but one way. Through the Narrows, past Cape Diamond, and a landing west of the city.'

'It's the only way, as I see it,' the major said, 'though I know that Brigadier Townshend does not agree. And, apart from getting the Fleet through the narrows, it has its difficulties in that there are cliffs to scale. In fact, we are to set up a camp, *here*, below the Montmorency Falls, and I think an attempt will be made against Beauport. Like you, I think it will fail. If it does, then it remains for us to essay a landing somewhere

near the Anse du Foulon. To do that we need a really good
chart of the river from St Laurent, where we are now, to Cap
Rouge. How long do you think that would take?'

'Is this a good enough outline of the river to use as a base?'

'We'd never get a better. It only needs scaling up and the
soundings pricked in.'

'That will not be simple, in these Narrows. We will have
to do the soundings at night, and run through the tide-cycle
at least twice. We already have a tide-gauge set up ashore
here, but to run through all the soundings – say a month,
with eight boats out every possible night. And a week after
all that, to work up the figures. It would require authority
from the admiral, since we should need boats and double
crews from at least four ships.'

The major got up to go. 'The general is seeing the admiral
now,' he said. 'Captain Simcoe is with them, and Captain
Palliser. I really came here with a message from your captain,
to ask you to attend. For though the attempt against Beauport
will be made, the General has no faith in it. In his heart I
believe he knows we will have to run the narrows and land at
the Anse du Foulon.'

The chart was not complete until the third week in August,
when twelve copies were made by Major Hollands' draughtsmen. Taking the soundings was very difficult, for the river
opposite the city was barely a thousand yards across, having
narrowed from more than six miles only thirty miles upstream. The downstream run as the tide fell was like a mill-
race, yet this turbulent channel had to be sounded again and
again, at every state of the tide. And this under the very guns
of the Citadel.

The boats making the soundings could not work unpro-
tected; almost every night the river was the scene of some
savage little fight. Boats were lost and men died in that service,
and up and downstream the river banks of the St. Lawrence
flickered and glared with war. General Wolfe scorched the

earth for miles on either side of the city, both to distract
Montcalm's attention from the charting and to spoil his food
supplies, bearing in mind that the battle for the city might
run into a second season. For so badly had the French run
this rich Province, concentrating on the lucrative fur trade,
that they could not grow food enough for their need even in
peacetime.

There had been attempts at landing, as the major had fore-
told, but all had failed: at Beauport, at Montmorency, and at
Pointe-aux-Trembles. Only at Montmorency had there been
a partial success. A camp had been set up there, and General
Wolfe had made it his headquarters.

But that was over now. During the first week in September
the camp was struck, and using the new chart and the tide-
table that accompanied it, ship after ship slipped through the
narrows, protected by the batteries set up around Point Levis.
Meanwhile, smaller ships were sailing up and down off Beauport, bombarding the French a long cannon shot and threatening a second landing. Though they may have suspected a
ruse, the French dare not ignore this threat, and at least half
of their regiments would be held there.

As for those ships going upstream, the French never suspected they were going to cover a landing. If General Montcalm thought about them at all, he imagined, perhaps, they
were sailing to attack a food convoy, coming down from
Montreal by boat.

James was only one of dozens of masters and lieutenants
who commanded a cutter or launch in the landing. The boat
was crowded with the kilted figures of his shipmates of the
year before, the Seventy-Eighth Highland Regiment. Each
man sat with his firelock loaded and on half-cock held between his knees, a hand cupping the pan to keep the priming
dry. The moon was in its first quarter; James had only to
glance at it to know the exact state of the tide. The figure of
the tide-table he had helped to make was fixed in his brain.
The seamen rowed at ease, with muffled oars. There was no
fear of any undue noise from this carefully picked crew.

Then came a long hail from the northern bank: *'Qui vive?'*
James nudged Lieutenant Fraser of the Seventy-Eighth,
sitting beside him.

'La France!' the Scotsman replied. Then, in a low voice
to James: 'I hope they have no password.'

'They never have,' replied James. 'Answer them again.'

'La France – et vive le Roi!'

'Vive la France!' came from the shore, and they swept on
towards the landing.

James was looking out for the marks he was to land by:
two lamps hung in the rigging of schooners on the far bank.
Keeping these in line, he could not fail to reach the agreed
beach. Dozens of other boats were going the same way; the
landing would be in some force. Surely the French could not
fail to hear what was going on?

Early as they were, the General and his staff were on the
beach before them. James waited long enough to see Lieutenant Fraser join up with another company of the Seventy-
Eighth and begin to scale the steep banks. They were scarcely
cliffs, but difficult enough to climb in the darkness. Then he
re-embarked on the long row back to the *Pembroke*. The
river seemed as thronged with traffic as the Pool of London
yet still there came no rattle of firelocks from the shore. At
the ship he changed crews, swallowed a pot of coffee well
laced with rum, then embarked more soldiers. By now there
was a crackle of small-arms fire along the Heights, but nothing
of any great significance.

Four times in all James made the passage that night, with
a fresh crew each time; for him there was no relief. The last
passage he made with a twelve-pounder gun cocked up on the
thwarts, mounted on a field carriage made by the shipwrights.
Dawn was breaking on the beach by the Anse du Foulon
when they got this awkward load ashore. There was another,
brought in by the launch, and it took the united efforts of the
two boats' crews to get them both up the steep diagonal path
someone had found. Then there was the powder and shot to
bring up.

James began to lay and serve one of the guns himself, taking orders from a major of the Artillery Regiment. Suddenly

they heard the sound of distant cheering. 'Sounds like some-thing!' exclaimed the major. 'Damn this smoke! That's the worst of being a gunner, a man never gets close enough to the front to see what's going on. Runner! Get away smartly up to the front, find Colonel Mackellar, and see what that cheering's about. It might be the end of the war!'

'We'll cease firing until we do find out, anyway,' he said companionably to James. 'Can't see our targets in this smoke. We'll give it a chance to clear.'

Minute by minute the noise of musketry ebbed and the sound of cheering swelled. 'Those are English cheers, any-way,' said the major. 'That's a good sign. Ah, my runner! Well, man, what is it?'

'Colonel Mackellar says to cease fire, sir, and to pass the word along. The French have broke, sir, an' we've won the battle, sir! Oh, yes, sir – an' the General was hit three times, sir. In the belly, sir.'

'God rest his soul!' cried the major. 'The poor devil.' He drew a handkerchief from his cuff, and blew his nose loudly. 'Well, I only hope this city of Quebec will be worth it. Wolfe was as good a soldier as ever lived, damned if he wasn't!'

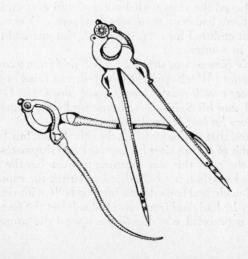

9 Newfoundland

HMS Northumberland,
At Halifax,
Oct. 12th, 1759.

My dear Elizabeth,

You will have heard ere you read this of the *Glorious News* of the great Victory we had over the French before Quebec last Month, and regret, as do we all, the Lamentable death of our General Wolfe. I saw much of him from time to time in Association with my Duties, and found him to be a most Polite and Affable Gentleman and Much belov'd of his Men. So the City is now in our Hands, but the French still have Great Numbers of men under Arms, at Montreal and other Places, but we all expect the Wars will be ended in these Parts next year.

And that was a white lie, James reflected. No one in the Fleet believed the wars with France would ever end; in this century there had been more war than peace. War was something that endured for ever, it seemed. But one had to sound cheerful in a letter.

Captain Simcoe was struck by a Ball fir'd from a canoe-load of voyageurs a Week after the City fell, and Died in the Hospital ashore two days later from Loss of Blood. His Death was Peaceful, and his Spirits were borne up by the knowledge of the Victory he had Helped to earn.

Aye, and that was more wind, thought James, but Elizabeth had a habit of asking after his captains and shipmates, and he told her the news this way meaning to spare her the truth. It had been buckshot, not ball, that had struck the captain, and his belt-buckle had been driven into his belly with the charge. Certainly he had died from loss of blood, but the fact that his death was peaceful was due to the opium the surgeons had

90

given him. After waiting on his captain in the stinking hospital ashore, James devoutly hoped that his own death would be quick, and in the open air.

We sail'd the 'Pembroke' to Boston and Paid Off into the Dockyard there, and I was appointed to the 'Northumberland 74', Capt. the Lord Colville. At the same time Capt. Palliser shifted to the 'Shrewsbury' and was order'd to the Levant, so that I have lost two good friends from the Fleet.

I shall be Here at least for another year, I fear, but Apart from not seeing you and my friends, I am not Unhappy. I have my Mathematics and my Chart-Making, and there are Worse places than Halifax to Spend a Winter. (Though not much worse, James reflected. He had heard it referred to as the fundament of the universe.) *I was much divert'd at your account of Deb's wedding, and it would have given me Great Pleasure to have danced a country-dance with you, though you would have had to Instruct me in the Figures. Never yet have I attended at a Ball, though as a Lad I skipped a Passable Hornpipe.*

Adding his signature – *Affect'ately – James Cook,* he folded it in with one to Robert Batts, then dropped the letter and one to his father into the mailbag outside the wardroom. It was years now since he had seen his father, or any of his family, though they had kept in touch by letters.

At first, James was somewhat in awe of having such an exalted being as a blue-blooded lord for captain. This feeling soon passed, for the captain wore his nobility lightly enough. He was another of the new breed of captains encouraged by the great Lord Anson, men who were navigators and seamen themselves – and who before the turn of the century would render the rank of master redundant. Lord Colville took a great interest in James' chartwork, though he did not have enough knowledge to help with it. But he did recognize its value, and during the winter, a spacious temporary deckhouse was set up amid-ships for James to use as a draughting office.

Here James and Major Hollands spent some pleasant and industrious days. With a tin coffee-pot gurgling on the stove, they could laugh at the sleet and snow lashing past the windows; the deckhouse was so weatherproof that James shifted

his cot and took to sleeping there. And it was here that James
acquired his first real knowledge of that fascinating art,
Mathematics. The late Captain Simcoe had bequeathed him
an unwitting legacy: he had loaned James two books the
winter before, the *Compleat System of Astronomy* and the
Young Mathematician's Companion, by a philosopher called
Leadbitter. James had struggled through both, though he
found parts very hard going. But Major Hollands had helped
him in his studies, and these books had been his constant
companions for a year. Without them, in fact, James doubted
whether he could have charted the St Lawrence at all. Captain Simcoe's effects had been packed and sent back to his
family by the *Porcupine,* and it was some time after this
James found he still had the two books. He could not now
send them back until the spring, and to send them then would
be to cripple himself intellectually. There were no book-
sellers nearer than Boston, and heaven alone knew when he
would get there. He kept the books, vowing to send them
back to Mrs Simcoe the minute he could provide himself
with other copies.

The French did not surrender Canada without another
year of fighting. Early in 1760, they came very near to re-
taking Quebec, driving General Townshend (he had been
brigadier under General Wolfe, and was appointed Governor
of the city after the battle) back into the city and summoning
it to siege. This was in April, when there was still ice in the
river, and Townshend and his men were weak with scurvy
after a winter on salt beef and dried peas. It might have gone
worse for the English had the French not been short of both
cannon and powder. Both sides were looking to the river, for
ships to come to their relief. Thanks to their charts, the English came first. Upstream in the middle of May came the
Vanguard 74 with frigates *Lowestoft* and *Diana.* Again the
high banks of the stream echoed with cannon-shot, again the
wreaths of powder-smoke drifted through the trees. Sullenly
the French withdrew from Quebec, and fought a series of
rearguard actions westward.

Five months later, the end came on the *Place d'Armes* at
Montreal. Never again would the *fleur de lys* flaunt over the

citadel of Quebec or the forts at Louisbourg and Montreal.
James' own part in the wars of 1760 was confined to a single
action in Chauleur Bay, in the Gaspe Peninsular near Resti-
gouche. Here Captain Colville, Commodore of a force including the *Phoebe* frigate and three sloops-of-war, trapped
four French frigates bringing relief to Quebec. James was
detailed to take these French prizes into Boston, over summer
seas under easy sail. And in Boston he found a bookshop and
got himself copies of Mr Leadbitter's work, and so was able
at last to clear his conscience by sending his long-borrowed
copies back to Mrs Simcoe. He inscribed his own name into
his new books with something of a flourish.

So, as 1760 merged into '61, Canada lay firmly in English
hands. English garrisons sat in Quebec, Montreal and the old
French frontier forts, engaging in an eternal guerilla war
with hostile Indians. The *habitants* grumbled, lit their pipes,
and settled down under a new rule that allowed them to re-
tain their own language, laws, and religion.

James remained in the *Northumberland*, which for two
years settled into a fairly uneventful routine of patrols and
minor expeditions to wherever a pocket of French resistance
showed itself. During this time, mathematics, astronomy, and
chart making largely occupied his mind. And the vexed
question of the calculation of longitude was an endless topic
of debate in the wardroom.

The finding of latitude at sea was no great problem: James
himself had been able to do this ever since he was a second-
year apprentice in the Walker brothers' colliers. Longitude
was quite another matter: it could be calculated ashore, given
a few clear nights for the making of lunar sights, but this
method was impossible for a ship moving over the face of the
sea. Longitude was somehow linked with the concept of time
– so much was clear – and time itself was a concept only beginning to be studied. James thought it a pity that the great
Newton had never taken an interest in the calculation of longitude. The solution of the problem would be of immense value
to navigation and trade, but it would only be solved by a great
mind. There was much discussion about the prize of ten
thousand pounds offered by the Royal Society for an accurate

method of determining longitude at sea. There were those
who declared the prize would never be claimed, but James
thought otherwise, though he was convinced it would take a
genius to solve the problem. Its solution would be of immense
value to navigation and trade. *He* was no genius, that he
knew, so he gave himself up at this time to the work he knew
he could do well.

The lack of even the simplest charts for some quite well
used trade routes was his concern. There should be charts of
roadsteads and harbours and ocean routes that showed prevailing currents and winds – for in many places, currents
changed with the seasons. There were captains who had
made their own charts of certain seaways, but these they kept
to themselves as trading secrets, passing them on to apprentices under a vow of silence. The Spanish and Portuguese
were among the greatest offenders in this, but no maritime
nation was entirely guiltless of the practice. It would be the
dawn of the Golden Age of navigation, James thought, pur-
suing his new dream, when a man could obtain an accurate
chart of any stretch of water that would float a ship. Now, he
lost no opportunity to chart strange harbours, and produce
a number of charts which almost satisfied his own exacting
standards.

In August, 1762, when peace talks had already begun in
Paris, *Northumberland* and the attendant frigates *Diana* and
Phoebe were taking on firewood and water near Placentia,
Newfoundland. And that month, six big French frigates
under the command of Admiral de Ternay slipped out of
Brest under cover of a summer haze, bearing a large body of
marines. The English gave chase but de Ternay swept south,
outsailing them. The next morning, the French were alone
on a wide summer sea. They were reported some time later
from Praia, in the Cape Verde Islands, a position so far south
that it was logical to assume their destination was India. But
when de Ternay cleared from Praia, he turned west, then
north. It was still August when he turned up before St
John's, Newfoundland.

As he had expected, the French Admiral found no ship of
force in the harbour, and no regular garrison ashore. His

marines landed almost unopposed. His task was the easier in
that St John's was largely a summer fishing settlement. There
were not above fourscore permanent inhabitants, and nothing
that could be called a town. Yet to hold on to it until the
Peace was settled would gain for France at least one port to
offset the losses of Louisbourg and Quebec. For in Paris, it had
been suggested that each side should keep any colonies taken
in the war.

It happened that a Portuguese who had filled his hold with
bacalhoa earlier than usual in the season crossed de Ternay's
track in mid-Atlantic, and reported the sighting when he
arrived in the Tagus. By good fortune, Admiral Graves was at
Lisbon in the *Antelope*, with Captain Palliser of the *Shrewsbury* and the frigates *Calliope*, *Maenad* and *Daphnis*. Within
twenty-four hours of receiving the report, the little English
fleet was at sea. At Halifax, they had fresh news of the French.
Word of de Ternay's descent upon St John's was brought in
by English fishermen. As they sailed north, the Admiral called
a council in his flagship.

'It would help considerably if we knew where Commodore
Colville and *Northumberland* stood,' he said. 'Up north somewhere. But where?'

'He might be at St John's already,' Soames of the *Daphnis*
suggested.

'He might be.' The Admiral gave the suggestion some
thought. 'However, one of those fishermen told me of a place
where King's ships put in for wood and water – Placentia,
Newfoundland.' He made up his mind. 'It's worth a try.' He
turned to Captain Savage of the *Maenad*. 'Yours is the fastest
of our frigates. I'll give you orders for Commodore Colville,
and you will look for him there first.'

The lookout in *Northumberland*'s maintop narrowed his
eyes. 'Ahoy, the deck! Sail ho! Looks like a frigate, sir. One
of ours.'

The Commodore came up. 'Frigate, hey? Must be trouble
somewhere.'

James hurried to collect the Navy List from his cabin and

got back to the quarter-deck just as the midshipman called:
'Her number is two-four-nine, sir.'

'Two-four-nine . . . *Maenad,* twenty-eight guns, Captain
Savage,' James read out. Listed here as one of the Levant
Squadron. – That will be Admiral Graves' command, sir.'

Lord Colville nodded. 'He's a long way off station, to be
sure. Pass the word to back top-sails, Mr Cook, while we hear
what *Maenad* has to say.'

What had begun as a leisurely summer cruise for *Northumberland, Diana* and *Phoebe* developed into a race against
time. The four ships made a fast passage of five days to St
John's. They arrived to find that Admiral Graves had been
compelled to engage the French, even though he was outnumbered by four ships to six, and had the heavy seige guns
set up ashore directed against him. *Antelope's* and *Shrewsbury's* riggings were in ruins from bar- and chain-shot. But
two of the French frigates had struck their colours and three
more had broken off the fight, under orders from their
Admiral. De Ternay was a brave man, but he knew when
he was beaten. With a line-of-battle ship and three fresh
frigates coming up fast he had no choice at all. He fought
his own ship *Foudrouyant* to a standstill to give the three
least damaged of his fleet a chance of escape. He himself did
not escape, but as he ordered the Golden Lilies to be hauled
down and surrendered his sword, he saw that the last of his
three frigates had disappeared over the skyline.

It took three more days and a deal of hard work to reduce
the little garrison ashore. Then Admiral Graves held a council
in the great cabin of *Northumberland.*

'I think we have done very well,' he said. 'Your coming up
when you did, Colville, turned the tide. You might think we
lost three prizes, but if you had not come His Majesty might
have lost four goods ships.'

'And the prizes, sir?' Lord Colville asked. 'I usually send
mine into Boston.'

Admiral Graves considered. 'This war will be over come
the spring; there's no sense in putting any more money into
those American colonists' hands than we need to. No, it's
Deptford for the prizes, and you'll have to find the crews.'

Lord Colville nodded. 'Will you be sending an escort with them?'

'I suppose I'd better. Captain Savage – you can take your *Maenad* to look after them.' The Admiral turned back to Lord Colville. 'No doubt you'll send good lieutenants as prize-masters? None of the ships are very sound.'

'I'll put lieutenants in two of 'em, yes. But I'll put a master in the most damaged. My Mr Cook. He's far and away the best seaman I have.'

'That's not the James Cook that was with me in the *Pembroke*?' Captain Palliser broke in.

'The same. He's been out since late '57. I have a fancy that he wants to go to England to marry.'

Captain Palliser looked at the dark-green shore and the waters of St John's harbour. There was work here for James Cook, if he could be talked into doing it. He took an elegant pinch of snuff.

'Indeed I might have a word with him before he sails.'

Coming up the London River, James looked on it with new eyes. It was muddier and narrower than he remembered; his eyes had become accustomed to broader reaches and bluer waters. He glanced up at the gaff of the *Semiramis*, where the blue ensign flew above the golden lilies, token to the world that he was sailing a French prize. How crowded the river was! Indiamen, coasters, lighters, hoys – and, of course, colliers. Stubby-rigged little Geordie coal-cats, low in the water going up, high in ballast coming down. What ships they would have been to take up the uncharted St Lawrence, with its swift tides and sudden shoals! They would have taken the bottom fair and square, sitting upright and undamaged until the tide floated them off.

There was one yawing across the tide now, the *Grace Amy*, with the mate at the wheel munching a pasty, and a couple of 'prentices sunning themselves on top of the deckhouse. He thought of his own first passage up this same river back in '46, and the anchor-watch with Andrew Ferguson. Andra had become a father two years ago, and was beginning to put on

a rare belly at his tavern in Halifax. It took a great deal to wear
out an old collier hand! Maybe, if he himself had not volunteered into the Navy, he might have been eating a pasty at
the wheel of a collier, with a name like the *Grace Amy* or
some such. Instead, he was bringing in a French prize to
Deptford, a prize with an outlandish name that no one on
board knew how to pronounce. Well, that was the way of it.
He had not done so badly. He had saved much of his pay and
all of his prize-money, and just around the next reach was
Wapping, where Elizabeth lived. He would see her tomorrow, speak to her father, then put his fortune to the test. He
felt his heart thumping and there was a tightness in the chest
he had never noticed when he faced French gunfire. Elizabeth!

10   *The Surveyor-General*

'. . . wilt thou have this woman to thy wedded wife, to live together after God's ordinance in the Holy Estate of Matrimony? Wilt thou love her, honour and keep her . . .'

It was the same church where he had stood sponsor for Elizabeth at her baptism. James liked the way the curate pronounced the words of the marriage service, the book open in his hands, though obviously he knew the passage by heart. The church was filled with Elizabeth's relatives, and though there were no kin of James present, there were many old friends and shipmates.

The wedding breakfast was held at the *Prospect* inn. James, feeling stiff in his best uniform and a high neckcloth, sat beside Elizabeth at the high table while speeches were made and toasts drunk. They had taken over the entire ordinary at the *Prospect*, and there were drink and victuals enough to provision a ship. Elizabeth cut the first slice of the bridescake with his sword, and then there was the bride-ale itself, a mighty brew from Mr Whitbread's brewery. But what really added spice to this wedding was the fact that everyone knew the war was really over now.

Through the crowd of guests came a tall gentleman, elegant in civilian clothes, to shake James' hand.

'Captain Palliser! You honour us, sir!' James said. 'May I present my wife? Elizabeth, my dear, this is Captain Palliser, of whom I have told you so much.'

Hugh Palliser bowed. 'Your servant, ma'am!' Then, over a glass of madeira and a slice of bridescake, he asked Elizabeth if he might have a private word with her husband. 'It will take no longer than five minutes, I promise!' he told her.

Elizabeth smiled and moved away, and the Captain came straight to the heart of what he had to say. 'Tell me, Mr Cook,

99

what plans have you made for yourself now the war is ended?'

'I have not really thought about it, sir. At present I am on half-pay leave from *Northumberland*.'

'You can forget her, Mr Cook. The French Navy is in ruins, and I doubt if any of the bigger line of battle ships will re-commission in the spring. They'll be laid up in ordinary, until they either rot to pieces or the next war breaks out. This always happens! Shall you return to the coasting trade?'

Should he? James hesitated for a fraction of a second, then spoke the words that settled the whole of his future career. He remembered the sheer, slogging hard work of the colliers, and the fact that, although he had sufficient funds to set himself up in a share of a ship, he was out of touch with that life now. There was something else, too: there would be little scope to exercise himself in mathematics or chartwork, carrying coal.

'No, sir – not that. I have been long away from it. I would sooner stay in the service.' He spoke slowly, as if his mind were not quite made up. It was hard to draw his mind away from the gaiety of the wedding to thoughts of the future.

'But you fear there may not be a place for you – is that it? I think there may be, and that is why I am come to see you today. It is very likely that I will be appointed Governor of Newfoundland, at St John's. If this happens, I would want you on my staff.'

' 'Tis very kind of you to make the offer,' James replied, 'but I fear I would not assist you greatly as a shore officer. I am too long trained as a seaman.'

'Who mentioned shore service? I had in mind the work you did in Halifax and before Quebec: survey and chartwork. There is a deal of that required along the Newfoundland coast, as you must know.'

'On your staff – as surveyor?' Of all the appointments in the Service, this was one James most desired. 'Sir, I can scarce believe it! I would be most honoured.'

'It's not certain yet; we would have to find excuse for appointing you, but that is what I want. It would mean a summer on the coast, leaving here about March, and returning to London around October, with the winter to work up your

charts.' He pulled a gold watch from a fob pocket. 'I was on
my way to Greenwich by water – an appointment with the
Governor – but I thought I would drop in to see how you felt
about the matter.'

'You were fortunate to find me, sir. We plan to leave for
the north tomorrow, to keep Christmas with my father in
Yorkshire.'

'About how long do you plan to stay?'

'Until just after the New Year. Five weeks or so. 'Tis not
worth making the journey for less.'

Captain Palliser, a Yorkshireman himself from the northern
dales, smiled at the mention of the New Year. 'Let us hope
it will be a successful New Year for both of us. You will be
returning to these parts?'

'Not far away, sir. We shall be living in a house I own
near Mile End.'

'Well, when you get back, look for a message from me at
the Agent's here.'

Betty Cook peered into the looking-glass of the bedroom
at the Holborn inn where she and James had spent their
wedding night. Everything that had happened yesterday had
been so right. The wedding and the breakfast, and Captain
Palliser coming with such a wonderful offer of employment
for James. . . . Think of it! She would have him at home every
winter. She looked at the reflection of her face. She saw no
difference at all from yesterday – yet surely there must be one.
Yesterday she was a spinster; today she was a married woman.
. . . Mrs James Cook! There was a sound at the door, and she
fell to dressing her hair. This was no time for woolgathering;
the coach for the north was leaving at five. James had already
gone down to see to their baggage.

The coach reached Hatfield, a distance of twenty-two miles,
in three hours after setting off from Holborn.

'I declare my head was whirling at the pace we travelled!'
Betty told James as he helped her to climb down.

The red December sun was just level with the winter fields,
and glowed cheerfully on the yellow-brick houses of the little

town. Inside the inn where they had halted for a change of
horses, husband and wife sipped hot coffee together.

'Delicious!' Betty said as she tasted it.

James smiled. 'There's a tot of good Jamaica rum in it, to
keep out the cold.'

'I never had that before! But then, these last two days have
been so filled with new things . . . '

'For me, as well as you, my love,' James told her gently.

'Oh, James! I had quite forgot – you must be feeling things
strangely, too!'

In five days they travelled half the length of England, and
came at last to Ayton, beyond York. It was full seven years
since James had last seen his family. Both his parents had aged
considerably. His mother and Elizabeth took to each other at
once, and the first night they all sat up talking and talking
until well past midnight.

James did not regret the money he had spent on their wedding journey. He showed Elizabeth all the places he recalled
so well: they visited Aunt Alice at Newton, and he talked of
the day he and Jonty had climbed Roseberry Topping. They
went to Staithes to see the Sandersons, and enjoyed a good
fish dinner. Christmas they kept at Ayton. James met brothers
and sisters he had not seen in years – Elizabeth never did get
all their names straight in her head. As she mingled with the
family, her high London voice sounded clear above their
north country speech. James' deep voice had lost much of
its Yorkshire accent over the years; he had not realized it until
he came home again. They had a noble Christmas dinner:
roast goose, roast pork, and plum-pudding with rum sauce.
And a week later they saw the New Year in at Newton, with
Aunt Alice. Then seven more days, and it was time to return
home, to the house in Mile End which James had seen for
the first time just before his marriage.

Robert Batts had looked after James' property carefully.
There was fresh paint and wallpaper, and one of the new
cooking ranges had been installed in the kitchen. It was a
comfortable rather than an elegant house – but it was their
own, and its upkeep was not beyond the half-pay rate of four
shillings a day of a master, Royal Navy. They had a maid, a

girl recruited from the local workhouse, and when it was time for James to go to sea, Elizabeth had arranged that one of her young half-sisters should come to keep her company.

James was busy until the end of January, settling in and arranging his affairs. He made a new will, and checked his affairs with Robert Batts and his prize agent. He was surprised at the size of his fortune. Apart from the house he was living in, which was reckoned to be above two hundred pounds in value with the furnishings, he had over four hundred pounds in cash or in various ventures. He was astonished; he had never thought to be worth so much, and all gained by careful living and a little luck in the matter of prize-money! Nor had he reckoned in the worth of his books – there must be at least a hundred pound laid out on those. It was not a fortune, but it was more than most men possessed in their early thirties. Why, it was more than enough to buy a share in a collier!

About the middle of February, he received the expected letter from Captain Palliser (only it was Sir Hugh Palliser now, with a ribbon and star to set off his well-tailored uniforms). It contained an appointment for James to be at the Admiralty the following Tuesday at ten o'clock.

James went by water, wrapped in his boatcloak against the raw winter weather. He walked from the river up Whitehall, with the old Palace on his right. Though he had never been to Admiralty before, he knew it was near the top of Whitehall, not far from Cockspur Street and the Royal Mews. Then he was at Admiralty Yard, turning in at the gateway with the posts crowned by winged sea-horses, smiling to himself at the conceit of the artist who had fashioned such an appropriate symbol for the white-winged Royal Navy.

One of a pair of elderly watchmen – both worn-out seamen by the looks of them – rose from a hooded chair in the entrance-hall and inquired his business. Introducing himself, James asked for Captain Palliser.

'Aye, aye, sir! The captain said you'd come asking for he. If 'ee will kindly come this way, sir!'

So James was ushered through a series of dark corridors into a great room, forty foot square at least. It was simply enough furnished with a long oval mahogany table and a great

many chairs. There was a fireplace under a marble mantel at
each end of the room, and two tall windows gave a prospect
over the Horse Guards Parade towards St James' Palace. The
walls were hung with stirring pictures of sea battles. He had
little enough time to take this in. There were four gentlemen
present, standing backs to the fire warming their coat-tails.
Two of them, Sir Hugh Palliser and Admiral Sir Charles
Saunders, he knew; the others were both civilians.

'Ah, Mr Cook!' Sir Hugh came across, hand outstretched,
'Very civil of you to be so prompt. You and Sir Charles are
acquainted, I know. May I introduce you to Mr George
Grenville, the First Lord, and the Viscount Barrington, Treas-
urer to the Navy?'

Mr Grenville was dressed in a plain brown worsted suit of
clothes, but my Lord Barrington was gorgeous in a maroon
coat, yellow waistcoat and buff breeches. James made his bow,
wondering what had brought him, a simple master, into such
distinguished company.

The admiral took charge of affairs. 'We are met here, quite
informally, merely five gentlemen with a common interest in
the sailing of ships at sea,' he began. 'Three of us have actually
done a great deal of such sailing, while Mr Grenville and my
Lord Barrington have to answer to Parliament for the results,
and to foot the bill. And for the past four years we sailors
have had a deal to do, sailing in waters that were either very
poorly charted or else not charted at all. Am I correct?'

'Aye, aye, sir!' murmured Sir Hugh, while James nodded
his earnest agreement.

'And I believe it to be true,' Sir Charles continued, 'that
there is no office in Admiralty responsible for making good
this lack of charts?'

'Not as yet,' said Mr Grenville. 'The matter has come up
before the Board many times, of course, and the project
received strong support from the late Lord Anson. He, of
course, had as much experience as any man in sailing un-
chartered waters; it was very much his wish that a Cartographic Service should be set up. But there were so many
other things that my Lord had to set right . . . abuses in the
Dockyards, victualling . . .'

Aye, James thought, old Lord Anson had done right well by the Service. Sir Charles and Sir Hugh here were both officers he had trained. Anson himself had suffered from Admiralty when it was as corrupt as a body could well be. He had taken *Centurion* – a sixty-gun two-decker James remembered at Quebec – round the world, being the second Englishman after Frankie Drake to do it, and had made a great name for himself by bringing her back loaded with Spanish treasure. It had made his name, and he had used his reputation and influence to better the Service. When he died, only last year, he had seen the Navy that was his pride triumphant over the French from Canada to India.

'Very true,' said Sir Charles. 'In some things Lord Anson's work is completed, but in this matter of cartography it is not yet even begun. Tell me, do either of you gentlemen see a way clear to setting up a Cartographic Office in Admiralty in the near future?'

'I doubt it very much,' said Lord Barrington. 'With a war newly won, and no fresh hostilities in prospect, it would be most difficult to get funds for such a project out of Parliament. You know what those Commons are like! There'll be ships laid up by the dozen, and seamen paid off by the thousand. It's the same at every Peace.'

'Lord Barrington is quite right,' Mr Grenville said. 'This is no time to propose setting up a fresh Department in Admiralty. Nothing can be done without funds, and we shall be pared to the very bone. I agree about the necessity for good charts. The best thing I can suggest is that we have something ready to launch for the beginning of the next war, when the Commons are in a generous mood and the purse-strings are loosened.'

'A gloomy view,' Sir Charles said, 'especially as this matter of cartography is essentially a peaceful pursuit. It would be of great benefit to trade, for instance. 'Tis a pity it has to wait upon war, seemingly, to furnish the funds for it.'

'You asked a question, sir, and we answered it,' Lord Barrington said. 'We do not like the answer we gave any more than you do.'

Sir Hugh said: 'As I see it, we are all agreed that the

Service needs a Cartographic Office, but that Parliament is unlikely to vote funds to pay for it until we have a new war. But I have a suggestion. As you know, gentlemen, I have been appointed as Governor and Commander-in-Chief, Newfoundland. There is little permanent settlement there, but a large summer population of fisherfolk, coming and going. I sail to take up my appointment next month, and I will spend six months of the year there. As Governor, I come under the Foreign Office, but as Commander at St John's I shall be serving as rear-admiral under Sir Charles.'

'That could be awkward,' murmured Mr Grenville.

'It will not be,' said Sir Charles. There is no reason why we should clash. Sir Hugh will not fly his flag at sea, and I shall not tread on his toes ashore. But what we had in mind was to set up a local office of Cartographer General, and begin by making good charts of Newfoundland waters. Which is why we have got Mr Cook here.' He turned to James. 'Mr Cook, what sort of vessel would you need to work on a coastal survey during the summer in Newfoundland waters?'

All the time they had been talking, James had been thinking. 'Nothing very big, sir. Something like one of the schooners they use for fishing off the Banks – about seventy or eighty ton. With about a dozen crew, sir, all staid men for preference.'

'And who is to pay for this?' asked Lord Barrington.

'I have thought of that,' said Sir Hugh. 'All I require from Admiralty are the services of Mr Cook and three or four master's mates, used to inshore work. We can give you the names of volunteers. The ship I shall provide, in the first place, from my own pocket, but I will pay for it by a levy imposed on the fishermen for the use of wood and water. It will, of course, be entered locally on the Navy List.'

'And the remainder of the crew?'

'Local volunteers, Mr Grenville. We shall enter them into the Service for local waters only, and pay them all as able seamen, at a special local rate.'

'You see the advantage of this plan, Mr Grenville?' said Sir Charles. 'It is something of a bow at a venture. By way of Mr

Cook and his master's mates we build up the skeleton of a
Cartographic Service. If it is a success in Newfoundland, I
shall institute something of the same sort for the coast of Nova
Scotia, so that when the time comes and the funds can be
got there it will stand as a beginning, at least.'

'And the charts you make – I take it they will be made in
the winter, when survey of the coast will be impossible? How
will they be sold?'

'That is still under discussion,' Sir Hugh told him. 'But
they will probably be made available through the Royal
Society, which has a suitable printing press. Or from Mr
Scales' press – he printed the charts for Lord Anson's book.'

'I like that plan very much!' said Lord Barrington, smiling.
'We get good surveys, well-printed charts – and the Colonial
Office foots more than half the bill without knowing it!'

11 *The Transit of Venus*

James Cook, Engineer and Surveyor to the Governor of New-foundland and Labrador, sat in his cabin in H.M. schooner *Grenville*, meticulously checking four pages of closely written calculations that represented as many weeks of spare-time work. It was October, 1766. The *Grenville*, named for the First Lord of Admiralty that had made her work possible, had finished her summer survey of the coast, and was lying in St John's doing a quick self-refit before crossing the Atlantic for the winter. *Grenville* was fast and handy, and with any luck should make the passage in about six weeks. This was James' fourth season in command, and he knew how to get the best out of her without straining anything.

Four summers now he had taken *Grenville* up and down the coasts of Newfoundland and Labrador, sounding the known havens and looking for new ones. The task had become his life. The years varied little; the winter at home in Mile End, on full pay working up his charts, then the boisterous spring passage to the coast. The summer spent surveying, with a midsummer visit to St John's to revictual, then the autumn passage back to Deptford or Chatham. A good life, with the results clear to be seen in the additions to the Admiralty Sailing Directions and the charts on sale from Mr Scales' shop in the Minories. And, then of course, there was his steadily growing family. There should be three children when he got back. He wondered if the newcomer would be a little girl, or a brother for Nathaniel and young James.

The ship was quiet, with work secured for the night and an anchor-watch set. James was proud of both his ship and crew. The *Grenville* had been the *Sally*, Salem-built in Massachusetts for the cod-fishing off the Newfoundland Banks. Fast and handy, she was an ideal vessel for close inshore

survey work, well worth the £328 15s she had cost. She had
made six crossings of the Atlantic without ever losing a spar.
Although she was but seventy tons in burden, James would
willingly have taken her around the world. He carried a crew
of twenty-one. Three master's mates, two midshipmen – one
was a cousin of Betty's, young Isaac Smith, on his first voyage,
a sailmaker, a carpenter, a blacksmith, a cook and a dozen seamen. A big crew for such a small ship, but there was employment for every one. Every seaman had to be a sound leadsman,
and trustworthy; often two or three men were detached from
the ship to sound out some small inlet, working from a dory
by themselves for a few days. Some of the hands had been
with the ship since she was commissioned in '63, and James
was proud of the fact that he never had to award a flogging
to anyone.

He finished his check as the afternoon wore on, and began
to make a second copy of the document. It was interesting,
even to copy. Two months ago he had been near Cape Ray,
and there had been an eclipse of the sun noted in the Alma-
nac. It had occurred to him that he could observe it and use
the figures to estimate the longitude of the Cape, checking the
results with a series of the more orthodox lunar sights. Which
he had duly done. The resulting calculations were of no
practical value, since an eclipse happened so rarely, but they
had novelty and were a good check on the accuracy of his
lunars. They had the virtue of speed, since they were based
on the results of two sets of angles taken only minutes apart,
whereas he had taken three nights over the lunars. He thought
they would interest the gentlemen of the Longitude Commission, which was why he was sending them to the Royal
Society.

The problem of the determination of longitude was still un-
solved. James was of the opinion that Mr Harrison's chrono-
metric timepiece would give the real answer – until someone
could think of a way of firing a noon gun from Greenwich so
that the report would be heard simultaneously all over the
world! But the gentlemen of the Longitude Commission
seemed to think otherwise. They pinned their faith to a system of sights and formulas, with no mechanical device to sully

the pure realms of thought. James had copies of both John
Harrison's papers, and was especially impressed with the
second one, *Proceedings Relevant to the Discovery of Longitude at Sea*, published less than a year ago. He devoutly
wished he could lay his hands on one of Harrison's controversial instruments. They were at least as quick and accurate
as an eclipse of the sun, and much more accessible.

He finished copying out his own contribution to this controversial subject, sealed it with a wafer, then put it in the mailbag to go with his other correspondence in *HMS Niger*.
Purely as a precaution, of course: both ships were sailing on
the morrow, but they would not keep company for the whole
of the passage. Light winds would favour the *Grenville*, but
in a real blow the *Niger* would be the faster. She could go on
under reefed top-sails in weather that would compel the little
Grenville to lie hove-to.

'Howson!' James called for his seaman-servant. 'Take a
dory and run this mailbag over to *Niger*. No! On second
thoughts, I'll go myself. I want a word with the Governor.'

St John's was a summer station, with not above a dozen
families living there the year round. It was the custom for
the Governor to return to England for the winter. This would
be Sir Hugh Palliser's last journey as Governor. He hoped
soon to be flying his flag at sea again.

As he was rowed across the almost circular harbour, James
opened the mailbag and took out his letter addressed to the
Longitude Committee. Maybe he could get Sir Hugh to deliver it in person.

Niger was fitted as a flagship but was not carrying an
admiral, so that Sir Hugh had very spacious quarters. James
found him on the sternwalk admiring the sunset.

'I have got used to this place,' he told James. 'I find it strange
to think that I shall not be back in the spring. So many of my
friends will be here – yourself, and all the others.' He turned
into the cabin. 'Tell me, Mr Cook – do you never wish for a
change?'

'A change, sir? I can't really say I want one, not so long as there are charts to make of this coast. I like the work. It suits me well – regular pay, my own little ship to command, every winter at home! 'Tis a seaman's dream, sir!'

'Well, let me know if you ever feel like a change,' said Sir Hugh, 'and I'll do what I can. Is there any small thing I can do for you now?'

James produced his letter and explained the contents, much to Sir Hugh's interest.

'You say you determined the longitude of Cape Ray with only two sights, taken minutes apart? That sounds almost incredible.'

' 'Tis all written down in the paper, sir. Mind you, I took the sights ashore – there was none of this scend-of-the-ship, and an arm through a backstay to stand steady enough to hold the quadrant! And it could only be done if there were an eclipse of the sun.'

'Granted all that, it was still only two sights in a few minutes. May I open this copy and study your mathematics on the passage home? Thank you. Rest assured I will deliver this myself should we be first to arrive.'

They were standing at the open stern-windows when a longboat pulled around the stern, a liveried boat's crew at the oars and as passengers a well-dressed young civilian and some officers.

'You are taking a civilian passenger, sir? A gentleman?' James sounded surprised.

'He came out with the ship,' Sir Hugh said. 'I heard he is a college friend of Mr Phipps, our third lieutenant. For some reason Mr Phipps studied at Oxford before entering the service, and his friend, Mr Banks, is a great botanist. As he is also very rich, he can afford to indulge his hobby.'

'There are very rich men who do worse things, Sir Hugh,' James remarked. 'He looks an amiable young gentleman.'

Sir Hugh gave James a shrewd look. 'So he is – unless he be crossed. He lodged at Government House for a few days while he was making his botanical expeditions into the woods. I should not care to be on the wrong side of him a few years hence. It is to be hoped that he sticks to botany and does not seek to enter politics!'

There seemed to be no reply to this. James prepared to go. But Sir Hugh had something else to say. 'The ship's officers have asked me and my staff to dine with them at six o'clock,' he said. 'I trust we may have the pleasure of your company? I was about to send a message across to *Grenville* when I saw you pulling over.'

James glanced down at his weather-stained uniform. 'With respect, sir, I should like to be excused. This is the best uniform dress I have with me, and it is not fitted for good company. Also, I want to sail with the first of the ebb, just after midnight, and I gave no leave to my crew. It would look ill if I were the only one to dine out of the ship.'

'You're a conscientious man, Mr Cook. I had forgot you were sailing on the tide. I shall miss your talk amongst all this youth and fashion. And I should have enjoyed seeing how you and Mr Banks got on together.'

'How do you mean, sir?'

'Because, although he is younger than you, you are men very much of a kind. *You* have a passion for charts and soundings, he has a passion for plants and flowers. You would either get on famously together, or else fall to quarrelling.'

James smiled as he took his leave. 'Then, sir, I should think we would contrive to get on together. I do not think I would ever have a serious disagreement with a young man of wealth who spends it in the pursuit of knowledge for its own sake.'

The *Grenville* made a passage of six weeks to the Thames; by mid-December, James was back at home at Mile End. It was a true family home now, filled with the sounds of healthy children. Nathaniel was three, small James a year younger, and now they had a sister, Elizabeth, born about the time that James was leaving St John's. The attic floor had been transformed into a nursery for them, with barred windows and a stout gate across the stairhead to prevent falls. The thick drugget laid on the floors did not entirely drown the patter or their tireless feet.

They had a staff of three now: a cook, a general maid, and a nursemaid. It was as well that James' pay of eight-and-fourpence a day was maintained the year round, while the specialist allowance of one-and-eightpence a day paid while he was actually at sea came in useful for extras. Of course, there was the income from his savings in addition to this, and Betty had a tiny portion of her own. James considered himself moderately well-to-do.

The back parlour of the house was made over into a sanctum for him, with a baize-covered door to keep out the household noises. He always enjoyed those winters at home: a morning spent at work in his pleasant little back room, then a midday dinner eaten with Betty and whatever friend had happened to drop in. Then more work in the afternoon, and the evenings spent either by themselves or with friends. Most Sundays they went across to Wapping to attend church with the Batts. After church, James and his father-in-law would go down to the *Prospect Inn* for a draught of ale, while Betty would return with her step-mother to help prepare a great sprawling family dinner which they ate about two o'clock.

Once or twice a week, James would hire a hack at the local inn and jog into the city, either to visit the chart-printers or to take his latest amendments to the Sailing Directions into Admiralty. He could have taken a wherry and gone to Whitehall Steps by water, but he chose to ride. The exercise was good for his liver.

During this winter, his paper on *Longitude Determin'd by a Solar Eclipse* was published in the *Transactions* of the Royal Society, which led to James becoming involved in correspondence with some of the Fellows on points of the mathematics he had used. Christmas came, and the New Year, and James was less in his study now than at the dockyard, where the *Grenville* was undergoing her annual refit. There was a fine week about the end of March when he took Betty and the two elder boys for a three-day shake-down cruise into the Thames

Estuary. It was the first time he had done this, and both boys
seemed to take to the ship very well. By the first week in May,
Grenville was back on station, out of St John's, on the eternal
task of surveying the harsh coasts of Newfoundland and
Labrador.

About the end of May in that same year, their Lordships of
the Admiralty were discussing an old problem. Although it
had nagged at various generations of sea rulers, it had quite
suddenly become acute with the collapse of French colonial
power in Canada and India.

Was there or was there not a Great Southern Continent?
If there was, did it have cities and men ready to trade with
the known world? There had been stretches of coast, long
stretches, sighted and even landed on from time to time, but
they had been desert. However, all these stretches of coast
ended in a query; none had been linked into a complete whole,
either island or continent. Now it looked very much as if the
French were determined to recoup their North American
losses by solving the mystery, and taking possession of whatever was there for the golden lilies and Louis of France.

There was a certain Colonel de Bougainville who was in
the South Seas in command of a frigate, *La Boudeuse*. He
was a determined and brave man; had there been a few more
like him at Quebec, the lilies might still have been flying over
the Citadel. That he was a soldier in command at sea was not
so very strange. The French still held to the old custom of
giving a command to a prominent soldier, with a sailing-
master to navigate the ship under his orders. This practice had
only died out in the British service during the recent past.
James Cook's rank as master was a survival from those days.

Following Commodore Anson's circumnavigation in the
Centurion, several English ships had been into the Pacific,
searching for the unknown eastward limits of what Tasman
and van Dieman had named *New Holland*. The Englishman
Dampier had visited the west coast of this inhospitable land,
at the end of the last century, and his report was most un-

favourable. But that the west coast was desert did not necessarily mean that the unknown east coast was the same; the difference between the east and west coasts of southern Africa, lying in almost the same latitudes as New Holland, proved that. Since 1762, three captains had been sent half around the world to try to settle this problem. They had learned practically nothing.

True, Captain Byron in the *Dolphin* had not gone specifically into the Pacific; his mission had been to the South Atlantic to try to re-locate Pepys Island, in which he had failed. At the end of his abortive quest, the Magellan Strait had been close under his lea, and the Pacific had drawn him like a magnet. After that he had done nothing, except make his way back to Europe *via* the Philippines and the Cape of Good Hope faster than man had ever done it before. That his orders told him to search the Californian coast for a half-mythical Drakes Bay meant little to Foul-weather Jack Byron, nor the request that he should seek a north-east passage around Canada. He was too independent even to try.

Captain Carteret had sailed a half-rotten *Swallow* into the South Seas with instructions so vague that it was no wonder he found nothing. Their present Lordships considered he had done very well to get back at all. At least his track-charts would show a future voyager where *not* to look.

The *Dolphin* had made a second voyage, under Captain Wallis, and was newly returned with better fortune than the other two. New lands had been discovered, but they were islands, not a continent. Captain Wallis' discovery was the talk of the town – or that part of the town that was disposed to talk of philosophic geography. The Society Islands, he had named them, in honour of the Royal Society, which had sponsored the voyage. As he described them, they seemed an earthly paradise. Well-wooded and fertile, lying north of the tropic of Capricorn, they knew neither autumn nor winter, but had a climate where spring merged into summer and back again to spring the year round. They were inhabited by folk with a high degree of primitive culture, the veritable Noble Savages so beloved by the philosophers.

'I'm afraid we shall have to send another ship into the South Seas,' Sir Charles Saunders, the First Lord, declared. 'These islands of Wallis' make it imperative. As soon as the French hear about them, they'll have a fleet at sea, looking for more.'

'We must have a good pretext for sending out a ship,' said Sir Hugh Palliser. He was serving as Third Lord, while he awaited a suitable sea-command. 'And we must send a very good man with it.'

'Well, it won't be Foul-weather Jack Byron,' said Admiral Graves, the Second Lord. 'He's taking over your last appointment at St John's.'

'Filling these long exploring appointments is the very devil,' complained Sir Charles. 'The young captains don't want 'em in case they get passed over while they're away, and the older ones no sooner get out than they're on their way home!'

Then little Mr Stephens, the secretary, spoke. 'Sir Hugh said something about a pretext for another voyage, First Lord. There was a letter from the Royal Society a month or so ago asking for ships to be sent to observe a transit of Venus. Three ships they asked for, as I recall. It was endorsed by the Longitude Committee.' He got up and tugged a bell-rope. 'It is in my chambers.' A messenger answered the bell, and was sent for the letter.

'The Longitude Committee!' exploded the First Lord. 'They've been sitting long enough. I wonder they don't admit that fellow Harrison has fairly won the award, and quit trying to solve the problem with lunars and mathematics.'

'I entirely agree, First Lord,' said Sir Hugh, as the letter was passed to the head of the table. 'But if we can use these mathematical gentlemen to mask our real purpose – what's the harm?'

The letter was passed round, then Mr Stephens spoke again. 'I would say that gave you a good pretext, my lords. But – what exactly is a transit of Venus?'

'A passage of the planet Venus across the face of the sun,' Sir Hugh told him. 'As an eclipse of the sun is a passage of the moon. Only it is much rarer.'

There was one in '61, said Sir Charles. 'But I don't know if anything was done about it.'

'I can answer that,' said Mr Stephens. 'We sent out two parties. One to St Helena, and one to either Timor or Sumatra. I could look it up.'

'No matter,' said Sir Hugh. 'I can recall what happened. They had dull weather at St Helena that day, and saw nothing. The other party were taken prisoner by the French, in spite of the safe-conduct they carried from Paris.'

'You seem to have studied this subject, Third Lord,' said Sir Charles. 'When was the one before that?'

'A long time ago,' Sir Hugh answered. 'I cannot recall the exact year, but I think it was before the King's wars with Cromwell. There will not be another in our lifetime.'

'That *does* give us a good pretext,' the First Lord mused. 'I see the Society want one ship to go to Spitzbergen, one to Hudson Bay, and one to the Marquesa Islands. – Where the devil are they?'

Hastily, Mr Stephens rang the bell and sent for a chart of the Pacific, with the Marquesa Islands shown vaguely just below the equator.

'And where would these new Society Islands be?' asked the First Lord.

'To the South and West of the Marquesas,' said Sir Hugh. 'By gad, gentlemen! If the transit is visible there – in the Society's Islands – 'tis the perfect pretext!'

'Spitzbergen?' said the First Lord. 'Hudson Bay? We must send to all three places, to keep up the deception.'

'Spitzbergen is not easy,' said Sir Hugh. 'It never has been. But I suppose we could charter a Dundee whaler to put a party ashore there. What time of year is the transit?'

'June the third, 1769,' said the Second Lord, glancing at the letter.

'Well, we can do as you say, Third Lord – charter a whaler, and make a great to-do about it. Now – Hudson Bay?'

'Foul-weather Jack is at St John's, and there is the *Grenville*, fitted and crewed for the work. He could send the *Grenville*.'

'And the main venture. Could we use *Dolphin* again?'

'I fear not, sir. She is presently being surveyed, and is so rotten she may be condemned out of the service. Even if she is not condemned, her refit would take a very long time.'

'Let us take another view,' suggested the Second Lord. 'Let us decide the man to command, and let him choose his ship. There is no war pending; the choice is wide enough.'

'You gentlemen would note that the Society are asking only for a ship and crew,' said Mr Durrant. 'They favour a Mr Alexander Dalrymple in command.'

'Never!' said Sir Charles. 'No civilian sails in command of a naval crew while I'm First Lord!'

'It has been done before,' Mr Stephens said timidly.

'Aye – and caused mutiny. There was that fellow Dampier, and after him that star-gazer, Halley. They both caused trouble, and for very small results.'

'That was eighty or so years ago,' the Second Lord pointed out.

'Human nature hasn't changed in eighty years,' replied Sir Charles. 'No, if we send a ship at all, the captain and crew are all to be of the service. They can send an observer, if they like, but he travels without rank. And I won't have that fellow Dalrymple, either.'

'You know him, my Lord?'

'Met him in Lisbon once. He's no sailor, though he has been out to India for the Company. He's studied navigation and seamanship, both on paper; he'll talk your head of about either. He has the wildest theory about a great southern continent bigger that Europe and Russia combined, when any look at the chart we have here will show that if it exists it must be in latitudes as high as – as – Spitzbergen! He's had a lawsuit with the Company, he's fought a dozen duels, and he's got the gout. He's not fit to command a cockle-boat, let alone a King's ship.'

'Quite so, Sir Charles,' Hugh Palliser broke in. 'But it is agreed we use this pretext to send down a ship, the real reason being to forestall the discovery of a Southern continent by the French?'

'Aye. But damme if I'll accept this fellow Dalrymple even as an observer!'

'No need for that, sir. I think we have the men under our hand – both the commander and the observer.'

'You have someone in mind?' asked Sir Charles.

'I have, sir – and you know him, too. A prime seaman, a good mathematician, a skilled cartographer, and a sound astronomer. In addition, experienced in command, trustworthy to a fault, and not ambitious for the future.'

'By gad, Palliser – a very paragon of all the nautical virtues. You say *I* know him?'

'You do, sir. He is James Cook of the *Grenville*, doubtless taking soundings off the Newfoundland Coast this very minute.'

'I remember him. Yes, he would do very well. But is he not still only master?'

'He is. He refused a lieutenant's commission only a couple of years ago, because it would have meant giving up his chart-work. So you see – he is not ambitious. But he would not refuse promotion for a voyage such as this.'

'Cook – Cook? Tall fellow, rather small head – brown eyes, carries himself well. Very sober.' Admiral Graves nodded.

'And what about the other – the observer?' The First Lord inquired.

'A young man called Joseph Banks. Very rich, with a passion for botany. Member of the Society, too. We took passage back from St John's in the *Niger* together.'

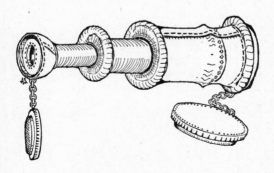

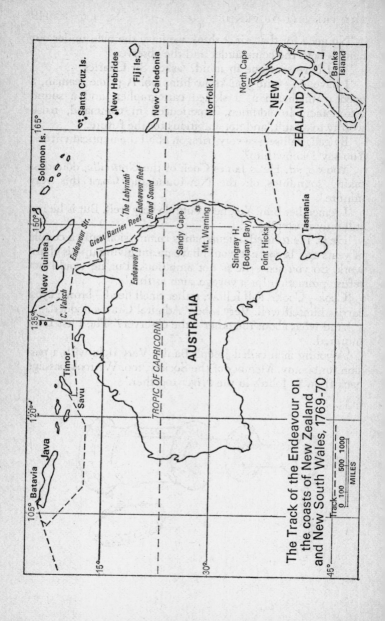

The Track of the Endeavour on
the coasts of New Zealand
and New South Wales, 1769-70

MILES
0 100 500 1000

Track ———

Batavia
Java
Timor
Savu
105°
120°
135°
150°
165°
New Guinea
Solomon Is.
Santa Cruz Is.
New Hebrides
Fiji Is.
New Caledonia
Norfolk I.
C. Valsch
Endeavour Str.
'The Labyrinth'
Great Barrier Reef
Endeavour Reef
Broad Sound
Endeavour R.
Sandy Cape
Mt. Warning
Stingray H.
(Botany Bay)
Point Hicks
AUSTRALIA
TROPIC OF CAPRICORN
15°
30°
45°
Tasmania
NEW
ZEALAND
North Cape
Banks
Island

12   *The Long White Cloud*

Saturday, 7th October, 1769, Lieutenant James Cook wrote in his log. *Gentle breezes and Settled weather. At 2.00 p.m. saw land from Masthead bearing W. by N., which we stood directly for and could but just see it from the Deck at Sunset. . . . Midnight. Brought to and sounded, no Ground with 170 fathom. At daylight made sail for the Land.*

Sanding the writing, he closed the book and put it in its place in the upper right-hand drawer of the desk. Then he locked the sloping top, caressing the smooth mahogany. Dear Betty – this luxury, a field-officer's campaign desk, had been her gift to him when he was commissioned lieutenant and appointed to *Endeavour.* Major Hollands had owned just such another in Halifax, years ago. James had always admired it. In those days he had never thought to own one, and sit at it as a commissioned officer and captain of a real ship under the King's colours. Yet here he was.

'You will think of me every time you sit at it to write your log,' Betty had said as they made their farewells. She was clumsy then with their fourth child, and her poor ankles were badly swelled this time. Yet James could still see the eager girl in her that had welcomed his gifts of carved dolls or Canadian furs.

'I will think of you a deal oftener than that,' he had replied. 'Both think of you and pray for you, my love. It will be a longer time than usual. I hate to leave you like this.'

'It will pass,' Betty had replied, her voice brave but her eyes bright. I knew that when I married a sailor I should not see so much of him as I would had I married with a – with a – '

'Flour-miller?' he had suggested, and they both laughed. Deborah's pompous husband – an alderman now, and sidesman at St Jude's – had become a family joke between them.

That had been their farewell, nearly fifteen months before. The child Betty had been carrying would be more than a year old, learning to stand, gnawing rusks with new-grown teeth. It would be at least another year before he saw it, and by then it would be talking. It! A fine way for the father of four children to speak of his youngest. He longed to know whether the child was boy or girl.

He sat and listened for a moment to the sound of the ship, creaking of timber and the gentle harp notes of the wind in the rigging. A reflection of the sun on the sea swayed across the deckhead, and the ship had a heel to the weather side that was unnatural, to say the least. There was not enough wind to make the sturdy ex-collier heel at all. One of the reasons James had selected the ex-*Earl of Pembroke* for this voyage had been the stability of the type. That, and a collier's enormous carrying capacity for its tonnage. He took his hat and went on deck. As he thought, the weather shrouds were crowded with men gazing at the long line of blue, white-capped mountains that filled the western skyline. It was their weight that was causing the list.

'Mr Gore!' James told the officer of the watch, 'I'll have the ship trimmed to an even keel, if you please. I don't believe all those people in the rigging have duty aloft.'

Mr Gore gave an order through his speaking-trumpet, and the rigging cleared like a miracle, *Endeavour* swaying over and taking up a slight list on the lee side. James studied the distant shadow of the shore. His telescope lens brought the looming mountains closer, but disclosed no detail. They were high mountains all right, but they might be at some distance from a low shore. It was, James was sure, an absolutely uncharted coast, uncharted and unseen. All his instincts were for caution.

'Have the ship brought to every hour, Mr Gore, and take a sounding.'

'Aye, aye, sir!'

From the corner of his eye James saw Mr Banks approach, and sighed inwardly. Everyone had his cross to bear; James sometimes thought his was the presence of Mr Banks. Although they had never come to actual words, there was a distinct conflict between them. It arose from a difference of opinion concerning the purpose of their voyage. James had carried out the first part of his orders to the letter; an observation of the Transit of Venus on Otaheite for the Royal Society. Now he was engaged purely on Admiralty business, to determine the extent and nature of the lands charted by Abel Tasman the Hollander, and named by him New Zealand. He was almost sure that the cloud-capped land ahead of him was an eastern coast of Tasman's New Zealand, an island and not a continent. It was his business to find out.

Mr Banks was of a different opinion. He did not appreciate James' clear-sighted view of his task. His consuming passion for botany (in James' opinion scarcely a fitting occupation for a grown man, although he certainly had a right to spend his own money as he saw fit) led Joseph Banks to try to turn this voyage into nothing but a plant-collecting excursion, to the detriment of serious geographical survey. Knowledge of what grew on a distant shore was certainly useful, especially if it could be eaten, but it was more important to the navigator to have a chart of the coastline.

'Good morning, Captain!' Mr Banks was at his elbow. Would the man never learn sea-manners, though James? He should know by now, after all his voyages, that a captain had no existence on the quarterdeck unless he spoke first!

'Good morning, Mr Banks. What do you make of our landfall?'

'Nay, sir – you should know the answer to that. I thought I had convinced all the afterguard that we must encounter Mr Dalrymple's *Great Southern Continent* somewhere hereabouts?'

'I am not convinced, Mr Banks. Especially as we have been sailing over part of Mr Dalrymple's *Great Southern Continent* for the past fortnight.'

'Indeed? What do *you* think it is, sir?'

There was the slightest hesitation between the last two words of the question, not quite enough to make it insolent.

'I think it is part of Abel Tasman's New Zealand, and I am inclined to believe it an island. But time will tell. My orders are to circumnavigate it, if possible.'

'Circumnavigate it? That will take months! What of my collection of specimens?'

'They will keep, Mr Banks – and you may be able to add to them. We will have to land from time to time, if only for wood and water.'

'You will be wasting our time, sir!' Again that hesitation. 'Mark my words, that is nothing but a long peninsular, stemming from a continent farther south.'

Diplomatically James replied, 'You may be right, Mr Banks, but it is my duty to prove it, one way or the other. Fortunately for us, we have the summer coming on, seeing that we are sailing under Capricorn.'

James turned to speak to Mr Gore and Mr Banks rejoined his Swedish travelling companion, Dr Solander. Presently they were joined by Mr Sporing, who also claimed to be a Swede, although from some things he had said in the mess, James was inclined to the opinion he came from Abo in Finland. He had travelled enough in the Baltic to know this, but kept it to himself. Finns were held to be unlucky aboard ship. But young Herman was a nice enough fellow, and a very handy instrument repairer.

Wherever Mr Banks was, you could not help being conscious of his presence. There was an arrogance about him, an assumption that his great wealth set him above the rest of mankind, and that there was nothing in the world his money could not buy. Sometimes there was a certain bombast in his manner, and despite his customary charm he could be callous on occasion.

So far the death rate on this voyage had been very light. They had sailed with near on a hundred souls on board, had lost five by death and recruited four in their places. Three of the deaths were by accidental drowning and two by freezing. These last were two of Mr Banks' servants, both negro and acquired by purchase. Mr Banks was no more concerned about their deaths than a farmer would be about two of his pigs, except to lament the waste of money. Their deaths had been entirely due to this botanizing passion of his. Mr Banks and a party had been landed on Tierra Del Fuego to collect plants, and the two poor blacks had been separated from the main body without any means of making fire. The others had made a cheerless enough camp with a fire, but the two negroes had huddled together and frozen to death in the night. Mr Banks had been very high-handed about the whole matter, but James was pretty sure that if he had been ashore in charge of such a party, poor Richmond and Dalton would still be with them.

Now Mr Banks had two new protégés, acquired in Ota-heite, Tupia and a small boy, his servant, who had no name at all so far as James could find out. Mr Banks had done well on Otaheite, James had to admit. He had been put in charge of all trading with the natives, and had served the ship very well. But he would persist in joining the natives in their odd rites and ceremonies, taking of his shirt and breeches to wear bark cloth and paint, and making very free with some of the women. James had wanted to refuse a passage to Tupia and the lad, since he suspected that all Banks wanted of them was to make a raree-show in London. However, he had to admit that Tupia was worth his keep as a pilot and interpreter as long as they were in waters where his people had sailed. Banks professed friendship for the solemn Otaheitan, but James thought it an odd sort of friendship that would take a man thirteen thousand miles from his homeland to set him up on show as a Noble Savage.

The Noble Savage! There it was again, the beloved fiction of the philosophers: take a man away from cities and civi-lization, and see his true nobility shine forth. Once it had been the Noble Red Man of the North American woods and rivers – the philosophers had not seen the sights James had seen there. And James could not see that these Society Islanders were a great deal better. They almost certainly practised some form of slavery, for there were two distinct sorts of folk on the islands, a taller, lighter coloured ruling class and a smaller and much darker working class, and there were tales of canoes being launched in the blood of human sacrifice. And undoubtedly there was cannibalism on some of the islands, though to be fair he had seen no evidence of it in Otaheite.

James took a last look at the distant coast. There was but the lightest of airs; the ship had bare steering way on her. Unless the wind freshened they would be twenty-four hours before they closed the coast. He called for his servant, Howson, to serve breakfast, and decided to eat it in the quiet of his cabin. He was a little weary of the endless, and sometimes ill-informed, speculation in the mess.

It was a meatless breakfast, a savoury porridge of scraped coconut meat, dried currants and crushed biscuit, with a pint of wort to drink with it – coffee was a luxury that had not been with them for months now. James wondered if there would be coconuts on this new shore. He doubted it; they were too far to the south. Coconuts were a fine precaution against the scurvy, and the men liked them, which was a blessing.

He ate with the bowl in his hand, walking about the cabin, with the chart-table opened and the very latest of the South Pacific charts weighted down on it. This showed voyages as long ago as those of Quiros and Torres, a hundred and sixty years before, right up to what had been learned of de Bougainville's journey, just before *Endeavour* sailed. Every voyager to these parts had been looking for one thing, the Great Southern Continent which philosophic geographers held to be necessary to balance the terrestrial globe against the mass of Europe, Africa, Asia and North America in the northern hemisphere. The later explorers had not studied each other's voyages very closely, James thought. Their tracks crossed and recrossed, all much too far to the north. If there was a continent at all, James thought it must mainly lie south of latitude 55°, and would have a climate like Greenland or Spitzbergen. Even colder, if one could judge by the summer weather he had met off the Horn. Though, of course, a man was foolish to judge a climate by a few weeks in only one season.

There was a tap at the cabin door. Mr Hicks, the First Lieutenant, looked in. 'Sunday, sir. Divisions as usual, sir?'

'Bless me, I had almost forgot. Divisions, most certainly. *And* Rounds! At four bells, please.'

'Aye, aye, sir!'

'And how is the cough, Mr Hicks?' Mr Hicks suffered from what James thought might well be a consumption, and his breathing was not helped by the fact that the cubby-hole of a cabin he had was on the deck below, three parts below the waterline.

'Much better now that I can sleep in the gig again, sir, since the pigs are all in the longboat. The night air seems to be soothing to it, sir, in spite of all the surgeons say.'

Mr Hicks withdrew, and James undressed and knotted a towel round his middle. On the deck below was a minute bathroom, with the drainage arranged below one of the two sternports. Here, with soap compounded of the salt beef fat, which James would not permit the hands to eat, and wood-ashes from the galley stove, a man could have as fine a bath as he wished, provided he did not mind unlimited salt water and crouching to keep his head below the five-foot-high deck beams.

Howson had laid out clean duck trousers and a linen shirt, and James took a worn uniform coat and his belt and sword from the closet, since this was a matter of ceremony. He took the prayer-book from the desk – another gift from Betty – and found and marked the psalms and collects for the day. With John Gathrey's fiddle and a few good voices to carry the tune, the psalms usually went over pretty well.

Divisions and Rounds, a good Sunday dinner with a tot of rum, then a Make and Mend for the afternoon. The men had earned a little ease after six weeks of beating against the everlasting westerlies of these parts. And no doubt there would be anxious days and hard times enough when it came to surveying that new coast that lay to the westward.

James was not yet really worried about the ship, but they had touched no civilized port since Rio de Janeiro – and much good that had been to them. Before they faced another winter so far from home, he would have to find somewhere to heave her down and bottom-clean, and set up the rigging afresh. Suddenly he thought of his cousin Jonty, who had planned

to become a nabob of the coasting trade, and who had died
so young. He recalled his own words to his cousin, of sailing
for weeks without sighting land. With a little shiver, he
reflected he was doing just that.

The ex-collier bark creaked and groaned as it laboured
slowly over the gentle swells. James was glad he had been
able to persuade the Committee to purchase her into the Service, rather than having to take some old sloop-of-war. Slow
the colliers might be, and cramped, but not as cramped as a
sloop-of-war. And at least *Endeavour* could take the ground
on an even keel, if she ever had to.

He went into the wardroom – general mess and workroom
for twelve officers and supernumeraries, and not a very big
space at that. Colliers ran narrow at the stern and the wardroom was only about eighteen feet by twelve, although the
light during the day was excellent from the five stern-windows.
Mr Gore, having come off watch, was eating breakfast in company with the master, Mr Molyneux, at one end of the table,
while Mr Banks and Dr Solander were eating theirs on a
corner at the other end. Three of the supernumeraries, Mr
Parkinson, Mr Buchan, and Mr Sporing, occupied the centre
of the table. They had finished their meal and were busy at
the eternal task of pressing and classifying the plant collections.

'Good morning, gentlemen,' James said. 'I trust you will
be free to attend at Divisions this forenoon?'

Joseph Banks looked up from his plate warily. 'Certainly,
Captain – if you wish it.' He clearly cared neither for the ceremonial nor the religious side of Divisions. James had wondered whether he were a Freethinker. Many of the fashionable
philosophers were inclined this way, he knew.

'Mr Green' – this was the astronomer sent by the Royal
Society, the only civilian in the ship not employed by Mr
Banks – 'I shall be taking a round of sights for longitude tonight, if the weather serves, and I would be grateful if you
would run a check on my observations.'

'A pleasure, sir. Er – I take it that is an unknown coast
ahead?'

'To the best of my knowledge, yes, but we shall know more when we have worked out our sights.'

James returned to his own cabin. From the spar-deck came the sounds of preparations for Divisions and Rounds. Glancing at his watch – a gift from the Royal Society, and a very good timepiece it was – he saw that he had at least forty minutes to spare. He took down William Dampier's *Discourse on Winds* and settled down to read for a while. Despite the early hour, he caught himself nodding over the book and was a little ashamed of himself. The fact that he had supervised the midnight soundings himself and had been on deck at first light was, he felt, no excuse for drowsiness. That was the duty of any prudent captain with an unknown coast ahead. He decided he would turn in during the afternoon; it was just possible they would find themselves in soundings at sunset, and if this happened the silent hours would be tricky, to say the least.

As a background to Master Dampier's excellent prose, James heard the shuffle of bare feet on deck as the hands were mustered. Red watch to larboard, Blue to starboard and White drawn up athwartships, abaft of the foremast. Three watches were unusual – most ships were watch-and-watch – but except for the time when they rounded the Horn, James had been on this system since they left the Channel. With so large a crew in such an easily run ship, it seemed foolish to remain on the old exhausting system. Three watches meant that every man could get eight hours' sleep every second night at least. The fact that his men were so well-rested was, James thought, one of the reasons why he had so little sickness.

The shuffling of feet died down to a murmur of voices – you could never keep Jack from talking in the ranks – and as James rose and assumed hat and swordbelt the first stroke of four bells sounded. Aloof and calm, he emerged on to the quarterdeck as the last stroke was dying away.

'Ship's company – attention!' Mr Hicks called the order. He turned and raised his hat to James. 'Ship's company present and ready for inspection, sir. All hands on deck except the magazine sentry.'

'Thank you, First Lieutenant,' James replied, as his retinue gathered behind him – Mr Hicks himself with Mr Orton, Mr Molyneux, Mr Monkhouse, and Mr Forwood; clerk, master, surgeon, and gunner respectively. 'I think Blue watch has the honour today. Please to request the other to be stood at ease.'

'Blue watch – off hats! Remainder, stand at ease!'

As the hats came off in one graceful sweep, James caught the waft of pomatum and macassar oil from thirty well-groomed heads of hair. This, mingled with the smell of fresh-washed ducks, was for him the very essence of Sunday morning Divisions.

Divisions was doubly pleasant that morning, with the interest of the new landfall ahead. James felt an almost fatherly regard for the ranks of fresh faces ranged around the half-deck. There was an odd family likeness among them, with their well-scrubbed white trousers and vari-hued shirts, each man with his hair drawn back into a short queue, stiffened with pomatum and secured by a leather thong. Some had the mark of the West India-man, a pierced left ear with a gold ring in it, a fashion taken from the Spanish and believed to strengthen the eyesight. James had as much faith in this belief as he had in another, beloved of the old Levant or East India hand, that tattoo marks conferred immunity from fever. All the seamen were barefoot, as they preferred to be, the shuffle of their horny soles on the deck sounding in contrast to the crisper tread of the officers and marines, who were either booted or shod.

It does not take long to inspect eighty-odd healthy men, even if the captain stops to exchange a few words here and there. James passed a word with Stephens, who, with Marine Dunster, had been one of the first two men he had ordered to a flogging on the cruise. For such a stupid thing, too: they had refused to eat the fresh beef he had obtained at the Azores, preferring the salt junk they were used to. So they had been flogged, twelve strokes each, and all for the good of their health. He wished sometimes there was some other way than flogging to keep order. James had an odd squeamishness about flogging; it was unknown in the coastal trade, where crews were small and ships run almost on a family basis.

He had ninety-odd on board *Endeavour*, and by no means all were volunteers. When the ship had sailed as the *Earl of Pembroke* there would have been no more of a crew than sixteen, and a third of those would be 'prentices. You could not ship a big crew and hope for solid quality right through. So – there had to be floggings on the deep-sea voyages. James had not ordered more than a dozen, and each of them light enough, and well deserved. Less than one a month. He had heard of skippers who would have two or three a week in a ship this size. His three-watch system meant he was able to order alternative punishments sometimes; much could be done by ordering a man to four hours' extra work each day, or stopping his grog. Some men had been known to ask for a flogging instead of having their grog stopped. When James did order the lash, he saw to it that the punishment was fair, that the nine-tailed lash was not a twelve-tailed one, and that the lashes were without knots or half-split buckshot clamped to them. His aim was not to scar for life.

He had been lenient even to the marines who had attempted to desert at Otaheite, realizing how strong the temptation must have been to young men cooped up in the monastic crowding of the mess-decks to desert to the warmth and friendliness of the women of Tupia's island. For this most serious naval crime he had ordered the very minimum punishment laid down in regulations: two dozen lashes – and he had remitted half of that. There was, after all, little point in laying on a punishment that was only going to make life harder for their comrades as the delinquents recovered from it.

Now it was time for prayers; he moved to where his lectern had been rigged for the quarterdeck rail. Taking out his prayerbook, he read the Order for Morning Prayer. Mr Hicks and Mr Molyneux read the Lessons, the psalms and collects were recited or sung – it was the 19th Sunday after Trinity, and James thought the second collect rather appropriate, and then Divine Service was over for another week.

'Rounds, sir?' asked Zachary Hicks.

'Yes, Mr Hicks. The orlop, the lower store rooms, and the cable tier, if you please.'

They dropped down the midships hatchway into the 'tween-

decks, then the lower deck and finally to the orlop, still attended by their retinue. Ahead of them went one of the
surgeon's loblolly boys, lantern in one hand and a brightly
polished silver spoon in the other. If this tarnished, it was a
sign that the air was too bad to breathe.

This morning the air was damp and heavy yet sweet enough,
thanks to the draughts from the windsails and the fires
burned at intervals in the well. Here all the woodwork was
whitewashed, and the bilge salty-sweet, like a tide-pool on a
rocky beach.

'She smells right sweet, Mr Gore.'

'Thank you, sir. I had a firepot burned in the well until
just before divisions.' The well was the very lowest part of
the ship, below the orlop even. A brazier of charcoal allowed
to burn there stirred up the sluggish gases that gathered in
the cleanest bilge.

'How are we off for charcoal now?'

'We still have just above two quintals, sir. Next time we
heave down the ship I would like permission to build a furnace and char some fresh.'

'A capital plan – we might even win ourselves a few gallons
of tar, at the same time. We are in the latitudes where we
could hope to find trees to yield tar and turpentine.'

'No doubt some of Mr Banks' people will set us right on
that, sir.'

'Just so!' James ended the conversation in a way that left
no opportunity for further discussion either of botany or Mr
Banks. He knew that both were something of a joke to his
foremast hands, but Mr Banks *was* nominated by the Royal
Society, and that same Society was paying handsome gratuities
to both James and the lieutenants. In James' case it was £160
per annum, a great sum indeed. A man owed some loyalty to
a Society which made such a generous gesture.

All was sweet in the orlop, the cable tier was dry, there was
no more than an inch or so of water in the well, and the
lower store rooms were in spotless order. There was a marine
sentry at the magazine, very sensibly stripped to his shirt with
his cross-belts over it. James asked Mr Forwood about the state

of the powder. Gunpowder absorbed moisture very easily; it
was impossible to keep it properly dry at sea.

'It's not what I would call bad, sir, as long as all we have
to face is savages in them galleys of theirs. I wouldn't like to
be at it hammer-an'-tongs ship-to-ship.'

James nodded. 'Well, summer's on the way, Mr Forwood,
and we'll be bound to find a beach to heave-down the ship.
You can begin making your plans to dry out the powder at the
same time.'

And that completed Rounds for the week. Up through the
mess-deck and back to the upper, past the galley where
Thompson, the one-armed cook, had great kettles of sea-pie
and sauerkraut simmering, as well as the traditional Sunday
duff. James felt an appetite. He had got the idea of carrying
sauerkraut from the Dutch and German fishermen at St
John's, and now he even liked it himself. Thompson might
only have one arm, but he had something even better than
two hands to a sea-cook: imagination.

'That smells excellent! What did you do with the salt
horse today?'

'Had it towed astern in the cage for twelve hours, sir. It
looks horrid, but it's almost fresh again, so long as it's cooked
quick. All the old pickle is washed right out of it, sir. I cut
off all the suet for soap, sir, an' the sea-pie has pepper an'
garlic to it, an' a crock of that Portugee Love-apple paste for a
relish. An' this week there's rum an' molasses i' the duff as
well as currants, in honour of the new land, like.'

So they reached the quarterdeck again.

'A very good inspection, Mr Hicks. Thank you!'

James gazed ahead, below the swelling courses and the sprit
and staysails. The long line of white-capped land almost required the eye of faith to place it nearer than it had been at
breakfast. But there it was, and almost certainly had never
been seen by a European eye before.

'I think this is an occasion to splice the main brace, Mr
Hicks,' he said. James knew that nothing pleased a sailor more
than a double tot of rum to mark some signal occasion. 'And
pipe *All Hands to Dance and Skylark* in the first dog-watch!'

13   *New Zealand*

For once James had been slightly out in his estimate of their speed. He had thought they would not close the coast until morning, but during the afternoon the wind strengthened and shifted and they struck a favourable current. By the end of the first dog-watch they were in soundings, lying at the entrance of a deep bay.

In the fading light James elected not to enter, but to stand off-and-on the coast all night, out of soundings to be on the safe side. They saw no sign of shipping, but there was no doubt that the land was peopled. After dark they saw two score or more of fires. James was not the only one aboard who felt a pang of home-sickness at these signs of domestic life.

They entered the bay with first light, sailing past cliffs at the entrance and seeing high hills in the well-wooded country beyond. No doubt now that this was settled country, and settled by folk with some pretentions to culture. Through the telescope the houses seemed to be well built of wood, with paddocks and tillage surrounding them, neatly fenced. And many of the folk ashore watching their entrance were dressed in long robes of some kind of cloth.

James had a curious, empty-bellied feeling as the anchor roared down in a shower of rusty flakes into ten fathom of water at the mouth of a small river. He had the sails brailed up and *Endeavour* swung slowly head to wind. They had arrived. James had no illusions about the nature of that empty feeling; it was fear. It was not fear for his own safety. It was the fear of a seaman whose ship is no longer fully under command, but embayed on what might well be a hostile coast. Fear for the lives and well-being of the near five score souls in his charge. Fear that he might fail to get the results of their joint labours back to Admiralty and the Royal Society. He knew the antidote – action!

'Mr Hicks! I'll have the yawl and the pinnace hoist out, if you please, with a swivel in the bows. And an armed guard in each all the time they are secured at the boom!'

'Aye, aye, sir!' Mr Hicks had anticipated this order; already the lashings were being cast off the boats as they lay in their chocks amidships. He glanced at a cluster of crowded canoes half a mile away. He hoped they would have no trouble.

'Mr Forwood! Please to tell off your gun's crews, and load all four-pounders with grape. And the swivels in the boats!'

'Aye, aye, sir! Grape it is!'

'No one is to fire without a word from me. In spite of the noise they make, they may be peaceable folk.'

Even as he said this, James had his doubts. The brandishing of arms and the shouting from the canoes did not sound peaceable.

'You appear to anticipate trouble, Captain.' Mr Banks had appeared beside him. 'I was hoping to be able to make an excursion ashore this afternoon. There must be plants growing here quite new to botanical science.'

James spoke stiffly. 'You will be able to make your collection in good time, Mr Banks. I must make sure of our defences first.' At that moment Tupia came up and said something to Mr Banks, who spoke the Otaheitan tongue well. 'What does Tupia say?' James asked.

Joseph Banks laughed. 'He says you do well to load the cannon, that those men over there are unfriends and most warlike. What they are calling to us is an invitation to come and be killed.'

James smiled. 'I confess that is what it sounded like to me, sir. And it is something we must try to avoid, else how will our results ever get back to England?'

'As ever, Captain, when it comes to our safety you have the right of it! Come, Dr Solander, we had better see to our pistols, although I hope we do not have to use them.' Saluting James, the gentlemen turned and went below.

Turning to Mr Hicks, James gave a final order. 'As soon as

the boats are in the water and all is secure, send the hands to dinner by watches. No need to clear for action, but have the men all shift into clean clothing.'

'We need firewood more than water,' Mr Molyneux, the master, told James as he dropped from the boom into the pinnace. 'But it looks very much as if we shall have to fight for 'em.'

'I hope not,' said James. He had worked out his sights with Mr Green, and found them to agree very well. He was some two degrees north of Tasman's Murtherers' Bay, on an east island. The land must be pretty narrow. 'We are not so short of either that we cannot go on for a few weeks longer on reduced allowance. We must hope for the best, and try to make friends with them.'

The pinnace seemed to fly through the water. James glanced down at Mr Banks, who looked very warlike with a pair of silver-mounted pistols thrust through a sash. He was paying no attention to the canoes with their noisy crews, but had his eyes set on the well-wooded shores they were approaching.

'There looks to be some good ship-timber there,' James remarked. He was mindful that Admiralty was becoming concerned at the run-down of timber-stocks in England. It took between five and six thousand tons of prime timber now to build a line-of-battle ship. Mast and spar timber had for a long time come from North America or the Baltic.

'I will look into it, Captain,' replied Banks. He looked casually at the gesticulating figures in the canoes. 'Those fellows look remarkably well nourished. We must try to find out what they eat in place of sauerkraut!'

They exchanged smiles at this; while the botanist realized the value of the long-preserved vegetable, James knew he loathed the taste. He felt anew the charm of the young man. If only he were not so self-willed!

They were pulling towards the mouth of a considerable river, with a steep bank on one side and a shelving beach on the other.

'Steer for the beach, cox'n. We may as well land as easily as possible.'

The pinnace grounded twenty yards from the bank and the shore-party was ferried to the bank in the yawl. The midshipman in charge of this boat was young Isaac Smith, that cousin of Betty's who had done his first year at sea in the *Grenville*.

'Thank you, Mr Smith,' James said when they were all ashore. 'I would be pleased if you would pull back into midstream and keep pace with us as we walk.' He called out to the pinnace: 'Cox'n! Lay on your oars at the rivermouth, and give us as much warning as you can if those canoes make to attack us!'

Walking for the first time on this new shore was a strange feeling. The weather was not unlike an English April day, but the birds and plants around them were completely alien. Even the greens were different, nor were the trees the same as those on Otaheite. As well as the strangeness, there was an air of menace on that shore; the usually nonchalant Mr Banks walked with hand on pistol-butt. James was relieved to see that he had them at half-cock. Many a good man had shot himself carrying fully-cocked pistols in his waist-belt.

They walked upstream a good quarter-mile and halted to look about them. 'Mr Smith' James called over to the yawl. 'Is the water fresh or salt?'

Young Isaac scooped up a handful to taste it, and spat it out. 'Very brackish, sir. Certainly not fit to drink.'

'Captain, sir!' said Trusslove, the corporal of marines. 'Are they not houses on the far bank?'

'Houses they are, Corporal!' said Dr Solander. 'And very well built. As good as the houses in Sweden.'

It was true; with their well-pitched roofs and carved bargeboards, the houses had an odd look of the Baltic about them.

'There are men over there,' James said, hailing the yawl to have themselves put across. 'We must try to get on friendly terms, if only to find out where their fresh water comes from.'

As they crossed the river the few men by the houses made

off into the woods. Bidding Mr Smith lie at a little distance
offshore, James and the others disembarked to have a closer
look at the houses. They were the most civilized dwelling any
of them had seen since leaving Rio de Janeiro the year before.

Though the seamen and marines seemed unconcerned,
James and the two botanists were inwardly stirred to think
that they were probably the first Europeans to set foot on
this new land. If this were indeed Tasman's New Zealand,
it was a part he had never seen, for it was an eastern coast
and he had seen a westerly one. Moreover, the Hollander had
made no landing on the mainland, though he had put ashore
on one or two islands off the coast.

James glanced at his companions. The botanists were
already plucking plants and grasses and stowing them in the
specimen cases that seemed as much a part of their shore-
going rig as hat and shoes. Gray, the bos'n's mate, was looking curiously about him as he stepped it out with his musket
at the high port, sniffing the unfamiliar land smells with
interest. Corporal Trusslove was keeping a wary look-out, as
he might have done on any hostile coast, and so were his two
marines. New Zealand or French Canada, James thought, it
was all the same to the men of the Duke of York and Albany's
Maritime Regiment of Foot. The four Jacks who made up the
party were looking about with interest, one of them already
chewing on a stem of grass. A run ashore was something that
came rarely enough to them. The last member of the party,
Tupia, was the only one who was showing any real emotion;
an expression of naked fear showed on his olive-skinned face.

The houses appeared to be deserted and they were within
fifty paces of them when there came the sound of shouting
from the river. They heard the sullen report of two musket-
shots on the damp air, then more shouting followed by a third
shot.

James drew a pistol. 'Back to the boats!' he ordered, turning
about and taking the lead from Gray. 'Smartly, there! On
the double!'

They reached the river bank at a jog-trot, to see the two
boats close together, holding off a group of canoes at the river

mouth. Ashore and a little way upstream, three men were dragging the body of a fourth towards the woods. When they saw James and his party they dropped the dead man and backed slowly into the shelter of the trees before the menace of the levelled firelocks.

James and the two botanists went to examine the body. It was that of a young man, strongly made and above the middle height, his skin a reddish bronze. Circular patterns were tattooed in a blue tint on his face, chest and arms. For clothing he wore a breech-clout of some felt-like fabric and a cloak of similar material across his shoulders. There were no weapons on or by the body. Tupia, braver now, came forward and gazed at the dead man, stirring the body with his foot.

'*Maori!*' he said 'He *Maori!*'

'What does he mean?' James asked Mr Banks.

After a short conversation in mixed English and Otaheitan, the botanist said: 'Tupia says that all the folk of this land are called Maori, although they are of many different tribes. They are fierce warriors; there is never peace between them. He says that when they fight they try to take their enemies captive, so that they can kill and eat them later on.'

James felt a revulsion as he looked at the well-fed body at his feet. 'Well, this one will make no more war. I wish he had not been killed. I had hoped to get to peaceful commerce with these − Maori, did you say − and this will not make it any easier. I think we had best get back to the ship at once.'

'We leave him here, so that his friends can dispose of the body after their usual fashion. − Just as it is!' James added firmly, seeing Mr Bank's fingers straying towards the cloak-toggle. 'If Tupia is right about these folk being man-eaters, we do not want them to get the same ideas about us, or to think that we would steal a dead man's cloak.'

They re-embarked and went down-river, the canoes giving way before them and closing in behind, but never coming nearer than a quarter-mile away. James was glad when they were under the guns of the *Endeavour* again. Not for the first time, he wished he were not responsible for an overeager young botanist as well as a whole ship and her company. He

had a horrid feeling that Mr Joseph Banks would have
brought the dead Maori back on board and pickled the corpse
in a rumcask to take home for the Society, such was his eagerness to get specimens of the lands they visited.

*Tuesday, 17th October, 1769: Seeing no likelihood of meet-
ing with a Harbour & the face of the Country Visibly altering
for the worse, I thought that standing further to the S. would
be loosing of Time which might be better employ'd in examin-
ing the Coast to the Northward. . . . The Bluff head of land
we were abreast of at noon I have call'd Cape Turnagain
because here we return'd.*

James finished writing and went on deck. Outwardly he
looked his usual calm self, but there was a gnawing feeling
of doubt in his belly. Please God, he had done the right thing!
He had been upon this new coast for nine days now; nine
days of constant anxiety. The experiences of the first landing
had been repeated over and over again; in all they must have
killed above a dozen of these Maori folk. With such reckless
bravery had these attacks been pressed at times that James
knew he was lucky not to have had deaths among his own
people. The brawls were not due to lack of understanding.
Tupia could speak to them and be understood; it seemed that
there was a strong similarity between the Maori speech and
the Otaheitan. One night they had three young lads on board
until morning, and they had seemed friendly and unafraid.
They had been set ashore with gifts, hoping that this would
lead to friendly commerce, but nothing had come of it. There
had been no trade. The Maori did not seem to understand the
amicable bartering so dear to the Otaheitans. They simply
took the cloth and other goods James had tried to exchange
for food and a chance to fill the water-casks. After nine days,
all they had obtained from the new land were a few cords of
firewood, and this had been got at the point of the musket.

Another reason for turning north was the time of the year.
October in these parts corresponded to a northern March, a
time of fierce gales and blustering weather. It seemed point-
less to thrust into the south-westerly gales when there was an

equally unknown coast to the north that could be explored at much less hazard to the ship. In two months' time summer would be with them, with the prospect of many weeks of settled weather. That would be the time to press to the south.

And there was yet a third reason for changing course. In the second week of November there would be a transit of the sun by the planet Mercury. The gentlemen of the Royal Society had not asked that this be observed, simply because there was no sure knowledge of land in the area where it would be visible. But if a landing could be made and the transit observed, then a longitude calculated from the results would put this new land on the charts firmly and forever.

Within a few days of the change of course came a change of fortune. The truculent inhabitants of the area around Poverty Bay, as James named their first landfall, gave way to a people no less proud and manly, but prepared to meet the newcomers in peace and friendship. Mr Gore was able to refill the water-casks, they found an abundance of wild celery ashore, and they were able to trade a little cloth for sweet potatoes. Once friendship had been established with the Maori, life was much more pleasant. On 4th November they entered a bay and prepared to observe this second transit.

'I take it that we will be here some days, Captain?' Mr Banks said.

James nodded. 'Today is Saturday, and the transit is next Thursday. We can top up the water-casks, get all the clothes washed ashore, heel and scrub the ship, cut firewood, burn charcoal – oh, we can do a mort of things!'

'And I may have a boat and crew? I must remind you, sir, that I have been afforded little opportunity as yet to make a collection of all the new things that are growing ashore.'

'And I, Mr Banks, have been afforded even less in making good the deficiencies of the ship.'

'That, sir, is your business! Mine is that the Society has charged me to make a collection of every new thing that grows on the coasts we should touch at.'

James drew a deep breath. There were times when Mr Banks' charm wore very thin indeed. 'There is no comparison between the two responsibilities, sir! Without the ship we stay

here, marooned half a world away on an unknown coast, and
not the entire Admiralty nor the Royal Society could do anything to rescue us. After I have attended to the immediate
needs of the ship I will put a boat and crew at your disposal.
It will be armed with a swivel, and the crew will also be
armed. Also, I shall require an undertaking from you to obey
the officer in charge in every particular affecting your safety
or that of the crew, as long as we remain on these unknown
coasts.'

'Indeed, sir! I would remind you that I am a civilian, and
not to be talked to like this!'

'That may well be, Mr Banks. But you are signed on board
a ship under my command, and I alone am responsible for
all on board.'

'Have a care, sir! You may be preventing myself or Dr
Solander from making discoveries of priceless value to science!'

'That again may well be, Mr Banks. I am aware that men
have made discoveries in the sciences that have caused their
names to ring down the ages. I hope indeed it may be so with
you and the good doctor. But I am also aware of this. If the
ship be lost, it will not be you or any of your party who will
bear the blame for the loss. It will be me – James Cook!'

Mr Banks had his wish, for *Endeavour* lay in Mercury Bay
eleven days. Most of the time they were at peace with the
Maori, except for one brush with a party commanded by Mr
Gore, when a warrior was killed by a musket-shot.

'I am most displeased,' James said when his lieutenant reported the matter. 'I thought we had done with that sort of
thing when we left Poverty Bay. I know we must protect ourselves, but please see to it that the firelocks are loaded with
bird-shot in the future, for the first volley at any rate.'

Strangely enough, this incident did not seem to affect the
Maori in any way. They were still willing to trade such food
as they could spare for cloth, but unlike the Otaheitans they
had no use for iron at all. Throughout their time on the
coasts of New Zealand, the explorers found no evidence of
the use of metals, in spite of the fact that the Maori made
excellent canoes and good houses. James and his crew never
came to like the Maori as they had liked the Otaheitans – a

gentle, happy people by comparison. And although they saw
no direct evidence of the practice, there was little doubt that
the Maori were cannibals. Mr Banks had bartered cloth for a
chisel which they were almost certain was fashioned from a
human shin-bone.

They found no beach on which to careen the ship, but she
was lightened and heeled so that much of the three-foot
growth of weed could be scrubbed off. Firewood and water
was got on board, and Mr Gore contrived a furnace that
yielded some excellent charcoal and a gallon or two of tar.
Oysters and other shellfish were there for the gathering, and
the cook contrived some excellent chowders. Mr Banks and
his assistants made a rare collection of new plants, including
at least five new kinds of scurvy grass and some ferns with
an edible root.

But for James, the deepest satisfaction came with the excellent observation they made of the transit of Mercury. Never,
so far as he knew, had the astronomers observed the transit of
both inner planets across the sun so far away from Greenwich in the same year. Whether or not Mr Bank's collection
of botanical specimens was complete, the gentlemen of the
Society would be gratified by this. With some pride he pricked
in the bearing of Mercury Bay on his chart; latitude 36° 47'
south and 184° 4' west of Greenwich. It was certain now that
he had sailed more than halfway round the globe; now every
league would be one more nearer home. And every day that
passed would be one less before he saw Betty again, and his
two sons and small daughter – and the child born since he had
set out.

14 New Holland

*Tuesday, January 16th, 1770. Variable light airs and Clear
settled weather. At 1.00 p.m. hauled close round the S.W.
end of the Island . . . and . . . at 2.00 p.m. we anchor'd in a
very Snug Cove . . . in eleven fathoms; soft Ground, and
moor'd with the Stream Anchor.*

And just as well, thought James, for the bottom must be as
foul as any ship's had ever been. The heeling and scrubbing
at Mercury Bay had only taken care of the growth 'twixt
wind and water; along the keel it must be more than a yard
thick. She had not had a proper bottom-clean since leaving
England, seventeen months before.

There were the sails and rigging to be looked to as well. If
necessary, new planks and sheathing could be cut and shaped
ashore; there was timber growing here very suitable for the
purpose, as good as any he had seen in Canada. But rope and
canvas were quite another matter. Stocks of both were limited,
and he knew of no place nearer than Timor or Batavia where
he could get more. Either of these was at least fifteen hundred
leagues distant, assuming that the strait south of New Guinea
and claimed by Luis de Torres existed, and other unknown
seas at that. If there were no strait, then the distance could be
doubled and the seas were still unknown.

Meanwhile, there was work to be done. James sent Howson to summon the first lieutenant, the master, and the warrant gunner.

'Well, gentlemen,' he greeted them, 'I think we have found
a suitable careenage at last. I shall require all the boats in the
water, with swivels and sentinels as usual, Mr Hicks. Mr
Molyneux, you and I will put off presently in the pinnace to

look for a suitable beach for our purpose. When we find it I want two carriage-guns landed and a small fort built. Mr Forwood might look after that side of things. Then we will lighthen ship. Master, you may land such of our sea store as might benefit from an airing ashore, while Mr Forwood can dry out our powder at the same time. And Mr Gore can set up his furnace and burn some charcoal — at a safe distance from the powder-drying, of course!'

There was a polite chuckle at the captain's little joke.

'Shall we set up new shrouds after the breaming, sir?' Mr Molyneux asked. 'We could do with them.'

'I know we could. But you know the state of the bos'n's store better than I do. And we'll get nothing new nearer than Timor at least. I suggest you renew every third lower and every other upper and t'gallant shroud, preserving every inch of old rope. We must keep some new in hand against future need, and the same with our canvas. We may have to win back all the way to England with what we have on board. Heaven alone knows what the state of naval stores is like on Timor or Batavia.'

Having given his officers enough orders for the day, James was about to return to his journal when he heard a volley of stones thunder against the ship's side and the sound of argument from the deck, Tupia's deep voice sounding loudest.

'What now,' he thought wearily. They had been on this coast above three months, and never a day of it free from care. He took hat and pistol and went on deck; he and his officers had not faced a Maori band for months now except with arms at hand.

It was a storm in a teacup. A double canoe filled with Maori had passed close, hurling rocks and insults at the ship. They had refused to trade, but had called inviting battle. One had sucked and gnawed a large bone before hurling it on deck. Surgeon Monkhouse had identified it as a human forearm, which had been cooked and which still had pieces of gristle and flesh attached. They were not far from the place Abel Tasman had called Murtherer's Bay, where he had lost a boat and four seamen. James wondered whether the seamen had gone into the cooking pot. Mr Banks wanted to keep the bone – he would – but James ordered it to be hove over the side.

For three weeks they lay in this pleasant place, which James took possession of and named Queen Charlotte Sound. The ship was lightened and beached, hove down first to one side and then the other. The bottom was scrubbed clean and the sheathing renewed where necessary from thin planking of local timber, then payed with a mixture of lime and tar. The lime they got by burning seashells.

The last English ship into the Pacific, the *Dolphin*, had been coppered on the bottom, to prevent the growth of barnacles and the attacks of the teredo worm. This it had done very well, but the copper had by some mysterious means eaten into the ironwork of the rudder and its pintles, so that in the end the cure had been well-nigh worse than the disease. James could have had *Endeavour* sheathed with copper also, but until the philosophers found out the reason why one metal attacked another he preferred to pin his faith to close-nailed tingles of elm or something similar, and the time-tried tar and lime.

Endeavour's rudder pintles were worn, too, but this was fair wear and tear, only to be expected after so long at sea. There was nothing amiss there that the smiths and armourers could not make good. When all the work on the bottom was done, the ship was hove upright on to an even keel again, and the top-sides and deckseams caulked with oakum and payed with tar. Then, while some hands painted topsides and deckhouses, the rigging was set up anew, and when the outside glistening with fresh paint the storerooms and 'tween-decks right down to the orlop were fresh whitewashed. Then, on a spring tide, she was kedged back into the water again, restored and ballasted with well-tarred boulders to make good the weight of the stores they had consumed.

It was arduous work, and went on from sunrise to sunset, but there were compensations. The men lived well while they worked thus, and they had that greatest of all sea luxuries:

unlimited fresh water. Enough to drink, to cook with, to bathe and wash clothes, or just to splash and skylark about in when work was done for the day. Every day a boat shot and hauled the seine-net – one day they drew in three hundred pounds of fish at a haul – and one-arm Thompson made some notable chowders.

James was not a little proud of the health of the ship. Apart from cuts and bruises, Mr Monkhouse rarely had a case on his hands. And Mr Banks was happy. He had the jollyboat and a crew of four with a midshipman – fresh-rostered every day – with a maze of creeks and inlets to explore at leisure. The botanists gathered so many specimens that it would surely take them all the way back to Plymouth to classify and preserve them. James sometimes went with him, to take a round of angles to be worked up later into a detailed chart of the Sound.

With the Maori they were on terms best described as an armed neutrality. But although the people were unfriendly and vaguely hostile, there was no treachery in their manner; they did not blow now hot and now cold. In many ways, James preferred this to the elaborate friendship of the Otaheite, with their name- and gift-exchanging and time wasting ceremonial. The Maori were much more direct. James felt that true friendship between two peoples with such dissimilar ethics and culture was not really possible.

Friday, February 9th, 1770, James wrote, while *Endeavour* dipped and swung over an easy swell. *Gentle breezes at S. and S.S.E., hazey Cloudy Weather. We continued our Course along shore to the N.E. until 11.00 o'clock, a.m., when the weather clear'd up and we saw Cape Turnagain bearing N. by E.E., distant 7 Leagues . . .*

An arm hooked through a backstay, James held the telescope on the hump of Cape Turnagain, satisfied that it was the same place that he had sketched and charted four months ago.

'No doubt about it, gentlemen!' he told the officers and scientific gentlemen clustered on the quarterdeck. 'That is Cape Turnagain, so we have sailed completely round an island.'

'You have put a vast piece of land on the charts, sir!' Mr
Gore exclaimed. 'Neither Captain Byron nor Wallis did anything like this.'

James felt a prickle of pride rising, and did his best to thrust
it away. Byron and Wallis had commanded the *Dolphin* in
the last two English voyages into the Pacific, and Mr Gore
had been a midshipman with both of them.

'Thank you, Mr Gore,' he said stiffly. 'I could have done
little without the aid of the ship's company.'

Mr Banks, however, looked doubtful. 'We certainly seem
to have circumnavigated an island, a very large one,' he said.
'But what of the land to the south of Cook Strait and Queen
Charlotte Sound? Might not that land be a peninsula ex-
tended north from a Great Southern Continent?'

James looked tolerantly on the younger man – by God, but
he never gave up! And, of course, what he said might well
be true. Well, now it was high summer, with some weeks of
settled weather ahead. It had taken ninety-odd days at sea,
with a fouled ship under him, to prove this northern land an
island. It should take much less with a sweetened hull and
summer weather to prove what this southern land was.

He called to the First Liuetenant. 'Mr Hicks! Please to put
the ship about, on a course south by a little west. We seem
to have been here before!'

Two days later they had dropped Cape Palliser astern (one
of the pleasures of being a discoverer, James decided, was be-
stowing the names of friends upon the features of a new land)
and were sailing south by west along a seemingly endless
coast. The ship seemed like a new vessel, answering easily to
the helm, no longer held half in check by the great growth
of weed they had scrubbed from her in Charlotte Sound.

Just a week since they had made the turn southward, James
wrote in his Journal: *Friday, February 16th, 1770. In the
P.M. had a light breeze N.E., with which we steer'd W., edg-
ing for the land . . . making like an Island . . . distant about 8
Leagues . . .*

But the curse of it was you could never be quite sure
whether it was island or peninsular – unless you did a cir-

cumnavigation, of course. James went on deck. There it was
– an island, to all intents, but he could not *prove* it. Given
unlimited time he could do so, of course. But he did not have
unlimited time. Nor would any captain on survey duty have
such a priceless commodity until some genius found a way
of moving a ship independently of oar or sail, which would
certainly not be in his lifetime.

Mr Banks and Doctor Solander were taking an airing on
deck. They were deep in classifying the specimens got at
Queen Charlotte Sound, and James had seen but little of
them for the past week.

'Good afternoon, Mr Banks.' He indicated the distant land.
'I cannot make up my mind whether that is an island or not.
What do you say?'

'You have proved me partly wrong once before at least,
Captain, so my opinion is pure guesswork. But, it appears to
me to be an island. Is there any chance of making a landing?'

James shook his head. 'I regret it cannot be, not at this distance from the shore and against this wind. I would like to get
closer to it myself, to settle this island business.'

'Nay, sir, we settled that – I said it was an island, you
remember?'

'Then I shall just have to take your word on it, Mr Banks.
Have I your permission to mark it on the charts as Banks
Island?'

The younger man's face flushed with pleasure. 'Sir, I am
honoured! I confess I had hopes that one or other of the new
plants we have found might bear my name – but an island
of such magnitude!'

*Saturday, March 10th, 1770. P.M. Moderate breezes at
N.W. by N. & N., with which we stood close upon a Wind
to the Westward. At Sunset the Southernmost Point of Land,
which I named South Cape, and which lies in the Lat. of 47°
19'S., Long. 19°12'W. from Greenwich . . .*

Not at all bad, thought James. Four weeks almost to the day
from Cape Turnagain, while it had taken four months to get

around the north island. True, the west coast of this one still lay ahead, and there was still a chance this land might prove to be a long peninsula jutting away from Tasman's New Holland, though unlike Mr Banks and Dr Solander, James did not hold this view.

Except for it being so far from England, this New Zealand he was putting on the map would be no bad place to found a colony. Taking a pencil, he began figuring out courses and distances. The quickest way out would be by the Cape of Good Hope, and the quickest way back by the Horn, which would give the advantage of steady westerlies for the round voyage. Waiting on the seasons, say a year for the round trip. It might have to be done, too, if only to keep out Fat Louis and the French. There were places in the north as fertile and beautiful as any in the world: the Thames River, for instance, or the place he had named the Bay of Islands. Both had good harbours, and with a stronger party than his the Maori would be no threat. The timber was good, except for mast-making, and there might even be suitable trees for that farther inland. The Maori were warlike and truculent now, but he felt they were good people at bedrock. Cannibalism? That might be overcome by introducing food-animals, and their lust for war might be countered by introducing beasts of the chase – deer, for instance. Hunting had always been a good substitute for war in the Old World. And the colonists-to-be might gain friends and headway by holding the balance of power between opposing Maori tribes, as the French had done with the Indians in Canada.

James shook himself out of his daydream. Time enough for such speculation when he was safely off this coast. He looked again at the calculations he had made concerning the length of the passages from England – four or five months, eh? Put another way, this meant they could be snugly back in England by Christmas! Back with Betty and his family, the house smelling of roast goose and plum-pudding, and the boys old enough to take an interest in his wanderings. He picked up the scrap of paper and let it fly through his fingers at the opened port. He must not let the roast goose of Old England get too strong a hold on his fancies while there was yet work to do.

Three weeks later, and they had run up the whole of the west coast of the south island, and were back in the entrance to Cook Strait. Tasman's New Zealand had proved to be two very large islands and a multitude of smaller ones. Much the same as the British Isles, in fact, but about half as big again, lying a little closer to the equator, and on the opposite side of the globe. A most satisfactory piece of chartwork, with a bonus thrown in by the observation of the transit of Mercury.

Most of James' orders from their Lordships had been carried out; and no one could blame him now if he took the easiest way home to give them his results. Yet there were still problems that plagued him. He felt the choice of a homeward route was not one to be settled by an arbitrary decision, but should be properly discussed by a council of officers. He sent Howson to summon them, and Mr Horton the clerk to take down the decision for everyone to sign.

James sat at his desk, the two lieutenants were perched on the narrow settle, and Mr Molyneux brought in a chair from the wardroom. Mr Horton sat on the only other chair, his writing tablet on his knee.

'Well, gentlemen, we are about to leave this coast. I thank you for the service you have done myself and their Lordships, and be assured I will mention you all in my Journals.'

'Thank you, sir! It has been a pleasure to serve with you,' responded Zachary Hicks. 'May we have smooth seas and fair winds for the homeward passage.'

'Amen to that, Mr Hicks! It is the matter of the homeward passage that has caused me to ask you here today. You may take it that this is a formal Council of Officers, and the decision we reach will be logged as such.' James continued: 'Up to now we have carried out all our orders to the letter. On Otaheite we observed the transit of Venus, and the outline of the New Zealand islands is firmly on the chart.' He paused. 'There is one more thing we were asked to do, at my discretion: to prove or disprove the existence of the Great Southern Continent.'

'Can we not do something in that matter too, sir?' asked Mr Gore.

'We could, by going home round the Horn and keeping to the south of latitude fifty degrees as much as possible on the way. In fact, that might be our quickest way home.' James addressed the Master, he being the most junior officer and entitled to give tne first opinion.

'The Horn? I don't like the idea, sir,' Mr Molyneux replied. 'Our hull is in very good shape, but our rigging is not. It will be midwinter when we reach the Horn, and God alone knows what the weather will be like.'

'We had stun's'ls set on the way here,' said Mr Hicks. 'From what *I* had heard, that was something I never expected.'

'Freak weather, it might have been,' said Mr Molyneux. 'I knew once a flat calm in the middle of Biscay in March, and the sun so hot the pitch softened in the deck-seams. But it was only the once.'

'It was midsummer when we rounded the Horn last, Mr Hicks – but as the Master says, it will be midwinter on the way back.

'May I ask a question, sir?' asked Mr Gore. 'Do *you* believe in the existence of this great continent?'

There was a little silence into which James dropped his reply. 'I can only answer your question one way. There *may* be a continent, but it must lie so far to the south as to be well-nigh useless to mankind.'

'I made two voyages in the *Dolphin* sir, and I've done as much reading on the matter as I could. I hold the same view as you do – and I believe we should do no good at all by sailing for the Horn. Put me on record as believing such a course to be a needless hazard.'

'Thank you, Mr Gore. That only leaves you, Mr Hicks.'

'I agree with the Master, sir. I don't think our rigging is fit to face winter gales. Like as not we should find ourselves dismasted.'

James nodded. 'And I concur, on both counts. So that leaves us with two alternatives. What about sailing for the Cape of Good Hope direct?'

'I'd rather not, sir,' said Mr Molyneux, 'and for the same reasons that I did not fancy the Horn. Going for Table Bay direct, we should be bucking the westerlies all the way.'

'And we'd find nothing,' added Mr Hicks. 'The very dogs in the street have quartered those seas, over and over again, ever since the Portuguese first rounded the Cape. The ice comes up pretty far north thereabout, sir.'

'Mr Gore?'

The young man grinned. 'I'd say no, sir. Fearnaught suits and sou'westers, and on watch and watch? Comfort for me every time, sir.'

'Then there is only one other way,' James said, a throb of excitement in his throat. 'Westward from here must lie the coast of Tasman's New Holland, which has never been seen. We could look for that, coast along it, then make for Timor or Batavia.'

'It would mean going north-about around New Guinea, by the Moluccas,' said Mr Gore.

'That is what every sailor to these parts has done,' said James. 'All but one, that is.'

'Who was that, sir?' asked the Master. He was a good seaman but did little reading.

'A Portuguese, Luis de Torres,' James replied. 'He reported a strait *south* of New Guinea, but no one has seen it since. If we strike this unknown east coast of Tasman's, and the Torres Strait proves to be a fact, then we are not so far from the Dutch Indies after all.'

'I'm for that!' said Mr Hicks. 'And who knows? It may be that this Dutchman's New Holland is the only Great Southern Continent there is!'

15   *Stingray Harbour*

On a Sunday morning – All Fools Day, to be precise – right
in the middle of Sunday Divisions, *Endeavour* finally dropped
Cape Farewell below the horizon. It was six months to the
very day since they had first sighted New Zealand. James
hoped there was nothing ominous in leaving it on this of all
days. He gave an inward sigh of relief as they left the rugged
coast. True, another unknown coast lay ahead, with an un-
proven strait at the end of it. But if the present weather held,
that lay about three weeks away. Meanwhile, they could en-
joy the luxury of day after day of plain sailing. The routine
for the passage was clear in his mind. Twice daily, at noon
and midnight, he would make a sounding. Weather permit-
ting, every afternoon he would shoot the trawl. The first
would give him warning of the approach of a continental
shelf; the second, with luck, should produce edible fish, or at
the very least some specimens of marine life for the delight
of Dr Solander.

James went through the routine of Divisions with a good
half of his mind on his own private thoughts, although anything out of the ordinary commanded his attention at once.
He had inspected Red Watch and found all well with it, but
midway through his inspection of White Watch his wander-
ing thoughts were brought up with a round turn at the
appearance of a young seaman. His complexion was a muddy
yellow, with a bright red flush on the sharp cheek-bones. His
eyes were unnaturally bright, yet had a weary look.

'Sutherland, isn't it?' he asked. 'What's the matter with
you, lad? Swallowed your quid?'

Most seamen chewed tobacco, some until the last moment
before the captain's arrival on Divisions, rolling the half-

chewed quid under the tongue for further use when the officer had passed on. To swallow either quid or juice was a fairly common occurrence and could half-poison a man.

'No, sir. I don't chew any more, sir. Don't seem to have the stomach for it these days.'

'Then you must be sick, looking as you do. Have you reported to the surgeon?' James knew the answer even as he spoke. Seamen dreaded the pills and purges of the surgeon almost as much as the thought of being wounded in battle.

'No, sir. But there's naught wrong with me, sir, except a bit of a cough. I eats hearty, sir.'

'Well, that's a good thing. But you're to see Mr Monkhouse, and you're to do as he tells you.' He turned to Hutchins, the bos'n's mate of the watch. 'Take Sutherland off watch-keeping and put him on day work for the present. Let him help the sailmaker; that will keep him in the open air. If Mr Monkhouse agrees, he's to rig his bed in the open whenever the weather serves.'

James sent for the surgeon that afternoon. 'What do you think is wrong with Sutherland, Mr Monkhouse?'

'I guess you know as well as I do, sir. Sutherland is in a consumption.'

'That's what I thought. Then I did right in ordering him to sleep above decks.'

'Quite right. I don't know that it will do him much good, but it will stop him transmitting it on his breath to the others. Not that I despair for Sutherland – his life may not be in any danger yet. After all, there is Lieutenant Hicks . . .'

'I know,' James said. 'He should never have sailed. But he holds up remarkably well.'

'He does. In fact, he is beginning to throw it off, I believe. As young Sutherland will, I'm sure, now that he's off watch.'

'We have lost no man by sickness yet,' James pointed out. 'By drowning and by mishap, yes – and one by overmuch grog – but these are accidents that can happen anywhere at sea. It would be a fine thing to sail right round the world, losing not a man by sickness.'

'That would be more than a fine thing, sir, if I may say so. It would be a miracle.'

Thursday, April 19th, 1770. James wrote in his long angular script. *In the P.M. had fresh gales to S.S.W. and Cloudy Squally weather with a large Southerly Sea . . . Sounded, but had no ground with 130 fathoms of line. At 5, set the Topsails close reef'd, at 6, saw land extending from N.E. to W. distance 5 or 6 leagues, having 80 Fathoms, fine sandy bottom . . . The Southermost point of land we had in sight I judged to lay in the Latitude of 38°0'S. in the long. of 211°7'W. from the Meridian of Greenwich. I have named it Point Hicks . . .*

And fittingly so, James thought, as he read over and sanded the entry, since Hicks had been the first to sight it. Though what he was going to do for names in the future he did not know, since he was sure that what Mr Hicks had sighted was the hitherto unknown east coast of Tasman's New Holland. That being so, there would be hundreds of miles of it. If the names he had already bestowed were to remain, the present Board of Admiralty and the gentlemen of the Royal Society were going to be very well remembered. His hands smoothed the dark mahogany of his desk, and Betty stole into his thoughts. It was still just possible he might be home by the back-end of the year.

On deck he went to larboard and surveyed this new coast. It was high in places, with a blueness quite different in degree to any he had seen on a mountain coast before, and he wondered at the cause. It was one of the things he doubted he would find out, since without horses they could not go very far into the interior. If the mountains were twenty miles in from the coast they might as well be on the moon, for all the exploration he could do among them.

He could not make the comparatively detailed survey here that he had made of the coast of New Zealand. There might be a great deal of it, since it might reach up all the way to New Guinea . . . but for the problematical Torres Strait. And time was against him. He was already twenty months out from England, with another four months at least for the homeward passage when he was clear of this New Holland.

(Incidentally, he would have to find a new name for it – no Dutchman had ever sighted this.) Time, cordage and canvas. All three were running out on him.

Ten days later. Another Sunday. Ten days sailing north-ward along a seemingly endless dreary and featureless coast. True, there were hills, but they were nowhere very high, and woods, but they were nowhere very thick. The one notable thing about the coast was its apparent lack of harbours, and the thundering surf on its beaches. Because of these no land-ing had as yet been made.

A landing was imperative if they were to save Sutherland's life. It was foolish, as he admitted to himself, to make such a fuss about one man dying of sickness. But he would be the first in the whole ship, and once he had gone – well, there would almost certainly be others. There was Ravenhill, the sailmaker, another Yorkshireman. He had an ill look at times. He had signed on as aged forty-nine, but he could well die of sheer old age, for in fact he looked to be well over seventy.

Mr Monkhouse held out little hope for Sutherland while they were still at sea. 'A week or ten days ashore, and I might save him. He needs fresh food to make new blood in him – underdone steaks, fish, fowl. Bleeding him might ease the fever, but that I dare not do. He'd never stand it in his present state.'

'There's no sign of the scurvy?'

'Not a sign, thank God! Otherwise, we might have half the crew down. No, 'tis the consumption – a wasting sickness – though God knows how he caught it.'

Then they had sighted the bay, running deep into the land, flanked by two low capes. Here were signs of human life. All along the coast they had seen smoke and fires, and once the figures of men on a distant beach, very black against the dazz-ling sand. They had stood into the bay on a Saturday after-noon. Now it was morning, and the yawl was in the water rowing towards the new land.

There was a swivel at the bows, and four armed marines under Mr Midshipman Smith as a guard. Six seamen man-ned the oars, and another two the swivel. Mr Banks and Dr

Solander were with them, of course, and Briscoe, one of their servants, and Tupia, in case he could talk to these new folk.

As they pulled towards the shore, James gave it a good looking-over. There was a beach so white it almost dazzled the eye, with sand-dunes behind it and then a wood with tall but thinly leaved trees. They were in a great bay, almost circular as far as he could see, about two leagues across. The entrance, however, was a scant half-a-mile wide, and invisible except from the south-west. He wondered if such bays were a feature of the coast: if they were, that would account for the fact that he had not seen them. Outside, the everlasting surf flashed white on the rocks to the north and south, but ahead of them the tide rolled in gently, breaking on the sands with the gentlest of ripples. Hills showed above the trees over toward the west, hills as blue as any artist ever painted in some fanciful picture of the Golden Age. They looked very far away.

Closer at hand the scene was less reminiscent of the Golden Age. In among the dunes showed several huts, very low and poorly built, while drawn up above the tidemark were a number of canoes, twelve or fourteen foot long. Along highwater mark a score of folk watched their coming. They were about the middle height, very slenderly built, and appeared to be completely naked. They were a very dark brown, nearly black, with curling hair.

'These are a different folk to any we have seen yet!' said Mr Banks. 'See, the men have beards. Try if they understand your speech, Tupia.'

The rowers lay on their oars fifteen yards from the water's edge.

'*Haromai, Taata, wahine! Awaii teraa?*' Tupia called.

An incomprehensible babble of talk followed this; the tones were not unpleasing. For some minutes Tupia tried to drive a conversation, then turned and shook his head.

'These men do not understand. They are different to those of *Ahinemoa* or *Toyipoanamn*. Tupia has not met with such men ever before.'

While he had been trying to speak to them, the women,

the older men and half-grown children had gradually retired into the dunes, but two younger men remained facing the newcomers. Their bodies were painted in odd patterns in white and ochre pigments, very like the crossbelts and accoutrements of the marines. They were armed with long barbed lances, a bundle of shorter spears and what appeared to be a thin flat club shaped like a Turkish scimitar. All these weapons were of wood.

'They are different to any I have ever seen, too,' said Mr Banks. In spite of his youth he had travelled much. 'And, I think, quite the simplest.'

James turned to one of the seamen. 'Throw out a handful of beads and a few nails,' he said. 'They may not know what they are, but they should know the nature of a gift. We might be able to establish some sort of friendship.'

Tupia and the seamen threw the offerings ashore, where they were hastily scooped up by the naked men.

As he watched them, James saw what seemed to be a gesture of friendship. He gave an order, and the boat turned in and approached the beach. At once the men ran down to the water's edge, making to hurl their lances. James aimed a musket loaded with birdshot between the men and fired. Running back, one made threatening gestures with his spears while the other picked up a large stone, hurling it so that it fell just short of the boat. A man may be killed just as well by a stone or spear, thought James. He picked up a second musket, aiming this time and peppered the stone-thrower's legs with small-shot. He seemed unaffected by the sting of the shot, though he showed some dismay at the sight of the blood-flecks from the wound. Then, covering themselves with small oval shields, both men followed their companions into the shelter of the dunes.

'Now, Mr Smith – put us ashore!' James ordered.

The midshipman jumped into the water with one of the seamen. As the yawl grounded, the two men reappeared among the dunes, sending some of the shorter spears whistling through the air with great velocity. One just missed striking Mr Smith's head; another stuck quivering in the

sand at his feet. James snatched up a third musket, and aimed
full at the body of one of the throwers. He fired, and saw
his target stagger and run back into the dunes. Sighing, he
handed the musket back to a marine to be reloaded. So much
for friendship once again, it seemed.

The midshipman stooped to collect the short spear from
the sand.

'Have a care, Mr Smith!' Mr Banks called out. 'It may be
poisoned. Wrap this kerchief round it!'

The shore party walked through the dunes into the woods
beyond. They were different to any woods James had seen
before, with very little undergrowth or grass between the
trees, and none of the mossy piles of leafmould of an English
wood. Some trees were shaped like those in the northern
hemisphere, but their foliage was a much darker green and
more glossy. Their trunks rose forty or fifty feet before they
branched, and were covered with a smooth integument with
darker patches that looked more like hide than bark. There
was no regularity or symmetry about the placing of the
boughs, and these hung down somewhat sadly, thinly leaved
so that they cast but little shade. They had a fragrance that
resembled the balsam of North America, but more pungent.
Their brown leaves lay dead on the ground, crackling into
powder under their feet.

'It is well on into autumn for these parts,' said Mr Banks.
'I would judge these trees to be in full leaf. So they must be
evergreen.'

The three botanists bent to collect specimens. Leaving two
men to guard their backs, James and the others pushed ahead.
They kept a good watch; Mr Banks might well be right about
the poisoned darts. But no folk appeared, and they went on
towards the little valley in the dunes where they had seen the
huts. These erections, some four feet in height, built of poles
and bark, were very different to the solid dwellings of the
Maori. They looked as if they would collapse at the first blow
of wind. In one of them they found four infants much of an
age sleeping in a heap like puppies. It was an innocent and
oddly touching sight. These folk must have no enemies,

thought James, neither man nor beast, to leave their children
so. He was confirmed in this opinion by a rack of darts, similar
to those flung at them on the beach, which all had dried fish-
scales on them, while around the fireplace lay the skins and
bones of large fish. He took a number of the darts, leaving an
equal number of bead necklaces in exchange.

'Water!' he said to his escort, thinking of the needs of the
ship. 'There must be some close by. Spread out and look for
it, but keep in sight of one another.'

They found it in a number of shallow sandy pits on the
shoreward side of the dunes, slightly tinged with salt but
quite drinkable. They were not yet really short of water, but
ninety odd men used close on half-a-ton a day, so that eight
tons had gone on the passage from New Zealand. James sighed
with relief. At least they could get firewood and water here,
and oysters, judging by the mounds of shells he glimpsed on
a midden. Some of the shells were big enough to be used as
dinner-plates. His thoughts turned to young Sutherland.

'Dunster,' he said to one of the marines, 'what sort of a bird-
shot are you?'

'I don't know, sir.'

'Well, here's your chance to find out. Take one of your
comrades, and shoot some of these parrots flying about. They
ought to make good eating enough; I'm sure Sutherland would
get some good out of a dish of stewed parrot-breast.'

'Aye, aye, sir! Shoot parrots it is, sir! About a dozen, sir?'

'As many as you can. You might like a few for your own
mess.'

'Aye, aye, sir! Try anything once, sir – that's my motto
these days.'

James smiled as he moved off on his hunting, thinking that
the few lashes he had ordered had done nothing but good. It
was Dunster who had been charged with refusing to eat
fresh beef at Madeira – and here he was on a new coast, cheerfully looking forward to a dish of boiled parrot!

The rest of the party left the hut with the puppy-children
still asleep. Apart from them, there was no other sign of natives,
and the woods were too thin to afford any concealment. Mr

Banks and the others were still botanizing, and James had
learned now that they could not be hurried once they had started collecting. He walked over to them to tell them he intended
to have a gun fired in two hours' time, as a signal for their
return. He found them laden with specimens already. 'Please
to remember, Mr Banks, that at least four of the guard *must*
have their hands free, to cope with any sudden ambushment,'
James said. 'And when the gun fires, it is to be regarded as the
signal for an immediate return.'

'I understand, Captain. Er – do you intend to stay long in
this place?'

'A week at least. Maybe longer. We have to wood-and-
water, and get enough fresh food to get Sutherland on his
feet again. You find this place interesting?'

'*Interesting*? You understate it, Captain! Never in all my
travels have I seen so much that is new! All of it is new –
even the birds.' The sound of Dunster's firelock sounded.
'What's that?' Mr Banks asked.

'Dunster and one of his mates shooting parrots for the pot.'

'I may have one or two as specimens?'

'Assuredly, Mr Banks! And you will let me know if you
find any edible vegetable?'

'Certainly. It would help if we knew what those blackfellows on the shore live from.'

'There is a hut down there with four sleeping children in
it, and a cooking-fire, gone out. They appear to live mainly on
fish and oysters, by the shells and bones.'

'Children!' Mr Banks exclaimed eagerly. 'I must see them.'

'Then pray, do not disturb them! We don't want a hornet's
nest about our ears. It would greatly assist us if we could be
at friendship with them.'

'To be sure, Captain. I shall but look, I assure you.'

Knowing Mr Banks, James was by no means assured, but
there was the wood-and-watering to see to, and that he could
only do from the ship. He walked between the dunes, calling
on the crew in the yawl to signal for the gig. While he waited
for it, he had time to look at the canoes on the beach. They
were the crudest sea-craft he had ever seen. Fashioned out of
bark skin, they were innocent of either frames or form-work

on the inside. At either end the bark skin was gathered up and
tied with a cord of the same stuff, while three or four rough
sticks of timber served as thwarts to hold the covering open.
Other timbers with a natural but uneven curve were lashed to
these and the two ends lengthwise, to serve as rough gun-
whales. It was a marvel to James that they held together, but
they must be stronger than they looked.

These must be very primitive folk indeed. Here was no
artistry, such as he had seen with Otaheitan or Maori arti-
facts. No carving, no inlay of shell, no evidence even of the use
of stone tools. Everything was of the very crudest construct-
ion. Some of the Maori canoes had a crew of fifty paddle-
men, and the Otaheitans built double canoes as big as small
ships, capable of long ocean passages. Compared to such
craft, these were indeed pitiful. If a sheer lack of culture was
a sign-manual of the Noble Savage, maybe they had found
that mythical creature at last.

'. . . suffer us not, at our last hour, for any pains of death, to
fall from Thee.'

Mr Hicks nodded to the bearer-party, and they scattered the
ritual handfuls of earth on to the hammock-shrouded body,
lying six feet down in this, the first English grave on the new
coast.

'Forasmuch as it has pleased Almighty God of his great
mercy . . . we therefore commit his body to the ground . . .'

James read on, careful of the words, for this was the first
time he had read the service over a shore burial. There was
another page and a half, the beautiful words falling on the
unresponsive ears of the marines and seamen, then the *Bene-
diction*, and it was finished. Mr Forwood mustered the firing-
party, five marines to one side of the grave, five seamen on the
other. At a little distance, a party of shock-headed blackfellows
looked on, curious as ever at the goings-on of the strangers.

'Marines – marines!' Mr Forwood gave the cautionary
words. 'One volley of blank – fire!' It crashed out, sounding
flatter than usual since there was only a wadding in the barrels
and no shot. 'Re-charge your pieces!'

Then it was the seamen's turn – the volley a little ragged
this time – and the marines once more. Mr Forwood frowned
at the second volley.

James thrust Betty's prayer-book back into the pocket of his
ceremonial jacket and walked back to the pinnace. He had
noted the blackfellows watching the burial, glad to see that
they were becoming tamer, though as yet he had never been
any closer to them than on that first day. On the second day
he had gone back to the place where they had seen the sleeping children, only to find the huts and darts had gone – the
necklaces they had left remaining. So far these folk had
proved to be shy and wild, but not hostile. It seemed that they
only wanted to be left alone in their noble savagery.

He told himself that he should not feel so depressed at the
death of a single seaman. The firing-party were marching
back to the pinnace in ragged time over the sands to the music
of a flute played by one of the marines, while his rear-rank
man carried both muskets. The tune was an old one, *Lilli-
burlero*, its arrogant gaiety striking the right note for the
occasion. It was traditional in the Service that grief for the
dead should be left at the graveside; James had already decided to splice the mainbrace that evening. That would cheer
up the lower deck as nothing else could, since there were no
wenches handy. As for himself – he would give a dinner-
party!

'I'll give a dinner in my cabin tonight, Mr Hicks,' he said,
'and we might roll the dice for a few turns at Hazard afterwards. Bring along one of the young gentlemen – anyone you
choose. And the Surgeon, and Mr Banks, of course, with one
of his gentlemen. I think that is as many as my cabin will sit.
Johnson can bake us a piece of that last stingray Mr Gore
harpooned. He has bayleaves, and there are oysters for a
sauce.' The liking he had acquired for fish at the Sandersons
had never left James. 'It's a mighty delicate eating fish for its
great size.'

'It is that, sir,' said Mr Hicks. He did not altogether share
James' fondness for stingray. Still, with plenty of oyster sauce.
. . . He looked across the quiet waters of the great bay. 'Have
you decided on a name for the bay yet, sir?'

'Not yet, Mr Hicks. I have been casting my mind about for some natural features to give it a name, as with the Bay of Islands. Have you something in mind?'

'No, sir – not really. I did just think of Sutherland's Point since he will be a part of it from now on.'

'It shall be so. But the bay itself – we have already almost run twice round the list of gentlemen to name it for.'

'You said a natural feature, sir. There's a mort of stingrays all about – big as dinner-tables, some of 'em. You wouldn't think of calling it Stingray Harbour?'

'Stingray Harbour? Thank you for the suggestion, Mr Hicks.'

And next day, after the dinner and a noisy evening at Hazard, James noted it down in the journal. But it never quite rang in his mind, and a few days later he scored it out and substituted Botanists' Bay. Nor did that have quite the right ring either. At last a good while later he altered it again to Botany Bay. That was the name it finally carried on the charts.

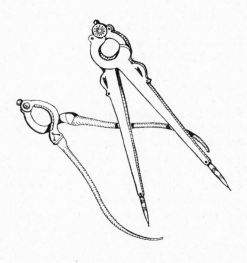

16   *The Labyrinth*

*Tuesday, May 22nd, 1770. At Noon we were by Observation
Lat. 24°19′S., Long. 208°5′ West from Greenwich. Wednesday, May 23rd, 1770 . . . Haul'd in close upon a wind, and
sent a boat ahead to sound; after making some Trips we
Anchor'd at 8 o'clock, a Sandy bottom . . .*

The official part of the Journal set down, the courses, bearings, and positions, James sat back and thought about his next
entry. It was a matter of human conduct. It was not so much
that Mr Midshipman Magra had slit the clothes from Mr
Horton's back as he lay insensible, but that he had seen fit
to slit Mr Horton's ears as well. That they had both been
drunk was some sort of official excuse, of course. But James,
an abstemious man himself, had strong feelings about any
man who drank himself into a stupor.

Justice must be done. Discipline must be preserved. Mr
Horton, as captain's clerk, ranked well above a midshipman.
James made a decision: he would disrate Mr Magra to able
seaman, then if there were any more horseplay involving
knives, let him beware. A midshipman was a warrant officer,
and could not be flogged, but an able seaman could be tied
at the gratings for any one of a score of petty crimes.

He set down the decision and looked back at the earlier
part of the two-day entry with some satisfaction. He could
not help but feel pleased at the distance run since leaving
Botany Bay. In seventeen days they had run through some
ten degrees of latitude. They were six hundred sea miles
nearer home. It certainly looked as if the wives and sweet-
hearts were hauling right strongly on the tow-rope. But the
satisfaction was tinged with caution: they could not possibly
hope to hold a pace like that all the way to England.

They had learned more at Botany Bay than the nature of plant life in this new land; it seemed that the Bay itself was almost a standard form of harbour on the coast. He had sighted several similar ones since, their narrow entrances giving on to a considerable sea-lake behind. The first two were within a score or so miles of Botany Bay itself. He had nosed into half a dozen since, always on the lookout for an easy watering place and not finding one. Now it was becoming necessary that they should find water, after seventeen days of coasting northward. Not even the best of crews could take easily to a short ration of water within sight of land. They were very close upon the southern tropic, Capricorn, when water would become even more desirable. So they anchored in Bustard Bay, named for the birds they found and ate there. The anchorage was not good, but it served; the water was not plentiful, but it was there.

'I shall need a deal of convincing there are any other kind of humans in this land,' James said, surveying the low bark shelters, the fish remains and the piles of empty shells by the warm embers of the fires. 'We are seven hundred miles from Botany Bay, and here we see exactly the same things: naked folk, no metals, no cloth, the crudest of wooden implements. These people are the most simple of any I ever saw, simpler than the Caribs in the West Indies, or the folk on Tierra del Fuego.'

'But, in fact, we have seen very little of this land,' Mr Banks pointed out. 'There may be places where the indigenous peoples have a much higher culture.'

James shrugged. 'Both Dampier and Tasman reported folk much the same as these away over on the West Coast – four thousand miles of sailing distance, at least. If men do not differ over four thousand miles, I think we are not likely to find much change in the eight hundred or so between here and the Torres Strait.'

'We might, sir. It happens in other places. There is much difference, for instance, between a Spaniard and a Dutchman in Europe.'

'There I find myself at odds with you, Mr Banks. There is

little real difference – each of them build cities and houses and ships very much alike.'

'Language, sir – that differs greatly.'

'For all we know, there might be a great difference between the languages these fellows speak and the ones Dampier met in the west. But do not speak of any more landings, Mr Banks. I intend to make the quickest possible passage from here to where I believe the Torres Strait runs south of New Guinea. All I shall stop for are wood and water, as we do here.'

'You know, sir, that I am charged by the Society to make the fullest possible collection of all natural history objects on these coasts? I cannot do that if you persist in remaining at sea all the time.'

James drew a deep breath. 'And I, Mr Banks, am charged by their Lordships with the command of this ship. If I put her wilfully at hazard I can be tried for my life. Already we are short of cordage, iron and canvas, which the most ingenious minds cannot fashion out of thin air, and which I cannot replace nearer than Batavia. With respect to the wishes of the Society, none of their requests can apply to this coast, since as yet they do not know of its existence. Already you have more specimens than you can properly preserve. Did I not hear Mr Monkhouse complain you had taken his copy of Milton and used the leaves for the pressing of plants? Enough, sir, is enough! There will no doubt be other voyages to continue where we must leave off.'

'So I am to tell the Society that you refuse to land me for my shore excursions?'

'You may tell the gentlemen of the Society what you will, sir! I shall continue to do my duty to my ship, my crew, and their Lordships of the Admiralty – in that order!'

Whereupon Mr Banks stamped away in a great pet. For the next few days, James knew, they would be on the most distant and formal terms, until Mr Banks would get over his ill-nature. He was really a pleasant little man, if only he could overcome his impression that his great wealth could buy everything in sight, including the services of one of His Majesty's ships. The fact was that this was a very crowded ship, and the voyage had lasted much too long a time. They could all do with a quiet run ashore in a civilized port, and the sight and sound of fresh faces and voices.

James reflected that he himself might have been a shade more diplomatic. He would have to find a careenage pretty soon, and have the ship hove down for another bottom clean. It was six months since she was last done in Queen Charlotte Sound, and weed grew fast in these waters.

Tuesday, June 12th, 1770. James wrote. He was dog-weary, and could only make his Journal entry with frequent references to the deck log. For the last few days they had been threading their way through a labyrinth of coral reefs, and inevitably they had run aground. *Fortunately we had little wind, fine weather, and a smooth Sea all this 24 Hours, which gave us an Opportunity to carry out the two Bower Anchors, one on the Starboard Quarter and the other right a Stern . . . and brought the falls in abaft and hove taut. . . . The tide we observ'd now begun to rise. . . . However, I resolv'd to risque all and heave her off . . . and about 20 minutes past 10 O'clock the Ship floated, and we hove her into Deep Water . . .*

He wiped the perspiration from his forehead. There, it was down: the story of a stranding that might bring him to a trial by court-martial if things went wrong. You could never tell. Who could know after all this time what the political wind was like in Whitehall? Admiral Byng had been shot on his quarterdeck by his marines for *Failing to do his utmost in the presence of the Enemy.* That was the charge at the court-martial, at any rate. In truth, the crime he had been shot for was that he had failed to satisfy the political masters of the hour. James mopped his brow again, and took a luxurious drink of the well sugared lime-juice he had indulged himself in once the ship was aswim again. There was precious little lime-juice left now, but James felt that if ever a man had earned a little self-indulgence, it was he. He had been aground for a full twenty-four hours, and they had refloated the ship. But – was the mishap not due in part to his own haste?

From Bustard Bay, where he had refused Mr Banks time for more shore excursions, was a full six hundred miles. They had made this distance in less than three weeks. Then they had come to the beginning of the coral reefs, beautiful deadly things that they were. Seen through Mr Banks' patent *Depth Telescope* they were another world of fantastic beauty, of gliding fish and bright seaflowers. From a ship's lookout they were a world of dreadful menace, with clutching fingers of coral reaching out to tear away the planking under the unwary sailor. He glanced back at the notes of the soundings in the journal; three fathom, four, eight, two-and-a-half, eighteen, and three again – there was neither constancy or pattern in them. This was the sea he had sailed through in quest of the possibly non-existent Torres Strait.

To be home by Christmas! Well, he could forget that, as far as the Christmas of 1770 was concerned. He could not forgive himself for sailing the night they had struck – yet it was bright moonlight and with two men in the chains and a full watch on deck they should have been safe enough. In this devil's labyrinth they could just as easily have struck by day. That would have looked even worse in the log.

Now that they were afloat again there was no question of sailing on. As soon as they raised the buoyed cannon and spare ironwork they had cast overboard to lighten *Endeavour*, she would have to be beached. They had a fothered spritsail over her bottom checking the leak, but that was a very temporary remedy. There was a day's work ahead, pumping the ship dry and getting the jettisoned gear aboard again. Mr Molyneux would have to take the yawl and go looking for a careenage at first light. Pray God he found one close by, even if it had no water! At need they could set up the still and make fresh water from salt, so long as there was firewood.

James heard the welcome gurgle as the pumps sucked out the last few inches of water from the well, and silently thanked God for it. At least the fothered sail was keeping most of the water out. They were afloat; they still had a chance. Never again would he drive a ship as *Endeavour* had been driven during the past six weeks. He made to take his hat and go on deck, but checked himself. What was to be done could be done by others as well as he, and there would be plans and decisions to make on the morrow that could only be made by him. As he turned instead to the welcome sight of his swing-

ing cot, he was aware of how tired he was, and that he had
been on his feet forty-two hours and more. Four hours in that
cot would be welcome indeed, before he was called at five
next morning.

James regarded the young man on the other side of his lectern, rigged on the quarter-deck as usual for the occasion of
Request-men, with some interest. Magra? The name interested him as did the man's appearance. That olive-skinned
face and the dark hair could have been Spanish. Or West
Indian, come to that. He spoke English with the hint of a
creole lilt in his tone.

The man was a fine seaman, and had done very well during
the stranding. James was now in some doubt about the assault
on Mr Horton. The clerk had been in the wrong too; no man
in his position should be drinking with the midshipman. He
looked at Magra again and turned to the master.

'You say that it was Magra who found the careenage?'

Mr Molyneux nodded. 'It was, sir. I was away with the
yawl and the gig, and we separated, and Magra took the gig
on his own. It had always been his boat, sir, before –'

'I understand,' James said. 'Able Seaman Magra. Three
weeks ago I disrated you when you seemed to have conducted
a wanton and foolish attack on the person of my clerk, Mr
Horton. The evidence was circumstantial, and I am aware
you have always denied the act. Since then your conduct has
been worthy of high praise. Mr Midshipman Magra, I am
pleased to restore you to your old rate – and I trust you will be
generous enough to bear no ill will.'

'Thank you, Sir. I'll not deny that I was bitter at the time –
but I have to admit that appearances were against me. Bygones are bygones, as far as I am concerned.' He held out his
hand, and they shook in friendship.

James staggered with weariness as he left the quarterdeck,
resolved that as soon as the ship was safely beached he would
give a full day's break to all hands. By God, they had earned
it. That four hours' sleep he had taken after they had got
Endeavour off the coral was the last time he had undressed
and turned in for six days. He had taken cat-naps since then,

never for more than an hour. God! how his legs ached! There
were muscles in his calves that felt like red-hot wires.

Endeavour River was by no means the ideal careenage. On
this coast it seemed such a place did not exist. The approach
channel was so twisted and narrow that James had been im-
pelled to buoy it himself, and the winds were so fluky it had
taken them four days to work the ship in – four days to cover
fifteen miles. In that time they had experienced everything
from flat calm to a fresh gale, dead ahead, and *Endeavour* had
taken the putty twice more. The first time the grounding was
slight, and she had slipped off easily, but on the second day
they had to wait on the tide, strike down masts and yards, and
raft them overside to lighten her. It was an exercise becoming
only too familiar to the wearied topmen, but it was well-nigh
the only way they had of lightening the ship. The tarred
ballast they had taken on in Queen Charlotte's Sound rested
for ever now on an alien bottom, as did six of the carriage
guns, lost when the buoys had carried away. The gun-wharf
at Priddy's Hard would have plenty to say about that. To lose
a gun was almost a capital offence in the eyes of the Ordnance
Board.

'You don't look too well yourself, Mr Monkhouse,' James
commented as he left the sick-tent. It was cool and shady
under the wind-stirred canvas, and the half-dozen invalids
were better already for their spell ashore.

It was a week after the first stranding; the ship was practically de-stored. In the middle of all the ordered chaos, James
had snatched a half-hour to visit the sick.

Mr Monkhouse did indeed look sicker than any of his
patients. His complexion seemed jaundiced, his breath was
foul, and there were ulcers at the corners of his lips. But he
assumed a jaunty air.

'Thank you kindly, sir, but I'll be all right after a spell
ashore. Fresh water and a still bed, that's what I need above
all. And fish – fresh fish, with a dash o' vinegar. My belly
revolts at the sight of salt food these days.'

James turned from the sick-tent and went towards the creek, which a couple of marines were deepening. On the way he met Mr Banks.

'Good morning, Captain!' Mr Banks sounded very cheery. 'And how long do you think we will be here?'

Of course – Mr Banks saw an indefinite spell ashore stretching ahead! 'A month, at least.' James told him. 'That will suit you, I fancy?'

'It will, sir – but I would not have had it so at the expense of such damage to the ship.'

'You saw where she was holed?'

'I have. Dr Solander and I were around the bottom this morning, looking for any new specimens of barnacle we might discover. We saw the hole in the planking – prodigious, sir, prodigious! If I may say so, an admirable feat of seamanship that we survived at all.'

When James had seen the great gnawed wound in the ship's planking, he too had been struck with wonder. It was so regular that it might have been man-made, worked with blunt tools. Had it not been for the rough knob of coral, broken from the reef and almost plugging the hole it had made, no seamanship or fothered sail or work with the pumps could have saved them. *Endeavour* would have quietly filled and settled down, to lie forever beside the lost cannon.

'We had a deal of luck, Mr Banks. More than we deserved, maybe. I should never have allowed the ship to take the ground in the first place.'

'Poppycock, sir! Very few could have done as well, and I shall not fail to bring the matter to the attention of the proper quarters when we reach England.'

There he went again, spoiling it all, talking as if the whole cruise was laid on just so that he, Joseph Banks, could fill the after-cabin with flowers and specimens.

It was Sunday, the third week in June, five days after they had beached the ship. The damage had been repaired on the starboard side, and the ship heeled to larboard so that the

carpenters could attend to that. James was taking a stroll
through the scrubby woodlands with the Surgeon. This was
midwinter in the south; the day was pleasant, with no insects
to plague them.

'You have seen no large animal in your time ashore, then?'
James was saying.

'Neither large nor small,' Mr Monkhouse replied. 'That's a
strange thing about this country. There seem to be no beasts
at all larger than rats.'

'Mr Banks thinks he saw dogs at Bustard Bay,' James said.

'Aye, there's such a thing as *wanting* to see things, sir!'

'Nay, that is unjust, Mr Monkhouse! Mr Banks is a most
careful observer. If he says he saw dogs, then I believe there
were dogs to see. After all, there were plenty of dogs in New
Zealand.'

'Aye, and the Maori ate them, when they weren't eating
one another!'

James laughed. 'True enough. But this beast, whatever it
was, was no dog. Sergeant Edgecumbe saw it, when he and
his marines were out shooting birds for the pot. Like a deer,
he described it, mouse-coloured, and proceeding in leaps, as
if at the gallop.'

'Rat-coloured, may be – and he having had a grog too
many,' Mr Monkhouse replied sceptically. 'But if there is
such a beast, Mr Banks will never rest until he has one put
down in pickle in a rum-cask to take home.'

'He'll not get the first one,' James assured him, 'not if you
pass it as edible. Fish is all very well, but we could all do with
a few good collops of red meat.'

Later that day, Mr Banks did catch sight of one of the
strange, mouse-coloured beasts that Sergeant Edgecumbe had
been the first to observe. It had a head like a hornless deer
and a long, heavy tail. It moved in a series of leaps from its
hind legs; the forelegs were clearly too small and powerless
to bear the creature's full weight. They were held at its breast,
almost in an attitude of prayer. The botanists also made contact with an old native man, his beard grizzled and streaks of
white pigment adorning his face.

'*Kanguru!*' the old man said.

Tupia said something in Otaheitan, but the old man shook his head, repeating emphatically 'Kanguru!'

'It's no use, Tupia!' Joseph Banks said. 'I don't know if that is the name of the beast, or whether he just is trying to say something else.'

'I think he a very foolish old man,' Tupia replied.

Joseph Banks shook his head. 'I don't know about that, Tupia. He might be a very wise one, since he can live and be content on so very little. We'll call the creature Kanguru. It's as good a name as any other for a beast like nothing else on earth!'

By whatever name they called it, kanguru made good eating, somewhere in flavour between hare and venison. Almost as good as the great turtles Mr Molyneux found among the coral outside the river, when he took out the yawl to prospect a suitable channel for their leaving. Once they discovered turtle and kanguru, the men of the Endeavour declared they lived like aldermen.

The sick recovered, outwardly at least, and the ship was patched and refloated again. But this was different to the refit six months earlier at Queen Charlotte Sound. Endeavour was sheathed with thin planks of elmwood, studded with iron nails, over a coating of cow-hair, lime, and tar. This did not prevent weed and barnacles resting on her bottom, but it did prevent teredo worm and other borers getting into the main planking. With such sheathing the ship might become fouled, but never rotten. As well as the actual hole made by the coral, much of this sheathing had been ripped off, and there was no suitable wood ashore to replace it. They did what they could, but iron for the fastening was running short. They would have to put to sea with a partly unsheathed bottom. That meant that in six months or less, the Endeavour would be riddled with teredo worm, and parts of the bottom would be so soft that a man could push a finger through it. The first place they could obtain iron and sheathing and new canvas and cordage was Batavia, fifteen hundred miles away . . . if the Torres Strait existed. If it did not, then Batavia was practically out of their reach, and they would leave their bones among this beautiful murderous coral.

Tuesday, August 7th, 1770. James wrote. His eyes were
reddened and sore from the glare of the sun on the everlasting
sea. (He must get some reading-glasses when he was again in
London, he thought – if he ever saw London again!) *Strong
Gales from the S., and I and several of the Officers kept a
lookout from the Masthead, to seek a passage between the
Shoals; but we could see nothing but breakers . . .*

It had been a dreadful day. Even when the sun was hidden
the glare persisted. And the unseasonable wind! In open
water it would have bowled them along at a good eight knots;
here, among the reefs, he had been compelled to anchor time
after time, since there was not room to lie hove to. To add to
the labour of constantly heaving in the cable he had to order
the top-masts sent down, since the windage they set up was so
strong in the gale that the anchors dragged.

In the teeth of the gale it was impossible to turn back and
seek another passage towards the Torres Strait. To the west
was the coast of the land he had named New South Wales,
barely visible. No one knew how far the coral stretched to
the east, but there might be hundreds of miles of it. James
knew that Mr Molyneux was all for riding out the gale at
anchor and then turning back. But this was a council of despair. James was sure the better course was to press on north-
wards. Torres Strait *must* exist!

The gales blew themselves out, the topmasts were set up
again, and the *Endeavour* crept on. Constantly sounding, with
a man in the chains on either side, they were piloted forward
with the pinnace ranging ahead to pick out the deepest chan-
nels. They anchored each night, with reefs sounding and
spouting surf all about them. There were days when they
sailed through waters of great beauty – which any of them
would gladly have traded for the grey seas of mid-Atlantic
and an October gale.

Their progress north on some days was as little as three
miles, rarely as much as twelve. They toiled like slaves for
every mile they won. However, they still ate like aldermen:
most days the pinnace, scouting ahead for a passage, succeeded in harpooning a turtle. But all of them longed for the

sight of a clear sea stretching ahead, unimpeded by the spouting of breakers, or the white bones of a coral reef menacing their advance.

And then – at last! *Wednesday, 22nd August, 1770,* James wrote, devoutly hoping he was not making a fool of himself. *Gentle Breezes at E. by S. and Clear weather . . . Having satisfied myself of the great Probability of a passage* (Torres Strait, please God!) *. . . I had in the Name of His Majesty King George the Third took possession of the whole Eastern Coast from 38°S. down to this place by the name of New South Wales . . . after which we fir'd three Volleys of Small Arms, which were answer'd by a like Number from the Ship.*

Well, he was *almost* certain of the strait, James thought, as he watched the carpenters nail the record of their visit to a tree on Possession Island. This was not the first place where he had taken formal possession of the new land. There were several landfalls along the coast where he had left similar records, in places as fit as Canada for English settlement. At least the blackfellows here would not scalp the colonists!

It would have to be hard work for all at first, of course. Everything would have to be brought from home until the land had been broken to the plough and the newcomers had learned the run of the topsy-turvy seasons. More than a very few would starve to death if they tried to live off the country, or else revert to the squalid way of life of the blackfellows. Mr Banks had found no real food-plants: a few antiscorbutics, but no grains, nor any very good grasses. They had found some very tough-shelled nuts at Endeavour River, but they were so ill to crack that a man would have his work cut out to feed on them. Mr Banks was very near the mark when he likened one stretch of country to the hide of a scrawny dun cow with the hair rubbing off.

'New South Wales!' Mr Banks repeated, as they turned from the memorial tree and walked back to the pinnace. 'What made you choose that name, rather than that of your own country? New Cleveland would have sounded well.'

'I don't know,' James told him. 'The hills I remember in Cleveland were a harsher kind than any here, except those we called the Glasshouse Mountains, below Bustard Bay. In Wales, in the south around Cardiff, I saw very similar countryside, on a smaller scale. Really, one name is as good as another.'

'Like *kanguru*!'

They laughed together, yet in truth James knew he had little to laugh at. He could not tell whether the string of islands ahead led to open sea, or whether they were still embayed by coral reefs. Even as he pondered, teredo worms were gnawing away at the ship's planking. And if they did not reach a port with some sort of comforts pretty soon, he was going to be short of a surgeon and a first lieutenant. Neither of them was looking very well – especially Mr Monkhouse.

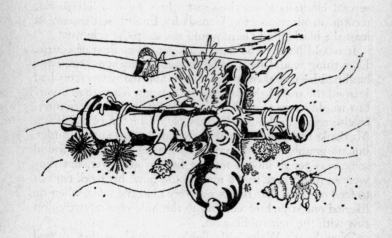

I7 *Batavia*

James was not really sure he had found the Torres Strait until Monday, the third of September, 1770. Divisions the day before had been held in an almost silent ship. Silent, that is, except for the clanking of the pumps, since *Endeavour* was making nearly a foot of water an hour. But she was out of sight of land in comparatively deep water, so that now there was no need for a leadsman in the chains at either side. Furthermore, in only six hours sailing she had logged twenty-seven knots.

Then land was sighted to the north; from its bearing it could only be New Guinea. Inwardly, James was jubilant since this proved the existence of the strait he had believed in all along. But his countenance showed very little emotion. Now it was almost a straight run to the westward for Batavia, with Timor on their way, where they might hope to get a little refreshment. They could do with this; they had sailed with only eighteen months' stores on board, and that was two years ago. Moreover, they were still on full allowance of food and water, although water had been rationed twice before on the passage. Apart from the loss of the cannon on the Endeavour Reef, he had nothing to worry about where stores or equipment were concerned.

They were sailing in six fathoms with little variation of depth, and the coast was about four miles away. James decided to have a run ashore. It seemed a pity to come all this way and not set foot on New Guinea. He looked into the wardroom, where the scientific gentlemen were engaged at their eternal preservation and classifying of specimens.

'I am thinking of taking a run ashore, Mr Banks. Would you and some of the gentlemen care to accompany me?'

'Willingly, Captain! But this is most unusual – mostly it is I who want to go ashore, and you who refuse.'

'I have my reasons, Mr Banks. I have observed several smokes, so the country must be peopled. We are within six degrees of the Line, so that there are likely to be coconuts. Where there are people and coconuts, there might well be pigs. We could do with fresh meat and greenstuff.'

'For the poor goat, as well as ourselves,' said Mr Banks. The goat had been shipped as a milk supply for the wardroom, and though she had long since run dry, she was a great pet with the crew. She, with a couple of sturdy cats, were the last survivors of the animals they had embarked at Devonport. 'Dr Solander and I will gladly come with you,' Mr Banks told James. 'Has this part been visited before?'

'By both the Dutch and the Portuguese, according to the names on my charts. But only rarely, and from the direction of Batavia. No one has been this way since the time of de Torres, in 1606.'

However, Mr Banks was not interested in history other than natural history, and was already on his way to collect his specimen case and pistols. He returned with Dr Solander just as the pinnace was being got into the water.

The shore was typical of a shelving coast: a dazzling line of beach with very little surf, and a dark-green belt of trees behind it. If there were hills beyond the trees they were hidden in a haze. There was no sign of human life. They felt the heat as they stepped ashore: a humidity that caused sweat to pour from their bodies, and made every movement a burden. As they moved up the shallow slope of the beach they saw dozens of footprints in the sand, all confused and overlaid one with another.

'They are quite fresh,' James noted. 'Since the last tide, anyway. Keep together, and keep away from the trees. We'll make our way along the beach, so that the pinnace can keep us covered with the swivel.'

Apart from the soft splashing of the sea there was silence, yet everyone could feel the presence of others than themselves. Suddenly, some of them leapt from the shelter of the forest, lithe brown men with close-cropped hair, very different from the blackfellows of New South Wales. A shower of small spears fell short of James' party, and while they launched them the natives whirled a short tube about their heads. This gave off puffs of smoke and showers of sparks, but emitted neither report nor missile. James raised his firelock, aiming to miss, and stirred up the sand at their feet with a charge of small-shot. Their attackers fled back into the forest.

'Back to the boat, gentlemen,' James said. 'No firing, unless they come to within spear-cast. No haste, either – they might well swamp us in a rush.'

This was true enough. Although they had seen only a small party, from the stirrings in the bush there were probably hundreds of men at call. At an order, the seamen bent to the oars, but lay-to outside the first line of the quiet surf.

'Well, it looks as if we get no coconuts today,' James said.

'No specimens, either,' said Dr Solander sadly. 'No doubt there are great differences between New Guinea and New South Wales. Those smoking tubes – I should have liked to examine them more closely. A weapon, perhaps? What do you think?'

'A magical device, more like,' Mr Banks said. 'A thing with no effect in itself, used to confer the notion of power on the flung spears.'

'Firepots or tobacco pipes, more like,' James said. 'The Indians on the St Lawrence in Canada carry a bark firepot, filled with smouldering tinder that will burn for a day or more. This could be something similar – but I am not prepared to find out at the risk of losing a man.'

'So! No coconuts – no specimens – no investigation!' said Dr Solander. 'I am disappointed, captain. We could have held off those fellows with the swivel and our firelocks long enough to have felled some palms and got a boatload of nuts – and doubtless some firesticks as well.'

James' voice was cold. 'Sir, that suggestion does you little credit. If I could have obtained nuts by trade or friendship I would have done so. But we do not need them so badly that I would risk life or do murder for them. Back to the ship, cox'n!'

Sailing during the next six days was a sheer delight. They

made as much as 120 miles between noon and noon, while on
the second day the leadsman could find no bottom with a
fifty-fathom line. For the first time in months they were out of
soundings. It was flying fish weather. Arrowing flights of these
silver sea-darts were seen constantly on all sides of the ship;
some even arrived gasping on the deck. They came in through
the open sternports, too, flapping among the specimens and
papers, and causing a great scuffle among the scientific gentlemen. A few were pickled in spirit for the edification of the
Society, but most of them found their way into One-armed
Thompson's skillet. Filleted and rolled in biscuit crumb, they
were judged to be in no way inferior to mackerel.

So they came to Timor. This was known to be part under
Dutch and part under Portuguese influence, and James had
hopes of getting some fresh victuals. At first it looked as if he
would be disappointed, although he soon made contact with
the Dutch agent. The local *rajas* were willing enough to trade,
but Mynheer Johan Lange was not.

'He is probably acting under orders,' James told Mr Gore,
who always acted as supercargo in these matters. 'Maybe he
does not recognize us as a King's ship; we do not look much
like one, I confess. We had the same trouble with the Governor at Rio de Janeiro, you may recall.'

'I have sailed these waters before, sir, as you know,' Mr
Gore said. 'The Dutch out here are all alike. They speak to
us fair enough in Europe, or even at the Cape, but here they
regard us as pirates. The truth is, I suspect they have never
forgiven us for taking New Amsterdam and calling it New
York.'

'Well, I cannot blame them for having long memories,'
James said. 'But you said you had a plan, Mr Gore. What is
it?'

'Simple enough, sir. I was with you this morning when you
gave the old *raja* a broadsword, and he indicated he was willing to trade. Then Mynheer Lange came up and spoiled the
deal.'

'Yes, I remember.'

'The Dutchman offered to take a party inland to see a spice
plantation, sir. Accept the invitation – Mr Banks and the

Doctor are agog to go – but find some pretext to leave me behind.' Mr Gore grinned conspiratorially. 'Left to myself, I
could do a good trade with the *raja!*'

They left Timor on a Friday, the twenty-first of September.
They had plenty of fresh buffalo beef for all – it ate well if
it were boiled long enough – while the hen-coops were tenanted again, so that there were eggs to go with the beef-steaks
for the cabin. In addition, there were two casks of a syrup,
lighter than treacle and scented with flowers. This went very
well with the Sunday currant-duff; on the messdecks the men
ate of it until their belts creaked.

They were clear of the coral, but there was another poten-
tial danger. Hereabouts the seas were rank with piracy,
especially along the Java coast. Ashore there was anarchy,
raja making war on *raja*; conditions were much the same as
they had been in Europe under the Vikings, eight hundred
years before. Although they fought among themselves, one
thing – the chance of a European prize – could effect a temporary alliance among these turbulent sea-kings. James kept
well clear of the Java coast, maintained a good lookout, and
had his four remaining cannon and all the swivels mounted.
The *Endeavour* made the passage swiftly and unseen.

On September the 30th, they were off Java Head at the
entrance to the Sunda Strait. James' hope of speedily reaching
the aid and comforts of a European port rose high. He was
now more concerned about the health of the crew than the
state of the ship if that were possible. There were more than
seventy men signed on before the mast, and half of these were
sick – not sick enough to be laid idle, but fit only for the
lightest of duties. Until she had struck on Endeavour Reef
they had a tight ship under them, and a half-hour in the
forenoon watch had been enough to keep her clear of water
for the day. She had made above twelve inches in the hour
ever since, which took fifteen minutes in the hour to pump
clear, day and night. One of the pumps was completely worn
out, while the other two were long past their best. The invalids were put to day work, and the hale men on watch and

watch. What James desired above all was a good fast run to
Batavia, and until their arrival off Java Head he looked like
making it. Batavia now lay only 120 miles away, at the other
end of the Sunda Strait. It took them nine days to cover it.
The winds in the strait were fickle and contrary; fifteen times
they had to bring to at anchor. In the torrid heat, heaving
on the capstan was killing work. More than one man collapsed
under the strain.

*Wednesday, 10th, according to our reckoning, but by the
people here Thursday, 11th October,* James wrote. He had
been puzzled by the difference between his and the local
reckoning of the date but soon saw the reason for it. Sailing
westward with the sun, he had gained a day when he reached
the 180° meridian, while if he had sailed east-about he would
have lost one. *At 4 o'clock in the P.M. Anchor'd in Batavia
road, where we found the 'Harcourt' Indiaman from England,
2 English Country Ships, 13 Sail of Large Dutch ships, and
a number of small Vessels* . . .

His thoughts flew back to his boyhood dreams. He would
never command an Indiaman, yet he had been where no
Indiaman had ever sailed. Sailing westabout, he had reached
the Far East by a back door. Ashore were the merchants of his
boyhood dreams in their spice-scented godowns, with the
leathern sacks of maravedis, ducats, and rupiahs. And he had
arrived in a leaking ship, so run-down that half his crew were
on the sicklist, and so many of his cannon lost overboard he
could not fire a fitting salute on his entrance. He sent Mr
Hicks ashore with an apology to the Fort, while he discussed
the Defect Report with Mr Slatterly, the carpenter. This was
long and detailed. James nodded gravely when he came to the
end of it.

'There's a great deal to do before the ship is properly sea-
worthy again, Mr Slatterly. If we can find a place to heave
her down, we can do the work ourselves.'

'We can that, sir! As we did at Charlotte Sound. Good for
the hands, too – living ashore, and a change of occupation.

Keep them from moping and keep them out of the grog-
shops.' He looked through the open port at the steamy shoreline.

The carpenter took his leave, and James made a fair copy
of the defect list, adding it to a letter for the Governor, re-
questing permission to heave down the ship and do the repairs
themselves. Then he went ashore and sought out a Scottish
merchant, a Mr Colin Duncan, and had his letter to the
Governor translated into Dutch.

'I doubt whether they'll let you do the work yourselves,' Mr
Duncan said. 'Ye ken the Governor and his officers take a per-
centage of the revenue from the dockyard as a perquisite?'

This did not shock James unduly; it was an accepted thing
that a government officer made what he could out of his office.
'That's a pity,' he said. 'The work would have given employment to the hands – the healthy ones, that is. I have a number
of sick, too, and a shore job might have help them recover.'

'Not in this place, it wouldn't,' said Mr Duncan. 'A man
has to be very strong to stand the climate here. You said you
had sick already. How many?'

'About thirty,' James told him. 'I shall have to find quarters
for them ashore.'

'You need look no farther, sir. I have a house empty and
on my hands, with a couple of godowns at the back that would
make good quarters for your men.'

So James took the house, which was pleasantly situated by
one of the many canals that wandered through the city,
Dutch style. That afternoon, Lieutenant Hicks, with Mr
Green and Tupia, took up their residence ashore, with a party
of semi-invalids preparing the godowns to serve as quarters
for their shipmates. Meanwhile, James paid his first call on
the Governor.

Mynheer van der Parra was Governor of Batavia. 'We will
do all we can for you, Captain,' he told James, 'but I regret
it will be impossible to allow your crew to do the work themselves. My government have very strict rules about the work
done in our dockyards.'

'I am twenty-seven months out from England,' James told

him, 'and I had the misfortune to ground my ship on a coral reef. She is making a foot of water an hour, even lying at anchor. I hope for speedy relief.'

'The work will be carried out as soon as possible,' the Governor assured him.

There was nothing further James could do about the situation except practise patience. He was acquiring a fine store of patience by this time.

Even at anchor in Batavia there were hazards to the ship. James had no sooner got back to the *Endeavour* when there was a violent thunderstorm. One of the Dutch Indiamen was struck by lightning and lost her mainmast. *Endeavour* was struck too, but during the forenoon Mr Gore and Mr Green had rigged the newfangled lightning-conductor. The bolt of electrical fluid ran down the copper cable and discharged harmlessly into the harbour, hissing like red-hot shot.

James was told it would be some days before there would be a vacant berth at the dockyard on Onrust Island, but meanwhile a working party was put aboard *Endeavour* to relieve the crew at the pumps, and arrangements were made for a daily supply of fresh food and schnapps. This last was almost as welcome as the food, for the rum was beginning to run short. James knew that while men would merely grumble over short rations on food or water, to cut short on grog was almost an incitement to mutiny.

Four days after their arrival a ship sailed for Holland, and James was able to get off a letter to Mr Stephens, the Secretary at the Admiralty, with a brief account of their doings up to date. It was the first time he had been able to communicate with London since he had written by the Lisbon packet out of Rio, two years before. Enclosed with his letter to the Admiralty was one for Betty.

My dearest Betty, he wrote, *this is a very brief note written in haste to let you know that I am Well, and that we have succeeded beyond all Expectation in the objects of our Voyage. I trust you and the Children are in good health, and that the Child you were Carrying at my departure arrived safely. How Strange it is not to know whether it be boy or Girl! I am writ-*

*ing this at the Desk that was your gift, where I daily write in
my Journal. So that you are ever in my thoughts, dearest
Betty. I will delay as little as possible after I leave this Place,
which cannot be Too Soon, and you can look for our Arrival
some four months after you receive this. There is a great
Convoy leaving here soon, and I will write you more fully by
that.*

He wrenched his thoughts back to the present. There was
much to do. The fit members of the crew were fully occupied
de-storing the ship and sending down the rigging in prepara-
tion for the refit. With the ship in a half-dismantled condition, James and his officers had all taken up their quarters in
the house by the canal, the anchor watch being kept on board
by one of the master's mates.

James' hope for a speedy refit once the ship moved to Onrust
Island was not to be realized. *Endeavour* was four full weeks
in Batavia before any work was done at all. However, he
could find no fault with the work once a start was made. The
workers in the dockyard were as good craftsmen as any in the
world.

It was now the wet season; it rained for some part of every
single day, and moulds and fungus grew on everything not in
constant use – spare clothing, shoes, tools. Keeping corrosion
at bay on metal instruments meant a daily overhaul; writing
was a burden. The hands stuck to the paper, sweat ran into
the eyes, blurring the sight. Everyone thought longingly of
autumn days in England, of crisp, cool weather, when butter
stood firm on the dish and there was not a constant hint of
taint in even the freshest food. The sun never broke through
the thick layer of cloud, and this, somehow, made the heat
harder to bear. The men sickened rapidly; when they arrived
in Batavia, about a third of the crew had been fit for light
work only; by now, only about a dozen were fit for any work
at all. James had been particularly worried about two of his
comrades: Mr Hicks, and Mr Monkhouse. Two days before
the ship was hove down to begin repairs the surgeon died, and
Jones, his servant, sought a discharge, intending to ship back
to Europe on a Dutch vessel. James let him go, shipping a

Danish seaman in his place, and promoting Mr Perry, the
surgeon's mate, to the vacant place. He could only be given
the acting rank, of course; the College of Barber-Surgeons had
strict rules about that. But his appointment would be swiftly
confirmed with the recommendation James intended to furnish at the end of the voyage.

Tupia died, and so did his servant, the boy-without-a-name.
In one way James was not sorry to see Tupia go, for he was
very touchy and quarrelsome, and had caused a deal of trouble
one way and another. He had been useful as an interpreter
in New Zealand, but had been a useless passenger since.
With him died Mr Banks' hope of taking a specimen of Noble
Savage to London. Not that Mr Banks seemed to care much
at the time; he was too ill and low in spirits himself to care
about anything.

A much greater loss was Mr Green, the astronomer. He was
the only one on board who was James' equal in the art of
mathematics. Now, of course, they were in known waters and
a fair impartial position check was not so important as it was
on unknown coasts. But it was a pity Mr Green could not have
lived to receive the thanks of the Society for his work on the
transits of Venus and Mercury. No astronomer, as far as James
knew, had been able to observe both in the same year ever
before.

Saunders, a midshipman disrated back to seaman for mis-
conduct, deserted a week before Christmas Eve. He had been
such a pest that James only made the most perfunctory efforts
to find him. Much more serious were the deaths of two seamen, Woodworth and Rearden, at Christmas. It was a cheerless Christmas that year, what with burying two of his men
on Christmas Day and more than sixty of the ship's company
too sick to attend at the churchyard.

But all things come to an end, even repairs to a ship in
Batavia. Two days after Christmas they left Onrust with
barely enough men to get in the anchor, and not enough to
handle the sails properly. James had been glad to see Batavia,
for the sake of the ship. He was even more glad to see the last
of it, for the sake of the men.

18 *The Melancholy Passage*

The Dutch charged foreign ships very dear for wood and water at Batavia. James took on only sufficient of either for a month, intending to complete his loading of both these necessities at Prince's Island, near Java Head. This was the usual practice with ships on their homeward run by the Cape of Good Hope. They reached Prince's Island ten days after leaving Batavia.

By then he had forty helpless invalids on board, with another ten at various stages of convalescence looking after them. The new surgeon, Mr Perry, rarely got more than a couple of hours of uninterrupted sleep, and with one exception every man on board had been sick in Batavia, including James himself. Mr Banks was so ill that he had been near death at one time. James was sure that only the will to live and see his collection of specimens safe at the Royal Society saved his life.

Every man was sick, that is, except Ravenhill the sailmaker, who had shipped when well over the regulation age. He now admitted to being seventy-eight, but from things he had let drop in conversation his shipmates were inclined to put him older even than that. No man of seventy-eight could have clear memories of the battle of La Hogue, for instance; it had been fought in 1692. Ravenhill's aged carcase was just about pickled in rum, and some of the seamen held that this was the secret for his continuing health: the fumes of the rum he took were so strong that disease was burned out of his body before it could gain a good hold.

Endeavour lay eight more days at Prince's Island, filling the water-casks and felling timber, hard work for a weakened crew. The island people were used to ships calling, and they were able to take on a supply of fresh fruit and meat on the hoof. They sailed, then for seventeen days drifted through the doldrums towards the south-east trade winds that would carry them to the African coast. Progress was maddeningly slow. Some days they would trap a flaw of wind and cover forty or fifty miles; other days there was a dead blistering calm, when they drifted with all sail set and the pitch bubbling in the deck-seams.

Thursday, 24th January, 1771, James wrote. He was dressed only in shirt and shortened trousers, and his hand, wet with sweat, stuck to the paper. Both ports were open in the stifling cabin, but his two candles burned steadily without a flicker. *First part Light Airs, the remainder calm. In the a.m. died John Trusslove, Corporal of Marines, a man much esteem'd by every body on board. Many . . . dangerously ill of Fevers & Fluxes. We are inclinable to attribute this to the water we took in at Prince's Island, and have put lime into the Casks in order to purifie it. Wind S.W. by S. Course S. Distance, 4°M. lat. 9°34'S., long. 256°50'.*

Trusslove! James could even now scarcely bring himself to believe that he had read the service for the big, slow-spoken Hampshire man. There seemed no way of checking the flux, even though they limed the watercasks and washed the mess-decks and 'tween-decks with vinegar. All they could do was keep things as sweet as they could and pray that there would be enough men still on their feet to work the ship into Cape Town.

A dreadful four weeks followed, men dying almost every day. One of the first victims was old Ravenhill, and his was, possibly the only death not a result of the horrible flux. He died drunk in his hammock, a half-empty bottle of rum in his grip.

'If he could have his other arm around the waist of a pretty lass it would have been the sort of death a sailor dreams of,' said Mr Perry when he reported. 'The crew are going to take it pretty hard. He was a sort of mascot to them.'

'I know,' James said. 'So he was to me, although he drank a deal too much. But he was a good sailmaker for all that. You must do all that you can to check despondency, Mr Perry.'

'I'll try, sir. It's about all I can do, now that we're run out of laudanum.'

But it was hard to keep up the spirits when almost every afternoon another weighted hammock was dropped over from the gratings. Stories began to be whispered of all the ships which had left the Dutch Indies for the Cape and were never heard of again. Maybe they would become just such another as the Flying Dutchman, who sold his soul to the Devil to save his life. It was said his ship had been driving round and round the world south of Cape Horn ever since, unable to get out of the clutches of the terrible westerlies.

No longer was the great cabin filled with earnest young gentlemen making pictures or classifying specimens – except for Mr Banks and Dr Solander, they were all dead. Dunster died, he who had once been flogged for refusing to eat fresh beef, together with three other marines. Mr Satterley and Mr Gathray the bos'n, honest craftsmen both, died within days of one another. And One-armed Thompson, the cook, had made his last Sunday duff, and was sadly missed.

Death raged through the ship like a grass-fire during the last week in January, and smouldered on through the first week in February. Then there were no deaths for almost a week, and James began to hope that the distemper had run its course. During the following week, three more men died. Then there was another lull, of eight days this time, but on February 27th three men died in the same day. James scarcely dared hope when no one died in the first week in March. They were in cooler latitudes by now, sailing close-hauled on the healing tradewinds, with windsails blowing the stagnant air from holds and 'tween-decks and the ship beginning to smell sweet again after the charnel-house stench she had taken on when the flux was at its worst.

There had been times when James really thought Mr Banks would have joined the death-roll. The deaths of his assistants had been a great blow to him, too. James and he had not always hit it off during the long voyage, and their philosophies often clashed, but James knew there was good stuff in the wealthy young man. He was taking the air in a hammock-chair one afternoon when James passed the time of day with him.

Mr Banks, who looked very weak, greeted him with a rueful smile. 'It's pleasant to find myself on deck again, Captain. I confess that at times I thought you were going to have the pleasure of burying me.'

'It would have been no pleasure, Mr Banks. We remain friends, I trust, in spite of having a difference of opinion now and again. I'm right glad to see you about again.' He paused. 'You will miss your young assistants, as I miss Mr Green.'

'I thought you did not approve of Mr Green wenching with the girls in Otaheite?'

'No more I did. But he was a fine mathematician; it seems a shame that so much talent should die unfulfilled.'

'You are a most forgiving man, sir. I confess I see few weaknesses of the flesh in yourself.'

James thought of the impatience that had led to *Endeavour* being stranded on the coral. 'They are there, sir. If they do not appear to you, it shows that my service in the Navy has taught me to mask them.' He leaned on the open rail, one arm through a backstay. 'Tell me, have you given any thought as to the origin of this flux which has ravaged us?'

'I have thought of little else during the past six weeks, when I was capable of thought.'

'Some on board say it was due to the water we got at Prince's Island.'

Mr Banks shook his head. 'I had the flux, and so did many others, when I came on board in Batavia. We did not have it when we arrived there.'

'So you would say the cause came to us in Batavia? Maybe from something we ate?'

'Captain, what did we eat there that we did not eat elsewhere? Moreover, ships coming from India brought it with them. It seems to me to be a disease of swamps and cities, when the two are close together.' He went on thoughtfully: I think the French philosophers may have a part of the truth, with their doctrine of the Noble Savage. The ills of the spirit do not affect the primitive man living a natural life. It might be that he escapes many of the ills of the body, until we meet him and give them to him. As we have to poor Tupia's folk, living in their ancient paradise on Otaheite.'

This was going rather deep for James' practical mind. 'Swamps and cities, eh?' he said. 'Drain the swamps, and the flux will disappear? With the rain they get in Batavia, I cannot see those swamps being drained in a hurry.'

'I've no doubt it could be done, captain. I have lands in Norfolk, and we have drained thousands of acres in that county. And when we drain the fens, the marsh fevers go. On the other side of the North Sea the Dutch have done the same. No doubt it will occur to them to do it in God's good time.'

Drain the swamps in Batavia! No doubt it could be done, James supposed, as charts could be made of every square league of the world's seas. But neither he nor Mr Banks would live to see it.

Saturday, 16th March. Moor'd the Ship and struck Yards and Topmast, and in the morning got all the Sick (28) ashore to Quarters provided for them, and got off fresh meat and Greens for the People on board.

'And please God,' James said to himself, 'that is the end of the sickness.'

On deck, he looked up at the slopes of Table Mountain with its coverlet of cloud, and sniffed the morning air. There was a dry spicy scent to it; it smelt healthy. There were no swamps in this part of Africa, whatever the tales might be about the Slave Coast. If the sick could recover, this was the place for it. Well was it named the Tavern of the Seas. Even the Dutch shore officials were more helpful and courteous here than in Java. They allotted him a house ashore to shelter the sick, and the weather was so mild and dry and bracing that even Mr Hicks and Mr Molyneux stood a good chance of recovery.

Table Bay was full of shipping, but an Indiaman – the *Admiral Pocock* – was due to sail on the morrow. That meant

a busy day for James and Mr Horton, the clerk. There were
courtesy calls to be paid to the Governor and the English
Consul, and things to be settled with the ship-chandlers that
would normally have been the master's business. With Mr
Molyneux laid sick, James missed Mr Gathray and Mr
Satterley badly – either of them would have made a good
acting-master. Mr Horton was a good clerk, but that was as
far as his talents went. James found his days pretty full on
his first arrival in Cape Town.

At the consul's house he met the captain of another Indiaman, the *Houghton*. Like many others in the service of John
Company, Captain Breaks occupied the tedium of his long
passages with study, and was greatly interested in mathematics and astronomy. He asked James to dine on board his
ship a night or two before he sailed.

'I envy you the voyage you have made, Captain,' he told
James. 'It was something to the ultimate benefit of all, not
just a venture to put more gold into the pockets of folk with
too much already.'

'There was little comfort in it,' James assured him, 'nor is
it likely to fill my pocket at all. There was a time when I
envied you this.' He waved his hand around the captain's day
cabin, where they were dining alone. It was panelled in teak,
the deck was polished with beeswax and spread with rich
Indian carpets. There were silk hangings at the ports, and
silver lamps burning scented oil. Only the breeches of a couple
of eighteen-pounders by the forward bulkhead showed they
were in a ship that might have occasion to fight.

'But not now?' asked Captain Breaks.

James shook his head. 'Not now, I have done very well for
a Yorkshire lad from a farm. I command my own ship, own
the house my family lives in, and one or two others besides,
and I like my work.'

'You are fortunate, sir,' said Captain Breaks, pouring James
a glass of madeira. 'As for myself, I take a great interest in the
mathematics of our profession – indeed, I have contributed
one or two little observations on longitude to the Society.'
This seemed to stir his memory. 'Stay! Did you not contribute

a paper to the *Transactions* a few years ago, on an eclipse of the sun? That was by one James Cook, as I recall.'

'I had that honour, sir – indeed, it might be that I owe my present situation to that same paper. I have always taken an interest in the determination of longitude.'

'And I! I believe John Harrison and his Chronographic watch has the best answer to date.'

'I had on board a Mr Green, sent by the Observatory at Greenwich to observe the transit of Venus at Otaheite, who knew Mr Harrison well. He went as assistant to Mr Maskelyne in the *Louise,* when one of the first timepieces was tested in a voyage to the Barbados in '63. He was loud in its praises.'

'Mr Green? He is on board with you? I would have had him to dine with us, had I known.'

'He died some weeks ago of the flux,' James told his host.

'What a pity! I heard you had the sickness on board. Had you much of a butcher's bill?'

'Twenty-eight,' James answered reluctantly. 'There were a half-dozen before that, but they were mostly by accident or drowning.'

'Twenty-eight! Out of how many, sir?'

'Ninety-four I sailed with. One or two of the twenty-eight were hands I picked up in Batavia. They came on board sick.'

'' 'Tis a very sickly place. All the eastern ports are, from Canton to Bombay. Last passage I did from St George I dropped twenty-one over the side. Luckily they were all of them lascars, so we did it in the early morning before the passengers were about, and I had not to go through the mummery of reading a service over them. You were really lucky to lose so few, sir. Some ships get into Table Bay at less than half strength.'

A fortnight before the *Endeavour*'s arrival at Table Bay, the frigate *Tamar* had sailed for England. She had been on station at Port Egmont in the Falklands, which were claimed by Spain but held by England. Hearing that the Spaniards were coming in great strength to take his ship and force their claim, her captain had left to lay the facts of the case before the

government in Whitehall. For all anyone at the Cape knew to
the contrary, England and Spain might already be at war.
James sincerely hoped not. If there was war *Endeavour* might
well be captured, and though as a survey vessel she was unlikely to be condemned as a prize, in the long run it might
be months or years before the two governments sorted out the
situation. Meanwhile, he and his officers would be on parole,
and the crew would be prisoners. And in a Spanish prison, at
that!

He knew nothing for certain about the war when *Endeavour*
sailed in the middle of April. Except for Mr Hicks and the
Master, his twenty-eight invalids were well on the way to
recovery. Two days out of Table Bay, Mr Molyneux died. As
James recited the service over him he felt a mixture of regret
and exasperation. Regret for the passing of an excellent seaman who might have gone far in the service, and exasperation
that Mr Molyneux had brought about his early end largely
by his own folly. He had been a most intemperate man, quite
unable to curb his passion for women and drink. He had
wenched and drunk in Otaheite, and James suspected he had
done the same at Charlotte Sound, and even with the poor
savage creatures at Botany Bay. In between he had never been
away from the rum-cask, and had taken a Javanese mistress in
Batavia. James recalled a Spanish proverb he had heard from
a fisherman in St John's: *Take what you want, says God: take
it – and pay for it.* Well, Mr Molyneux had taken what he
wanted, and he had certainly paid, poor soul. The shotted
hammock-shroud dropped feet first into the South Atlantic,
and the ship got under way again for St Helena.

May Day morning, and a pleasant fresh day, with a blue
sky and a pattern of white clouds. James crossed it off on the
calendar he had made. *Endeavour* was one of fourteen sail in
St Helena Roads. When he saw so many ships at this lonely
cross-roads of the sea, James was sure it meant war. To his
relief he was wrong. One of the ships was a frigate, the *Portland*, and another was a ship-rigged sloop, the *Swallow*. James
paid an official call on Captain Torrens of the frigate, to learn

he had been sent to escort the India convoy home in case war should break out.

'There was still peace when I left,' the captain said, 'and the strangest thing I've seen this passage was yourself coming in this morning. A collier, by gad! That Geordie's well off course, says I. Then I remembered hearing about your voyage – must be three years now, eh? . . . Did you find the Great Southern Continent?'

Captain Torrens was very like Sir Hugh Palliser, James thought, though a younger man. He smiled as he answered. 'That is not for me to say, sir. I charted two large islands, and eighteen hundred miles of continental coast, but they were in the wrong place for the Continent the gentlemen in London theorize about.'

'Two large islands, eh? How large?'

'About half as large again as the British Isles, sir. They are the lands Tasman glimpsed, but he only saw part of the west coast.'

'And you circumnavigated them?'

'Yes. It took near enough to six months.'

Captain Torrens just stopped himself from whistling in astonishment. Six months beating around an unknown coast. No wonder the ship looked a little worn and the canvas threadbare. Six months! 'You mentioned another coast, Commander.' (James warmed to the use of the courtesy title.) 'What was that?'

'The eastern coast of Tasman's New Holland, sir. I have given it the name of New South Wales.'

'Eighteen hundred miles, you say.'

'Maybe a trifle more than that, sir. Nearer two thousand.'

'Nearer two thousand! Dammit, man – do you realize what you are telling me? This is a greater discovery than ever Columbus made!'

'Nay, you flatter me, sir. I found nothing that was unknown. I only filled in gaps where others had been before me.'

'You have your charts on board?'

James nodded.

'I'd like to see them, if I may. Two thousand miles!'

He saw the charts next day. 'Fine work, Commander, fine

work!' he declared as they rolled up the last one. 'You'll be eager to get home now. Would you come under my orders, and sail with the fleet?'

'Delighted, sir,' James said. 'There's only one thing – I would not be much help if war should start and we run into trouble.' He told the story of the grounding on Endeavour Reef, and the loss of the cannon. 'I can only mount four guns out of the ten I started with.'

'What were they? Six-pounders?'

'No, sir. Fours.'

'But you could mount sixes, no doubt. I happen to know *Swallow* has two spares, and I could make over my two saluting guns – they're fours. And there's bound to be something on the gun-wharf ashore.' He chuckled. 'By gad, it'll be one in the eye for Deptford! You sail with ten guns, and come back with ten – only they're not the same ones! I wouldn't be surprised if they're still arguing about those guns in a hundred years' time'

James felt oddly comfortable being one of a fleet, the first time he had sailed thus in a ship under his own command. It was very pleasant not to have to make every decision himself, and to be free of arguing his motives with Mr Banks. As the slowest ship he left ahead of the convoy, but by nightfall he was lagging well astern. However, John Company's ships had the comfortable habit of shortening sail at sunset, so as not to disturb the slumbers of their passengers. By piling on all possible sail in the silent hours, James could contrive to be in the van by sunrise, to fall gradually astern as the long bright days wore on. But this sailing proved a great strain on both the worn rigging and the crew; after three weeks James was gradually losing ground. He was also much concerned about Mr Hicks. Mr Perry, well aware of his own lack of experience, said he would welcome a second opinion from an older man. So James signalled to *Portland* for permission to visit, and when the reply came had himself pulled across in the gig.

'Good-day to you, Commander!' Captain Torrens said when they had exchanged salutes. 'And what can I do for you this fine May morning?'

'Two things, sir, if you will. I would like to have your surgeon's advice on the treatment of Mr Hicks, my first lieutenant. He is in a consumption, an ailment of long standing, and my own surgeon is somewhat inexperienced.'

'Inexperienced? After all the sickness you've had?'

'He is recently promoted from surgeon's mate, sir. My first surgeon died at Batavia.'

'Ah! Well, that is easy enough.' Captain Torrens turned to a midshipman. 'My compliments to the officer of the watch. He is to pass the word for the surgeon to report on board *Endeavour* to examine a sick officer, and to see me on his return.' He turned to James. 'And your second request, Mr Cook?'

'Permission to part company, sir. Most of my top-hamper is well past its best, and I've only kept up with the fleet by cracking on with all I've got night and day, sir. You'll see if you look at my sails, sir. They're the best I've got, and I'm well-nigh ashamed of them.'

'On and off, I've been looking at them for days, Commander, marvelling that you've kept up so well. Surely that's a different foretop than the one you had set yesterday? What happened to the other?'

'Blew out during the night, sir, split from head to foot. The sailmaker and his mates are working on it now, but it's a case of patching over patches.'

'Then there's nothing more to be said, Commander – I'll push ahead and you may make your own way from here. I don't think I'll be more than three or four days ahead of you. Just in time to let them have the red carpet laid for the triumphant return, eh?'

'I don't know about that, sir, but both favours will take a load off my mind.'

'I can hold out very little hope, I'm afraid,' Captain Torrens' surgeon reported on his return. 'Mr Hicks has a great will to live, and that counts for something. But he is greatly weakened by the flux, and it is the weakness that is killing him.' He turned to Captain Torrens. 'If we could spare a dozen eggs, sir – they'd be the best thing in the world for him. You have a goat in milk?' James nodded, having taken on a milch goat at St Helena for the sake of his invalids.

'You can take all the eggs we've got, if it will do any good,' Captain Torrens said. 'And a chicken or two, since my steward tells me there are some that have stopped laying. I've not met Mr Hicks, but anything I can do to get a man home after three years – well, I'll do it!'

Two days later, for the first time since they had sailed from St Helena, there was no sail in sight. And in spite of the eggs and the the goat's milk and chicken broth, Mr Hicks died that same day. James, bareheaded as he read the service, felt the steady breeze stirring his hair, and thought of the thirty thousand sea miles he and Zachary Hicks had sailed together. Days like this, and days of storm, days of oily flat calm, days of sheer terror. The first lieutenant had been the only one to whom he could open his mind, in a sense his only friend. For a captain may share his thoughts with his second in command, but if he values his position and authority, he may speak on equal terms with no one else. James' voice sounded dry and unemotional, but inwardly he was shaken with sobs. Then the shot-weighted hammock slid from the grating into the kindly sea. Zachariah Hicks was gone to his long home.

It would be all plain sailing from here to the chops of the Channel, but James still did not know whether he would find England and Spain at war or peace. The sail drill of the crew was now beyond criticism, but their gunnery was another matter. With a full magazine, replenished at St Helena, and a full broadside of five-a-side once more, he gave Mr Forwood, the gunner, his head. Every day they exercised with the great guns or the small arms, and the ship became used to the squealing of the gun-trucks, the sharp orders of the gun-captains, and the flat crash of the broadside firing with reduced charges.

James had mounted his two six-pounders as a stern-chase. He was resolved to run as long as he could from any Spanish frigate, and he had old memories of what bar-shot could do to a bigger foe. So old barrels were weighted and flagged and towed astern as targets for the stern-chase. Twice, by a lucky fluke, they were struck fair and square, to disintegrate in a shower of splintered staves and a round of cheers from the lucky gunners.

Memory is a blessed thing, James thought, the second time this happened. Not a man now cheering but had lost a mess-mate on the voyage – and James knew well how deep and sincere such a friendship could be. Yet here they were, cheering their heads off over the destruction of six penn'orth of old barrel-staves and the prospect of the extra tot promised the lucky crew. One afternoon he reckoned up the total butcher's bill since leaving England. Ninety-four men had sailed; fifty-seven still lived. Thirty-seven deaths in under three years; an average of more than one a month. He hoped that what he had found was worth the lives it had cost. But on what scale did one measure a life like poor Zachary Hicks'?

There was one more death to come before they reached soundings, a death that touched James almost as closely as that of Hicks. Suddenly, out of the blue, Howson, his own servant, died. Howson had been with him since the days of the old *Grenville*. He was an orphanage boy, without family or home, and used to spend the winter months as general handyman at the house at Mile End. He had played with James' small sons and carved them toy boats to play with in the rain-water barrel. Decent, kindly, honest Howson! He had not even asked for a bed, but slung his hammock between two beams in the attic where they stored the apples and the winter pears.

The Downs in the second week of July, 1771, lay under a summer haze, with not much more than a mile of visibility. There was a light breeze from the west, dead foul for the Thames. Just a year ago, James thought, they had been in the Endeavour River. There had been plenty of times since then when he had never thought to rest at anchor in the Downs again.

'Shore-boat alongside, sir!' Mr Clerke called, pushing aside

the door-curtain. He had been promoted to acting lieutenant
when Mr Gore had moved up into Zachary Hicks' place. 'I've
made a bargain with him for half-a-guinea, sir. For Tilbury.'

'Excellent, Mr Clerke. I confess I've not got used to the idea
of bargaining with Englishmen again yet. Pass the word to
Mr Banks, please. I'll be up directly.' James looked round the
cabin that had been his home for three years. To leave a place
you had lived in so long was as if a part of you were dying,
he thought. There would be other ships and other cabins, but
three years of his life had been spent in this little space.

All his gear was packed. The low bench his desk stood on
was struck down, and the worn sailcloth cover for the desk
itself ready to slip on and be roped up. At that moment two
seamen appeared to take it off.

'Just a minute, Cox,' James said. He had suddenly remembered something.

Money! For three years he had not used any. At Rio,
Batavia and the Cape he had paid with Bills of Exchange; any
cash deals or bargaining had been conducted by Mr Banks or
Mr Horton. He opened the desk, and slid out one of the small
drawers under the lid. Yes, it was still there – two guineas and
a handful of silver and copper that had lain there since they
sailed in '68. It was a tangible reminder that he was back in
English waters again. The gold was bright enough, but the
silver was blackened and the copper green with verdigris. It
felt odd and heavy against his thigh as he slipped it into his
breeches pocket.

'You can rope up the desk now and bring it on deck,' he
told Cox. 'And be careful. Drop that in the water, and we'll
have to do the voyage all over again.' He was thinking of the
precious papers it contained.

Cox grinned. 'I wouldn't mind, sir – after a spell ashore.
Been a right pleasant commission, sir.'

James did not know what to say to this, so he went on deck.
Mr Gore was superintending the swaying down of the baggage.

'You can bring her up to Deptford when the wind serves,'
James told him.

'Aye, aye, sir. And – it's been a real pleasure sailing with you, sir. I'd do it again, any time.'

'After a spell ashore, I suppose?' James could not resist this.

'Well, naturally, sir. Three years is quite a time.'

'I doubt whether I'll be doing anything like this again – or you, either. If this war with Spain comes off, we'll both find ourselves in sloops-of-war or frigates, I fancy.'

Checking to see that Mr Banks was in the hoy, he dropped into the stern-sheets. The longshoreman touched his battered sennit. 'Tilbury, sir? Just about make it on the tide.'

Before James could reply the yards of the *Endeavour* were manned, right to some fool who stood unsupported on the main-truck, holding on by the standing part of the lightning-conductor. James hoped the iron was sound, and in spite of himself he grinned. Then came wave after wave of cheering as the hoy payed off under her great lugsail.

'Belay that, you fools!' he shouted. But it was one voice against fifty. The cheering went on.

19   *End and Beginning*

'Mr James Boswell, sir,' Amy announced. She was pink from the wash-tub and flustered at having to announce a gentleman of quality.

'Thank you, lass!' James turned from the chart-table set by the window. 'Mr Boswell – your servant, sir!' He looked regretfully at the half-finished chart of Charlotte Sound. 'To what do I owe the honour of this call, sir?'

He hoped the visit would be a brief one, but he doubted it. Mr Boswell was a loquacious Scotsman. They had met in the anteroom at St James', at the levee when James had been presented to the King. Mr Boswell had proved to be most curious about all aspects of the voyage of the *Endeavour*. But then, he had the reputation of being curious about almost everything.

'I am a messenger, sir,' Mr Boswell told him. 'I had the pleasure of taking supper last night with Mr Stephens, the Secretary at the Admiralty.' From a pocket he drew a rolled parchment, red-sealed with the familiar crest of the fouled anchor. 'We spoke at length about the achievements of your voyage, and of your long talk with the King. When I heard of your advancement in the Service, I begged to be allowed to bear the news to you.'

'My advancement – to be sure!' James was conscious of the eagerness in his voice. 'I am flattered you should think so much of me, sir.'

'I am not the only one who thinks highly of you Mr Cook. I am sure they all do at the Admiralty.'

But James was not so sure of this. The Royal Society had been very lukewarm about the results of the transit of Venus observations, and the supporters of Alexander Dalrymple were still insistent that a Great Southern Continent was waiting somewhere to be discovered.

The Scotsman made a clumsy leg, and handed over the parchment commission. 'I was to tell you it is already gazetted – is that the phrase – so that you may assume your new style straight away.'

James slid his penknife under the seal, unrolled the document and skimmed through the red-and-black lettered formal preamble. His heart sank a little when he came to the nub of the matter, though his impassive face showed nothing of his feelings.

   . . . *Their Lordships are Pleased to Appoint you* (he read) *to be advanced to the rank of Commander, with Effect from the first day of July, Seventeen Hundred and Seventy-One, A.D. And to be appointed to HMS 'Scorpion' for Holding Duties until such time as their Lordships otherwise Direct.*

Promoted Commander! So the Dalrymple party had carried the day, and his three years of toil had ended with this empty honour! For that was what James felt it to be. To be promoted Commander at his age was virtually to be put on the shelf. He would be left on the books of *Scorpion* for a few months, then quietly put on half-pay. No one under the rank of Captain had any real security in the Service.

'It is good news, sir?' Mr Boswell's voice was kind, if curious. This back-handed compliment was none of his doing. He knew nothing of backstairs politics in Admiralty. He could not be blamed for any part of the pettifogging economy of the Board. James picked up a decanter of madeira and filled two glasses.

'The best of news!' he declared, with a heartiness he did not feel. 'We must drink to the fact I am promoted to Commander.'

'I'll drink to it, but it is not enough!' protested Mr Boswell. It was said he made heroes of his friends; certainly he was very friendly towards James. 'You should have been Admiral at least – with a knighthood to accompany it. That is what my friend Doctor Johnson says, and he is far the wisest man I know.'

'Nay, sir. I may never aspire so far,' James replied soberly.
'Heights such as those are for the winners of battles or the
taking of treasure-ships, not for plotting coastlines or the
charting of reefs.'

James saw his guest to the door and handed him into the
waiting chaise, watching it as it bowled away down the street.
He re-entered the house just as Elizabeth came down the stairs.
She was still in half-mourning for their daughter, little Elizabeth, who had died shortly before James' return. He had not
seen the child she had been carrying when he left. It had
been a boy, Joseph, who had died after a month. But Nathaniel and young James were both thriving, thank God.

'Who was your guest, James? Not a messenger from
Admiralty? You are not bidden to sea again?' There was a
sad little catch in Elizabeth's high, clear voice, still young-
sounding despite nine years of marriage and four pregnancies.
That little catch twisted in James' heart.

'That was Mr Boswell, my love. I met him at the King's
levee. He brought me a new commission from Mr Stephens
at the Admiralty. What is known as a holding commission,
so that I remain on full pay while I work up my charts.'

'Not a promotion? You have been expecting that, my love?'

'Well, it is also a promotion!' James said drily. But you may
read it for yourself.'

'To be Commander!' she breathed. Then, more loudly:
'Oh, James! They have not made you post after all!'

'Nay lass I have done very well. I confess I had hopes, but
the Navy is a fighting service – and I am not a fighting seaman.'

'You have been in as many battles as most! At Quebec . . .'

'I was only one of many, lass. I have been master's mate,
master, and lieutenant, with my own command. Not many
who get aft through the hawse-hole ever reach so far.'

Elizabeth sank down beside him on the settle, taking his
scarred hand in hers. 'I know you have done well, dear
James. Far better than most men – better than any I know.
But I cannot help thinking that if you had put so much effort into the coasting service you might have owned your own
ship today, and been in a position to quit seafaring and

stay ashore to see your family grow up. You could have been
– what is your Yorkshire saying – a warm man!'

'But I am a warm man, my love! We own this house and
two others, and this promotion means at least two shillings a
day more.'

'I do not complain about that, James. What irks me is the
injustice. You are fobbed off with an extra two shillings a day,
while Mr Banks and that odious Dr Solander are lauded as
heroes everywhere they go. Mr Banks discovered this, Dr
Solander found that! Every news-sheet I read I find some
mention of them – and never a mention of James Cook! And
now they do not even make you post-captain!'

James saw the injustice of it, too. Mr Banks – and to a
lesser extent, Dr Solander – were being hailed all over London
as heroes. Every salon and drawing-room hummed with the
talk of Mr Banks' discoveries, astronomical, geographical and
botanical. And you might have thought that all these things
had been accomplished with the aid of a pair of magical seven-
league boots, for there was rarely any mention of a ship.
Joseph Banks was going to be a great man in his own field,
James knew that. With a few more years behind him, he
might learn sufficient humility to give credit where credit was
due. The collections of plants, the Otaheitan and Maori dress
and curios, and, above all, the beginnings of the Otaheitan
dictionary: these were enough to ensure the fame of any man.
Surely he did not need to take credit for the navigational and
geographical discoveries as well? It was a churlish act to seize
the credit for another man's work.

There was talk already of another expedition to the South
Seas, to settle for all time the existence of a Great Southern
Continent. It was said that Mr Banks was to have command
of it. James could not see their lordships at the Admiralty being party to that, after their experiences with men like Harvey
and Alexander Dalrymple. If Joseph Banks wished to command an expedition it would have to be a private one, and
however great his private fortune, the purchase of a ship and
its upkeep for two or three years – without hope of return –
would be a great burden.

Suddenly, James Cook felt sickened of it all. From boyhood

he had been led by a dream. That dream had fulfilled itself
in an odd way – and what had it earned him? Scarred hands,
wracked bowels, two separate lives, one at sea, the other briefly
ashore. As for Admiralty ever setting up an official Hydrographic Service – well, it would never come in his lifetime,
that was for sure. There would never be sufficient funds, in
spite of Sir Hugh and his friends on the board. In time of
peace there was no money allotted at all for anything but the
barest necessities, and in time of war everyone's mind was set
on prize-money. There was no prize-money in surveys and
charts. It would be a long time, if ever, before a Hydrographic
Office was set up.

Betty Cook was used to long silences between remarks from
her husband, although James himself was rarely conscious of
them.

'As you say, lass, they do not even make me post,' came his
long-delayed reply. 'What would you say if I resigned the
service altogether and swallowed the anchor?'

'Swallowed the anchor! But, my love, what would you do
then?'

James took a glance at his drawing-board; there was a good
living there, he knew. Betty followed his gaze.

'Turn draughtsman, James? That I cannot see. It is one
thing to draft your own soundings and make a chart. But can
you see yourself working from another's findings?'

Frankly, James could not. Yet there must be something.
Then Betty spoke again. 'What about that letter from your
father, James? About the new house he has built for himself?
Maybe there would be something in the north.'

'Farming,' James said. 'Anything but that. Had I wanted
to farm I had my chance to do that five-and-twenty years
back.'

'They build ships at Whitby,' Betty said thoughtfully.

'Aye, so they do!' James said. He saw over the lapse of years
the slips, ropewalks, rigging sheds, and sail-lofts of the ancient
port, and smelt the tar and brine of the waterfront. Another
doubt struck him. Was he ready yet to stay in one place all
the rest of his life? For that is what resignation from the ser-

vice could mean, unless he exchanged one form of sea-service for another.

'I have to acknowledge this,' he said, indicating the new commission, 'and at the same time I shall request leave to attend to family business. How would you like to travel? This time of year we might get a passage to Whitby in a coal-cat going up to refit. It would be quite comfortable, given good weather.'

'It would be very uncomfortable, given bad,' Betty retorted. 'Would it not be better if I had my mother care for the boys and we went by coach?'

James looked at her and smiled. 'Why not? I have nothing but pleasant memories of the last time we journeyed north. I shall write directly and ask for a month's leave of absence.'

'Oh, James!' Betty's heartshaped face was glowing. 'And this time I shall take an eartenware pig, to fill with hot water to put at my feet! And you must bring rum, to flavour the coffee at the changing-stops!'

James returned to his desk and cut a new quill to write his letter. He felt happier than he had been for a year and a half, happier than at any time since the stranding on Endeavour Reef. That had been the start of his real anxieties: the loss of the cannon, then the flux and the deaths of all those men, and now the ceaseless prating of little Mr Banks. He would not resign his commission – not yet. He would have to see how the land lay in Whitby, first. It might be better to stay on Thameside; maybe his father-in-law would know of something. In his mind's eye he saw the future: a house either in Yorkshire or London, with Betty and the children always beside him. Aye, it would be right pleasant. On the winter nights there would be no danger of being blown on to lee shores or hidden shoals. To James, the height of luxury was to lie snug in bed ashore of a winter's night, listening to a storm outside, knowing he had not to get up and go out on watch. He addressed himself to his letter writing. The street-sounds faded from his ears as he wrote, and in their place came the familiar old sounds of the Whitby water-front and the harsh mewing of the herring-gulls.

HISTORICAL NOTE

Soon after Cook's return from this first voyage of circumnavigation, plans were drawn up for a second voyage of South Sea exploration, to be made by two sloops to discover whether there was a continent in the South Pacific. In November, 1771, Cook commissioned the *Resolution,* and Tobias Furneaux was given command of the *Adventure*. The first plans included Joseph Banks as naturalist to the expedition, but after much controversy, he withdrew. The ships left Plymouth in July, 1772 and returned in July, 1775. During this voyage, the ships crossed the Antarctic Circle for the first time in history, and, having circumnavigated the globe in fairly high southern latitudes, Cook proved once and for all that no temperate continent existed in the Pacific outside the Antarctic Circle. Cook's second voyage was one of the longest and most dangerous ever undertaken, and *Resolution* suffered the loss of only four men in three years. Furneaux's crew did not fare so well; he came into conflict with the Maoris at Queen Charlotte Sound, and a boat's crew of two officers and eight seamen were killed and eaten.

During this second voyage, an account of Cook's first voyage in *Endeavour* was published in London; its immediate success made Cook a celebrated man. In February, 1776, he was elected a fellow of the Royal Society, was appointed at last to the rank of post-captain, and given the prized appointment of Fourth Captain of Greenwich Hospital.

In July, 1776, Cook left Plymouth in *Resolution,* having volunteered to command a third voyage with orders to sail *via* the Cape to New Zealand and Tahiti and thence to the 'New Albion' (the coast of Oregon) of Francis Drake, and to work up the North American coast in the hope of finding a passage

round the continent eastward, or round Asia westward. Charles
Clerke was given command of Cook's consort vessel, *Discovery*. Cook reached Adventure Bay, Tasmania, in January,
1777, then went by way of Queen Charlotte Sound and Tahiti
to the coast of Oregon. He made a vain attempt to find a passage to the Atlantic, first round Alaska, then west along the
Siberian coast. In September, he turned south to winter
in the Hawaiian Islands. He thoroughly charted Hawaii
itself, and spent some time at Karakakoa (Kealakekua) Bay,
where he found the natives friendly. Feeling that his presence made inroads on their stores of food, he decided to
move elsewhere, but sea gales sprang up and he was forced
back less than a week later. On his return, the bay natives
became hostile. They stole *Discovery*'s cutter, and on 14th
February, Cook went ashore with armed men to visit the
King and take hostages against the return of the boat. Fighting broke out between the natives and the landing party.
Four marines were killed, three others wounded. A cordon
of armed boats had been stationed round the bay; Cook, at
the water's edge, called to them to pull in. But he made the
fatal mistake of turning his back to the natives, and was
knocked down, held under water, dragged ashore and butch-
ered. The native village was fired and the inhabitants quelled;
Cook's remains were handed over to Charles Clerke and
buried at sea.

Following Cook's death, the King granted a coat-of-arms to
his family and a pension to his widow to honour his achievements. She was also presented with a special gold medal struck
in Cook's honour by the Royal Society.

So little is known of James Cook's wife that some writers
do not mention her Christian name. Those who do, call her
Elizabeth. Not all the authorities state that she was James'
god-daughter, but all agree she was a good few years younger
than her husband. She lived until 1835, dying at the age of
ninety-three and surviving all her children. She had six, three
of whom died in infancy. Nathaniel, the eldest, was lost at
sea, in the West Indies, the same year that his father was
killed. Hugh, the youngest, became a student at Cambridge

and died there at the age of seventeen. The only surviving son, James, a commander in the Navy, was drowned in Poole Harbour the following month. Their mother subsequently made her home with her cousin, Isaac Smith, who had served with her husband as a midshipman, and who rose to the rank of rear-admiral. On her death she left a fortune of £60,000, derived mainly from the sales of her husband's publications.

The italicized passages in the third part of this book are extracts from Cook's *Journal*, while those in earlier parts of the book are fictional. The Degrees of Longitude are as given by Cook. The International Date Line was not established in his day. The dates in the *Journal* conform with naval usage at the time, when the official day ran from noon to noon. March the 1st, for example, began at noon on February 28th and ended at 11.59 a.m. on March 1st.

*Some other Australian
Puffin Books
are described on the
following pages*

LONGTIME PASSING

Hesba Brinsmead

Longtime: that was the place in the Blue Mountains of Australia, in the heart of the Candlebark Country, where the Truelance family built their home. Edwin, the father, built the house himself, to an original and slightly lopsided design. Letty, the mother, planted a garden; and the five Truelance children had a world of rain-forest and bushland to explore. But they worked, too: they did correspondence lessons at the kitchen table, they lifted the turnip crop, and helped in the sawmill. Over the years, as they grew up, Longtime changed. More people came to settle there; Father got a motor-lorry to replace the bullock team; a forest fire changed the face of the country-side; a telephone line was put in; and, one by one, the children went to high school in the city, went 'down below' to Sydney, only returning to Longtime in the holidays.

This story, as told by Teddy, the youngest of the family, is based on the author's own childhood. Vital and gay and sad and funny, it is the story of a happy family and a vanished corner of Australia – for now, a busy highway cuts through the place where, not so long ago, Longtime stood, and the tall trees of the forest have melted away.

Longtime Passing won the Children's Book Council of Australia Book of the Year Award for 1972

For readers of ten and over

THE RUNAWAY SETTLERS

Elsie Locke

A true story of an Australian family who ran away to New Zealand and became pioneers. They had to go – it was the only thing to do with a father as drunken and brutal as theirs – so Mrs Small and her six children, Mary Ann, the four boys and little Emma, left their farm in New South Wales, changed their name to Phipps, and sailed away secretly.

But it was impossible to keep the children happy on the farm where the two elder boys were working to pay back the money for their fares, so they desperately needed a house and at last they found one – an old cob cottage, 'one room and a chimney' which they could have if they would cultivate the garden. And there, far out in the wilds, Jack woke the first morning with one joyful thought surging up inside him – 'Father will never find us here'.

The family's adventures with wild pigs and Maoris, the gold rushes which beckoned the eldest son Bill to try his luck, and Mrs Phipps' daring journey through the Southern Alps with a herd of cattle for sale, make this a story that will long be remembered.

For readers of ten and over

DOWN TO EARTH

Patricia Wrightson

Cathy was absolutely sure there was someone hiding in the ruins of the old house. Not that it really mattered, but they were going to pull it down and she had seen some funny goings-on. Gruff George Adams wouldn't believe a word of what she said, and boastful Luke Day and the others simply laughed at her. But one day Cathy was proved right, because she and George discovered a boy living among the ruins – his name was Martin and he came from another planet.

This story is about Martin and the friends who found him when he was on his first trip to Earth. He had to go back home before the next full moon, but before that some very interesting things happened. To start with, of course, no-one believed that Martin came from outer space: but what was the explanation of his green glow, his ability to squeeze himself into the smallest spaces or the way he bounced?

For readers of ten and over